LIARS

ANITA WALLER
PATRICIA DIXON

BLOODHOUND
— BOOKS —

ALSO BY PATRICIA DIXON

Psychological Thrillers

Over My Shoulder published August 2018

The Secrets of Tenley House published March 2019

Women's Fiction

They Don't Know published August 2018

The Destiny Series

Rosie and Ruby published April 2019

Anna published June 2019

Tilly published July 2019

Grace published October 2019

Destiny published November 2019

To me, to you, to me, to you.
This has been the fun way of writing a book,
so Trish and Neet have dedicated this one to each other!

Sometimes you put walls up not to keep people out, but to see who cares enough to break them down.

— SOCRATES

Love is like the wild rose-briar, friendship like the holly tree. The holly is dark when the rose-briar blooms, but which will bloom most constantly?

— EMILY BRONTË

PROLOGUE

I've been sitting here for over an hour now, staring at a blank sheet of writing paper and counting the petals on each of the daisies that adorn the border. They provided a welcome distraction, as did the two depressing news bulletins on Radio Sheffield, and that annoying yappy dog from next door. They were accompanied by my nagging conscience, an unforgiving voice that I could have done without, telling me to get on with it, have it over and done with.

The thing is, despite my burning desire to write this one last letter to you, I cannot find the right words, any words for that matter. How strange that after the thousands and thousands that have passed between us, when it matters most, I don't even know where to start.

Our last letter. That sounds so harsh, doesn't it, so final. Maybe that's why I'm dithering, avoiding the inevitable. I still can't believe this has happened, to us. It wasn't meant to be this way, was it? You and I were best friends forever, we made promises, swore oaths.

I wish we could start over, go back to the playground where meaningless squabbles were resolved over a shared Wagon

Wheel. Or the steamy canteen, one of us in the free-dinner queue, the other in the line of sniggerers who should have known better. We didn't care about our differences, did we, not then. Like a second-hand uniform versus the overpriced school outfitters, working on the shop floor while the other typed notes and never got their manicured nails dirty. At the end of the day, when the school bell rang or the shift finished, you were always there, waiting at the gate, the special face in the crowd.

Secrets, we had so many. Daft things like who was our favourite Bay City Roller or that we shoplifted make-up and spot cream from Boots. The bigger things, which at the time seemed huge, we guarded like treasure because they were private and sacred. They were our bond. Crushes, first kisses and sex. Fears and failures. Hopes and dreams. And yet in the end, one huge secret, carried for years, unshared, a burden I suppose, that became our downfall.

My conscience is back, reminding me there's another person at fault, at whose feet so much blame can be laid and even now I cannot bear to think his name let alone say it, but I will. Mike. That's where it began, when the rot set in. One man drove a wedge between us, poisoned so many lives, and by his very existence altered the course of what should have been.

I can't avoid it any longer, the inevitable. Otherwise I'll be here all day, twiddling this pen and staring at daisies. I know what I have to do now, before I write my last letter to you. I need to revisit the past, accept our mistakes and lay them to rest. This means facing up to the bad memories and cleansing my soul of the festering hate that burns inside for him, that despicable man. He's the one who really destroyed everything, who tainted our world and turned two women, lifelong friends, soulmates, into liars.

BOOK ONE 1978 – 1986

1

Ferme, La Chauvinais
Saint-Mar- la-Jaille
44540
France

20th September 1978

Dear Wendy, or bonjour, as we say on this side of the Channel.

I am here in France, safe and well and bloody knackered. I bet you never ever thought I'd be writing to you from an apple farm in the middle of nowhere but I am and I love it. Look at me with a Frenchie address!! This is where you send letters so copy it out exactly the same. I hope you are pleased to see that I'm using the fancy paper and envelopes you bought me – I bet you got them to make sure I write, but a promise is a promise and here I am. We are penfriends as well as best friends – fancy that.

I've got so much to tell you that I don't know where to start.

The journey was vile. I thought I'd never get here cos the coach stopped at every sodding town between Sheffield and Dover then I *honked up all the way across the Channel. I had to sleep in the station at Calais because I missed my connecting train but there were a few other backpackers in the same fix so it wasn't too lonely.*

The train ride down here was okay but took almost a day because I had to change a few times and I was scared to death of getting on the wrong one. I kept pointing to the tickets the agency sent and prayed that I was going in the right direction. I eventually hooked up with two other girls who were going to the same place (thank God) and one of them can speak a bit of French so I relaxed after that.

I was so relieved when we were picked up at the station but then the trauma continued when we had a scary but hilarious ride in the back of a smelly truck that bumped along the road. We thought the driver, Yves (the farmer's son who's a bit of a flirt) was trying to flip us off the back so we lay down flat and hung on tight. Apparently, he does that to everyone for a laugh, the weirdo.

We live in caravans at the back of the farm. They are okay, a bit basic but clean. Four people share, same sex only so there's no hanky-panky, not officially. I'll get to that in a bit.

All our meals are provided and at lunch and teatime we have bucketloads of wine – seriously, they drink it like water here but I'm not complaining. The work is hard though. We start at 8am and finish at 6pm but we do get nearly two hours for lunch which is like a feast. I've never eaten so much bread and cheese. Thank God I like veg because there's tons of it, and pig. We eat lots of pig in various forms because the farmer rears them. I refuse to eat brains and feet though. Just vile!

We get taken in trucks to the orchards which are so huge you could easily get lost. At first, the smell of apples was lovely but I've got used to it and I probably won't eat one ever again, I even dream about them and Harvey! Ha, I know your ears have just pricked up. He's from Wales but talks really posh and is here with a group of friends from university. They've been in France all summer, going from farm to farm, picking.

They spent August in the lavender fields of Provence which sounds like heaven and I bet it smells the same. I'm going to go there next year, and pick grapes too. From what I've heard, you can earn a decent wage if you keep moving and work hard. It's like the best of both worlds; you get paid, eat for nowt, are surrounded by lovely scenery, sun, sun, sun, wine, wine, wine and LOTS of men. Perfect. Not like dreary Sheffield. Sorry, I know there are nice bits, like where you live, but whenever I think of where I'm from I see grey and concrete and rain.

That's why I'm determined to keep on travelling like I planned. I've made a few friends and I'm hoping to move on with them once the picking season is over. Anyway, back to Harvey. He's really handsome, he's got long curly hair like Roger Daltrey, and a goatee beard – so cool. He's going to be an architect in his dad's firm once he qualifies. I can hear alarm bells ringing from here because you think I'm going to get my heart broken but I'm not.

My new friends have a different outlook on life than we have back home. It's like they are less worried about the things that tie us down and make us miserable so instead, they travel about looking for new experiences and adventures. Harvey believes in free love and I'm starting to believe in it too. I know he's going to go back to uni in a few weeks and I'll probably never see him again, so I'm making lots of hay while the sun shines. I will feel a bit sad when he goes but believe me, there's no shortage of replacements on the farm and those dotted around the area. Oh, and I'm trying really hard to parlez Français with the locals who seem friendly enough, especially the men, can't think why!!!!

You should see my tan. I wish I'd brought more hot pants but me and the other girls who I share with, they're called Molly, Jen, and Helen by the way, swap clothes all the time and next weekend we're off to the market to spend some of our hard-earned wages on new stuff. I've taken some photos but it might be a while till I get to the end of the roll. When I get them processed I'll send you one. It's a bit of a performance apparently because there's only one shop that develops film and it's in the next town and quite pricey.

Right, that's enough about me. I want to know all about married life, oh and will you send me a photo of us at your wedding? Did they come out nice? I can put it in my album with the ones of us growing up. I was a teeny bit homesick when I got here. I think that was down to exhaustion from the journey, but looking at our old photos made me feel better. I'd like one of me in my chief bridesmaid dress and you looking glam and virginal in your posh frock (yeah right).

So, come on, dish the dirt, do you have wild sex every night now you've got a place of your own and you don't have to bonk Mike in the back of his van? Have you turned into a domestic goddess? Does Fanny Craddock have competition? It seems so weird to think of you being wed, all serious and grown up. I honestly thought you and I would carry on being best friends forever and ever, and nothing would change which is so stupid. I know you were upset when I said I was leaving but I still think it was the right thing to do. Three's a crowd and all that, and let's face it, I've never been your Mike's favourite person so maybe it was time for a change. No matter what, you will always be my best friend, never mind how far apart we are.

Get me being serious and soppy.

Have you seen my Aunty Sue? Has she rented my room out yet? It wouldn't surprise me if she has. I wrote her a short note that I'll post with this but I don't expect she will reply. It was just to be polite and let her know I got here and so she can't throw it in my face that I didn't bother. You know what she's like, the grumpy old cow. The only thing she'll miss about me is the rent money. She was pissed off enough when I turned sixteen and the social stopped paying out so I suppose she'll have to get a lodger in, or cut down on the booze and fags. Serves the old witch right.

If you see anyone from school, make sure you tell them that I'm living it up in France and getting laid by sexy posh boys. When I send the photos you can show them how gorgeous it is here, and I'll try to get one of Harvey and his mates cos I swear they look like they're in Supertramp and everyone will be SO jealous.

It'll certainly shut them up when they find out that Nell Bradshaw from the estate has done okay and their sarky comments about me being from the children's home didn't stop me from having an adventure and getting away from that shithole town. Show the girls from the factory too, especially that bitchy Beryl. Has she had her sprog yet? I hope she looks like the back end of a bus and it's like squeezing a watermelon out. I'm never having kids; I'm going to see the world and wear hot pants and miniskirts till the day I die. Well, not quite but you know what I mean.

So, are you going to stay at the factory now you're legally wed or will Mike want you to be a kept woman? I realise he hates you working there. Perhaps he likes the idea of his domestic goddess waiting for him when he gets home!

Don't forget, tell me about your honeymoon and your house and how you've decorated it. I want to know everything, like what you've had for tea and about the weather and the latest gossip from the factory. Just because I'm not there anymore doesn't mean I can't be in your life. It's going to be hard being apart, that's the truth of it. We can't wipe away fourteen years, best friends since the sandpit, but I know we will survive. You've got Mike and I've got to get on with being a super hippy!

I know we made tearful promises before I left but that might have been the Babycham and Cherry Bs, we did drink a lot that night. I truly meant all of mine. You will always be the sister I never had, the best friend I could've wished for and no matter where I end up, I'll be thinking of you. You never let me down, not once. You stuck up for me and took care of me when I had nobody (apart from Aunty Sue who is worse than useless even on a sober day) and I will be forever grateful. The miles can't part us, not in our hearts.

I hope you will be really, really happy with Mike and married life is everything you wished for. If it isn't you can run away, leave the *laundry and Mike's socks, sod making shepherd's pie and hook up with me. The offer is always there.*

I've gone soppy again so I'll sign off and get this in the post. I hope you appreciate that I have to cycle three miles to La Poste (see I'm almost fluent already) but you're worth it.

Please write back really quickly.

Love you lots, miss you more. Your best friend forever,

Au revoir,

Nell x

2

Wendy sensed Mike's reluctance in handing over the letter, and she wondered what she could possibly have done wrong this time. It was a letter, for God's sake, not a bloody court order or something. She reached across, and he gripped it for a second too long.

'Mike!'

He let go, and stared at her. 'I thought we'd heard the last of her, as she's taken herself off to France.'

Wendy had, of course, recognised the pretty envelope, decorated with flowers, and knew he wouldn't be happy. She had deliberately chosen a distinctive stationery set as a leaving gift for Nell, hoping she would take pleasure from using it and write with details of her new life; she simply wanted them to not lose touch.

'Mike,' she said slowly, 'Nell and I have been friends since we were five. We're hardly going to write each other off because she's temporarily left the country.'

'I thought it was a permanent move.'

'I don't think so. She'll be back, she likes to try new things at times, and that's all this is.'

Wendy placed the envelope by the side of her plate, and instead of opening it, she picked up a piece of toast.

'You're not opening it?' It came out as a growl.

'Later. When I'm on my own.'

'When you're on your own? I thought we were married and shared everything?'

'Do we?' Wendy could feel the anger building. Mike had changed so quickly in the three months of their marriage, and she had decided to stop biting her tongue and become confrontational, or he would feel he could totally dominate her. Nell's letters, and Wendy hoped there would be many, would be her private domain.

He said nothing more. He picked up his lunch and newspaper, and stomped out of the kitchen. She heard the slam of the front door, and watched as he passed the front window heading towards his car.

She finished her toast and still she waited. She wouldn't have been surprised to see him return; he wasn't used to insubordination and it would prey on his mind.

The long finger clicked on the twelve telling her it was ten o'clock, and finally she picked up the letter. She hadn't wanted him to see the contents. She knew it would be Nell in despair. It had been a crazy idea, swanning off to France to find herself, and Wendy hadn't wanted Mike to get any hint of that. His sarcasm when Nell had told her of her plans had bordered on vitriolic, and there was no way she wanted him to have proof that his thoughts had been correct.

Wendy stroked the envelope. The daisy in the top left-hand corner had a big hand-drawn heart in the middle of it, and she couldn't help the smile that formed. She eased the envelope flap open, not wanting to rip it, and took out the letter.

Nell's familiar handwriting flew off the page towards her, and Wendy smoothed the folded paper carefully and placed it on the table. She began to read.

Ludicrous! It seemed her best friend was having the time of her life, getting all the sex she wanted, and picking apples! Wendy pushed her chair back and winced as it grated along the floor. It wasn't right – Nell should have been on her way back home by now, tail between her legs, in a different way, not the way she was describing it in her letter.

It seemed Nell was happy, enjoying the madcap life she had adopted, and was actually learning to speak French, possibly as a prelude to staying there long-term. But she couldn't... Nell had been Wendy's chief bridesmaid, and as such had certain responsibilities towards her best friend, like being twenty minutes away when she needed to talk, not in another bloody country.

She couldn't tell her in a letter how disappointing marriage was proving to be, particularly marriage with a man ten years older who was set in his ways and controlled by his mother. Wendy needed to talk face to face, but according to the letter, that wasn't going to happen anytime in the near future.

Wendy made a pot of tea and carried the tray through to the lounge. She placed it on the coffee table, poured herself a cup and took it across to the bureau.

She had placed an identical set of stationery in the bottom drawer, and she leaned down to remove it. They had promised to write their letters using their sets until there were no sheets left, and she eased out her first piece of notepaper.

Hillside
17 Langley Dell

Sheffield

27th September 1978

My dear Nell,

Thank you so much for your lovely letter. It arrived as Mike was leaving for the office, so we came back inside to read it. He was late for work, because we were so engrossed in your words. We think you are brave to change your life so completely, and I'm immensely proud of you.

Apple-picking sounds like such fun, and you seem to have quickly made lots of friends. Don't forget me, will you?

I love living in this house. Mike said I could spend whatever I wanted, and make it how I wanted it. The walls are cream now, and I've got beautiful velvet curtains in the lounge, lovely rich, dark green. It looks so much smarter than when he lived here with Margaret, no wonder he decided his best course of action was divorce. Everything was dark; dark brown curtains, dark beige walls, a hideous patterned carpet. I've changed all of that. I never mention Margaret, of course. Mike made it clear he didn't want her name spoken out loud. So I don't.

My kitchen has everything I could possibly need, which is good because I do lots of cooking, although not shepherd's pies! I'm not sure the people I entertain would appreciate pies of any sort. They're more steak people than pie people.

I've finished at the factory. Mike says I am more use to him at home, because of the dinner parties. Last week we had a couple of managers from his firm, along with their wives, and it really was a lovely evening. We had prawn cocktails for starters, and steak for our main course. I did baked apples for dessert because it reminded me of you.

Instead of my wage, Mike gives me an allowance. It's not as much as I was earning, but I don't have bus fares and lunches and stuff to buy, so it works out more or less the same. He's really sweet about it, pops it in a small wage packet every week so it feels like I am still earning.

I miss you, Nell. I always thought that when one of us married, the other one would be by their side. It hasn't happened, because you've disappeared to somewhere in France, with your apple-picking and your grape-harvesting, to say nothing of delicious lavender. How I envy you that, I love lavender so much.

I have a wonderful life, the one I always wanted, but how can I tell you about it if I can't talk to you? I guess your little caravan doesn't have a telephone in it?

And please be careful not to get pregnant. I should be the first one to have a baby, not you! You seem to be having a good time with assorted men, so I'm going to write it again. Please be careful, Nell.

Speaking of babies, Beryl had hers on the day I left the factory. She had a little girl, called her Tracy, but I haven't seen her because by the time she brought her in to show everybody, I had left.

I seem to be telling you about things I've missed, but honestly my life is really good. I have taught myself to crochet, so I'm going to make woolly things, maybe baby clothes one day, just not yet.

I think of you every day, Nell, and I hope you think about me. Mike asks about you all the time, so you see, you're wrong when you say he never really liked you. He does. I think he even admires you for having the courage to follow your dream.

I'm going to start and make notes for my next letter to you so I don't forget things that I need to tell you. This letter seems so short when I think of how much you packed into yours, but not much happens in my life. You even made the long journey sound exciting rather than tiring! Please take care, best friend, and always remember where your real home is, in Sheffield.

Much love

Wendy

The paper felt smooth in her hands as she folded it carefully before sliding it into the envelope. Wendy pulled Nell's letter towards her and copied the strange-sounding address onto the front, then flipped it over to write her own address on the back.

Wendy sat for a while deep in thought. *Hook up with me.* Words in Nell's letter that were tempting, but then she remembered the words spoken in church, and she knew she couldn't walk away. Michael Summers was her husband for better or for worse, and till death did them part.

She buried the stationery set under some folders, and closed up the bureau. It made sense to show Nell's letter to Mike, and maybe next time he wouldn't want to see it. In a year's time Wendy could start to be honest about her feelings, but at the moment she had to pretend. To lie.

She popped the letter into her bag ready for taking it to the post office. Having no idea of the cost of posting a letter to France, she thought if she got it weighed this time she could buy several stamps of the correct amount and hide them in the stationery set. Then she could write to Nell whenever she felt like it, and Mike would never know.

Chalet Montpelier
Rue de Ransou 78
1936 Verbier
Switzerland

January 4th 1979

Bonjour Wendy,

First off, I owe you ten million apologies for taking so long to reply. I got your last letter before we left France and in such a rush to leave. I was SO glad to see the back of that mistletoe farm. It was bloody freezing and I never want to spend November in France again. The misty mornings were picturesque but I swear the damp was soaking into my bones, so thank goodness Molly came up with our latest adventure.

I need to bring you up to speed properly because there was no time on the phone – it was literally eating my coins as I spoke to you.

Perhaps I should reverse the charges next time, your Mike would LOVE that! I'm sorry I couldn't stay on longer but I wanted to hear your voice and say happy New Year or bonne année. Did you have a good party? It sounded really lively at your house so I imagined lots of dancing and snogging when Big Ben chimed midnight. I'm so glad the mistletoe got to you in one piece. I wasn't sure it would make it, wrapped up in tin foil.

I have been wearing the hat you crocheted for me and I love the big flower on the side. Molly is so jealous and it's the one thing I refuse to share. I will keep it forever. Anyway, I need to tell you how we ended up as chalet maids in the most beautiful place on earth. You should see it, Wendy, the Alps are spectacular with little windmills and chapels dotted about. It really is like a Christmas card scene, or Heidi. We loved that film, didn't we? That day in the Roxy cinema, I never would have believed that in the future I'd be living in Shirley Temple-land.

Do you remember I mentioned Jen and Helen who we shared our caravan with? It turned out that they were more than good friends, if you get my drift. We were almost finished picking mistletoe when Jen and Helen went off together and neither me nor Molly fancied spending Christmas in a cold caravan so it was a choice between going home, or moving on. That's when we had the crazy idea to get on a coach and head for Switzerland. Molly had heard there were plenty of jobs to be had in the ski resorts as seasonaires (chalet maids) – and Bob's your uncle, here we are.

It's really hard work though. The people in the resort are mostly rich and expect their every whim to be taken care of. We get up at dawn to prepare breakfast then once they head for the slopes, we make the beds and clean the chalet. They've got a thing about cake and eat sodding tons of it so we have to bake one for tea – every bloody day! After that we get a few hours off and how fab is this – along with free board and lodgings we get a ski pass too. You won't believe it but I can actually ski – yes me!

I was rubbish at first but I'm getting the hang of it. No broken bones yet, but a sore bum now and then. It's a long day because we have to go back to the chalet about 4pm and serve them tea and cakey, then at 7pm we make dinner. As you know, I can't cook for toffee but I'm learning from Molly who used to work in a café, thank God. The Swiss food is really nice though – have you ever had fondue? You should serve it at one of your fancy dinner parties, or rosti or raclette. I know, I'll send you the recipes and you can say your cultured friend in Switzerland recommended them – that's bound to impress your posh guests.

By the way, I did take on board your warnings about getting up the tub so before I left France, I went to the doctor and he put me on the pill. It's so much more convenient and I don't have to rely on a man (or johnnies) either. I have taken control of my own body and it feels good. Are you on the pill? Or are you trying to make babies? Honestly, Wendy, you should get it. One little tablet in the morning sets you free. I've put it to good use while I've been here, I can tell you.

The ski instructors are hot and gagging for it (but so am I) and I'm currently having a fling with Luc, nothing serious because frankly there's no time. It's more a case of getting extremely merry on glühwein (beer to you Sheffielders) and then a bit of how's yer father then a few hours' kip. Not exactly romantic but far more exciting than a fumble under the dingy railway arches.

The season lasts five months and ends in April so we have made a proper plan and will be heading south and hitch-hiking to Spain. I really wanted to spend the summer in France because I'm desperate to see the lavender fields in Provence. I planned to send you some because I know how much you love it. One day I promise I will. Molly thinks it's more sensible to get bar work in Spain and then, once winter comes, we can head up to the Pyrenees and do the ski season there. There are so many places I want to go – across to Greece, maybe Turkey and Egypt, who knows. For now, I'm happy up to my knees in snow and cake and glühwein.

But that's enough about me. Will you try to send me another photo of you, and your house because it sounds so posh. I bet your mum and dad are really proud of you. So what do you do all day? Surely you must get a bit bored on your own or are you a lady who lunches? There are some truly glamorous women here who meet up for drinks while their other halves are skiing – that's how I imagine you now, sipping wine with the wives from the Conservative Club. I see Mike playing bowls on the village green with the old farts. He doesn't strike me as the athletic type. Only kidding!

I was surprised he asks about me – are you sure it's not to check that I'm as far away as possible? Maybe he's mellowing with age, like an old wrinkly has-been hippy. Will you say hello to him from me?

I hope you know I'm only teasing. I want you to be happy, Wendy, I really do and it sounds fab there. But you were always the clever classy one and destined for the typing pool whereas I had a feeling I'd end up on the production line putting ciggies in boxes. I wasn't far wrong was I? It sounds like your life is perfect and I'm glad for you.

Fancy Beryl calling her baby Tracy – unimaginative at best, I must say. If I had a sprog (which I certainly won't) I would give it an unusual name, maybe French. They have some lovely names here, and funny ones too. There's a girl who works in the supermarket and she's called Fanny! Poor thing.

You will be pleased to know that I have one more photo left on my roll of film and I'm going to get Molly to take a snap of me in front of the mountains, then I'll get some copies made and send them on to you. I hope they all come out. I'll post this letter today though, so you don't get the hump and think I've forgotten you. Like that's ever going to happen!

Molly has woken up so we had better get off to work. You'd love Molly, she's really good fun but not as much fun as you, so don't get jealous. You are still my best friend forever.

Please write back quicker than I wrote to you. My heart skipped a beat when I saw the daisy envelope – I hope it's the same for you when you get mine.

Lots of love,

Your Nell, always.

xxx

4

Nell read the letter through twice to make sure she hadn't missed anything out. It was hard to explain in writing everything that had happened but then again, she couldn't really afford to ring Wendy regularly and have a proper chat so this would have to do.

Sealing the envelope, Nell sighed as she listened to the sounds of Molly stomping about in the bathroom. Her room-mate had turned out to be a really good friend and Nell knew she wouldn't have survived so far without Molly's ingenuity and determination. But no matter how much fun they had, even on the twelve-hour coach journey from Nantes, across France and along the hair-raising roads into Switzerland, and despite the adventures they were planning, Nell missed Wendy more than she expected.

The worst time was after the apple harvest, once winter set in and the stuffy summer caravan turned into a depressing damp icebox. Nell thought she would die from the cold and with the arrival of dark nights, being stuck on a farm with bugger all to do, was utterly dismal. The looming spectre of Christmas forced Nell to face facts – she could either go home and admit defeat or come up with a plan. After much soul-searching the former was out of the question because after all, where would she stay? Her Aunty Sue wouldn't welcome her with open arms so the only other option would be Wendy, and gatecrashing her best friend's loved-up Christmas wasn't a brilliant idea. Not only that, Nell didn't want to be under the same roof as Mike because despite what Wendy said, there was no love lost between them. As far as Nell was concerned, he was still a creepy letch.

Poor Wendy had always done her best to smooth over the wrinkles but as hard as she tried, Nell couldn't take to Mike and vice versa. The thing was, Nell knew exactly why. How could she ever tell Wendy the truth? It would break her heart and anyway the messenger always took the bullet and Mike would love to pull the trigger.

It went back to an incident at the local golf club when Nell was fifteen. Aunty Sue was working there as a barmaid and after a while, managed to get Nell the job of pot-girl. It was only on a Friday and Saturday night but the pay was okay. All Nell had to do was clean up, collect glasses, then wash and stack them. It was here that she first came into contact with Mike who was a member. She first noticed his eyes on her as she wiped down tables, and now and then when he came to the bar and ogled her skinny legs as she filled the shelves with clean glasses. But it was the time in the tiny beer garden that freaked her out, when she found him alone having a smoke. Nell cleared the other two tables first but had no option than to approach his and get on with her job. She had no intention of chatting but he spoke first.

'Hello. Nell, isn't it?'

'Yes that's right, do you mind if I clear your table, has your friend finished his drink?' There was still almost half a pint of ale in the glass and Nell would get into serious trouble if she threw it away.

'No, leave it where it is. He's gone to use the bathroom. I must say you've certainly brightened the place up; us chaps do like to have something pretty to look at.' Mike smirked before taking a swig of his pint then a drag of his cigarette, blowing the smoke straight into Nell's face, causing her to splutter and cough.

It happened within seconds really, because once Mike had patted her back, apologising profusely as his fingers took on a more exploratory role, his hand slid downwards, over her bottom which he gave a hard squeeze before descending further, to the hem of her skirt and upwards in the direction of her knickers.

Nell was about to scream and push Mike's hand away when voices could be heard approaching and in an instant the probing fingers were quickly removed and wrapped around his pint. Overcome and trembling, her cheeks on fire while tears stung her eyes, Nell picked up her tray and barged past the two other men who were seemingly oblivious to their drinking partner's antics.

What made it even worse was that later, on the way home, when she told her Aunty Sue what had happened, Sue laughed loudly and brushed the whole incident under the carpet.

'Oh don't you go fretting over things like that, Nell. It's part of life, get used to it. Men are dirty bastards and will cop a feel whenever they get the chance. You mark my words, it won't be the last time some pissed-up bloke makes a pass.'

Nell stopped on the pavement, astonished by Sue's words. 'But he's a grown-up, he can't touch me like that.'

'But he has and they will, stop going on. You have to learn to laugh it off or give them a dig. Anyways, you should take it as a compliment... I would. Now stop dawdling otherwise we'll miss the chippy, get a move on.'

Nell had been dumbfounded and confused because no matter what her aunt said, what Mike had done was wrong and no way would she ever get used to it. The whole thing was embarrassing and disgusting, which was why she kept it to herself and didn't even mention it to her best friend, Wendy. Fortuitously, Nell was spared facing Mike again because two weeks later, Sue was sacked after the bar manager caught her slipping a bottle of vodka into her handbag and as a consequence, Nell lost her job too.

Eventually, the incident faded from Nell's mind and she did in fact get over it, right up until the moment in the pub when Wendy told her about the chap she'd met the night before, at the Conservative Club Summer Dance. Apparently he was dishy, a bit older but that didn't matter because her parents thought he was a catch, even if he was recently divorced.

'He should be here any minute, then you can meet him. Mike rang this afternoon and asked me out but I couldn't stand you up so I invited him along too. Wait till you see him, Nell, he's dreamy and you are going to be *so* jealous.'

'So, come on, dish the dirt before he gets here. I want to know everything about him so I can mark him out of ten... you say he's divorced. Bloody hell, I wouldn't have thought your mam and dad would approve of that.' Nell sipped her lager and lime then settled back to hear the juicy details.

'You know what my mum's like, the proverbial social climber, so being the son of the Con Club Chairman got Mike extra brownie points. Not only that, Colonel Summers, as he is fondly referred to, is a very upstanding member of the community.'

Nell sniggered. 'Colonel bloody Summers, you've got to be kidding.'

Wendy tapped Nell's arm and smirked. 'Stop it right now, no

taking the piss, I mean it. Then again, you should see the Colonel, he's got one of those twisty moustaches and wears a blazer with his regiment badge on the pocket, like a uniform and, he carries a cane.' Wendy giggled.

'This gets better by the minute. He sounds like someone off a sitcom.'

'Shush, we haven't got long, Mike will be here soon. Anyway, Mum says the Colonel's a magistrate and on loads of council committees so she's completely smitten and has been sucking up to his wife for ages. It seems she's a tough nut to crack, very private and a bit stuck-up. They went to dinner there once and Mum said the Colonel runs his house like a barracks, barking orders at his wife who scurries around doing his bidding.'

'Sounds wonderful... a right laugh a minute. But what about Mike? Please tell me he's not got a twirly moustache or is a trainee control freak like his dad, and what about his ex, how come they got divorced?'

'No, Mike's lovely and very well-educated. He went off to boarding school at seven because his parents were posted overseas and moved around a lot. Then he went to university and married a year after he graduated. According to Mike, they were just too young and the whole thing was a sad mistake which left him feeling like a failure. He said he found it hard to adjust to married life even though he longed for a happy loving home, you know, after being sent away to school so young. That's all he said really and I certainly didn't want to be talking about his bloody ex-wife all night. I had other things on my mind.' Wendy winked at Nell.

'At least he's got a softer side, not like his stiff dad, or down-trodden mum, for that matter.'

'I think he just needs a woman's love and to be understood. I bet it changes you, being away from your parents at a young age, the poor little thing.' Wendy had a faraway look in her eye.

'Oh, I get it. You think you're going to be the one who makes everything okay for poor Mikey-Wikey. Saint Wendy of Sheffield rides to the rescue. Pass me the sick bowl, quick.' Nell began making retching noises until she felt a hard dig in the side.

'Nell, stop it. He's here so behave. I mean it.'

With that, Wendy began to wave, far too enthusiastically for Nell's liking because in her opinion it looked a bit desperate.

Searching the faces in the crowd that were engulfed in a haze of cigarette smoke, Nell focused on the one heading in their direction, pushing his way through the bodies like a steam-boat parting the waves. He was wearing a polo shirt and blazer and at the time, Nell didn't notice anything else, he could've been wearing his underpants and stilettos for all she knew. Instead, her body froze as she fixated on his face, unable to believe who she was seeing. Once his piggy dark eyes dragged themselves away from their quarry, they turned to Nell and in a heartbeat, Mike's face stiffened, if only for a second. He recovered remarkably quickly and somehow smothered the panic Nell imagined he was feeling.

For the rest of the evening, Nell could only watch as Mike sweet-talked his way into her best friend's life, which going by the way Wendy was behaving, wouldn't take too much hard work. In the end, Nell threw in the towel, uncomfortable in the extreme, the proverbial gooseberry, so she made her excuses and left the lovebirds to it.

As she lay in bed that night, Nell was tormented by many things, the past mainly. Her aunt's uncaring words, the feel of those roaming fingers, that niggle of uncertainty that maybe she was being naive. In the present, she saw her best friend's pink cheeks and bright eyes as Mike lavished her with attention, and there was a nagging portent of doom, a strange sense of inevitability, a changing tide perhaps. But whatever it was, by morning, Nell had decided to keep her reservations to herself and observe quietly from the sidelines.

Mike would deny it, she knew that, and Wendy would be hurt and torn. Wendy's parents would stick the boot in too because they'd always looked down their noses at Nell. She was the bastard daughter of the woman who drowned in the canal, full of drink and drugs, the toddler nobody really wanted, who probably wouldn't make much of her life and had annoyingly attached herself to their precious daughter. It still hurt, deep down, that stain that marked Nell, through no fault of her own. At school it was like they expected her to fail, and with little guidance or a decent role model, Nell had only herself to rely on, and Wendy. If she had applied herself, Nell knew she was a worthy match for Wendy in the brains department but instead, she sought adventure and an escape.

Where Mike was concerned, Nell was fighting a losing battle because he was a wily adversary, especially when you threw love into the mix. He did his best to drive an invisible wedge between Nell and Wendy, any way he could, in case she spilled the beans; that much was obvious. Within months he had won the heart of Wendy, game, set, and match. It was to be a short engagement and they quickly set a date. Wendy's parents were thrilled, unlike Nell who felt sad but knowing how much her friend longed for a white wedding and fairy-tale honeymoon, who was she to deny her that, to ruin it all?

One thing Nell did know was that as soon as she'd done her duty on Wendy's big day, and no doubt caught the bouquet that would be launched in her direction, it was time to go. There was no place for her in Sheffield, not really, not anymore.

Attempting to shake off the past and her maudlin thoughts, Nell placed the letter in her bag along with her camera and fastened her boots. After Nell's doubts, it seemed that Wendy had made a good match, she was happy and that's what mattered.

Maybe that night in the beer garden was down to a randy pissed-up bloke fancying his chances, or maybe not. Mike still gave Nell the creeps and try as she might, nothing Wendy could do or say would alter that fact. It still rankled that nobody ever spoke about his first wife, it was forbidden, and he acted like she vanished, the memory of her erased, her name never spoken. Weird, just weird.

And what the hell was that about the pay packet? Perhaps it was a middle-class trend, giving your wife an envelope at the end of the week for services rendered. Surely Wendy could see the deeper connotations of that. Nell should have put money on Wendy leaving her job because she could see from a mile off that Mike hated her working at the factory, albeit in the offices.

But Wendy said she was happy, she had everything. It was there in black and white. Nell took the letter out of her bag and pondered on its contents. Would her comments about Wendy's stay-at-home lifestyle appear condescending or quarrelsome? Perhaps she should rewrite that page, just in case, but then again Wendy had questioned her love life and hinted she was being flighty, so it was only fair that Nell had her say where domesticity was concerned.

It had pissed Nell off that Wendy let Mike read her letters, but it made her giggle thinking of her comment about him playing old man bowls, he wouldn't like that. And she had said hello to him too, so Nell had the moral high ground, sort of.

'Sod it,' Nell said as she pushed the letter inside her bag and called for Molly to hurry up otherwise the posh lot would starve to death.

It had done Nell good taking a quick trip down memory lane because it reminded her of why she'd left in the first place. No matter how much she secretly yearned for Wendy, and fish and chips, Nell had to keep moving forward, no going back. She could do this. She could face the unknown, endure early starts and manage on her meagre wages. She could even deal with a smattering of homesickness. What she couldn't bear was the thought of anything bad happening to Wendy.

All Nell could do was hope and pray she was wrong about creepy Mike. Unfortunately, much as it pained Nell to accept it, Wendy had made her bed, and as the old saying went, she'd have to lie in it.

5

Wendy applied her make-up carefully, emphasising the blue of her eyes with the smoky blue eyeshadow and a touch of mascara. She had a follow-up doctor's appointment, then she intended heading into town and treating herself to some new clothes.

A recent twenty-first birthday gift from her parents had been money to get whatever she wanted, and even Mike had drawn the line at taking it off her. She leaned forward to add a little more mascara. He had been making noises about them starting a family, but she wasn't ready. She hadn't said no, that would have had repercussions, but she had remembered words of wisdom from Nell about the contraceptive pill.

She had blithely skipped off to the doctor for a prescription, but he had insisted on sending off a pregnancy test as she was a married woman. She had protested, wanting the tablets immediately, but he had been firm.

'If I gave you these, Mrs Summers, and you had already conceived, it could damage your baby. I won't take that risk. It only takes a week for the results to come back, so make an appointment for next Tuesday please, and then as soon as you've had your next period you can start taking them.'

And finally the day was here. Her ten o'clock appointment would change her life until she felt she was ready for a baby, and with her period due any day, she could start taking the tablets almost immediately. And this would be something else to tell Nell in her next letter!

I took your advice, my lovely friend, she thought with a smile. And if she could keep it hidden from Mike, she could simply tell him every month that she wasn't pregnant, but they would keep trying.

The surgery was full and after giving her name to the receptionist, Wendy sat. Twenty minutes later it was obvious the doctors had a backlog, and she glanced at her watch. She needed to be home by two at the latest in order to prepare Mike's evening meal. Luckily, it was only the two of them that evening, but it still required thoughtful preparation. She would have to cut short her shopping trip...

'Wendy Summers.'

She stood, smiled at the unsmiling receptionist, and headed for the door marked Dr Charlesworth. Wendy knocked, and pressed down on the handle.

Wendy knew her face had drained of colour. 'But I don't understand... I haven't missed a period!'

'Are you sure?' The doctor was treating her gently. It was clear from her reaction that it wasn't welcome news.

'Look,' she said, opened her handbag and took out her small diary.

'I'm due to start my period tomorrow, that's what that little red dot is, and I'm so regular I can almost time it to the hour.' She swung the diary around to show him. 'So if we take it back four weeks, you'll see that little red dot with a black circle around it.'

She counted out the four weeks, and the little red dot was there. The black circle wasn't. In panic, she counted back a further four weeks, and both the dot and the circle were clearly there.

The room started to swim around her, and the doctor gently eased her head forward. 'Keep your head down, and take some deep breaths,' he advised, and watched her carefully for a minute.

Wendy lifted her head. 'What do I do now?'

'You don't take the contraceptive pill, that's for sure,' the doctor said. 'I'm going to refer you for antenatal care, and around February time you'll have a brand new baby. Look, Wendy, I realise it isn't what you wanted at this point in your life, but it's happened. Go home and tell your husband that instead of your prescription, you're having a baby. It's obvious you've discussed contraception and decided the pill is a more reliable way and your particular way going forward, but you won't be taking it until after this baby is born. Will you be okay? You have a bit more colour than you did five minutes ago,' he said with a gentle smile. The news had really stymied her.

Wendy stood. 'Thank you, Dr Charlesworth. I wait for a letter?'

'You do, and they will give you your first appointment. Good luck, Wendy, and I'm sure when you both get your head around the news, you'll be absolutely delighted.'

Wendy walked home. She needed thinking time, and the news

delivered by the doctor had driven away thoughts of a shopping trip.

More than needing thinking time, she needed Nell time. For a few moments Wendy raged against her friend for leaving her; she had nobody to talk to other than Mike, and talking wasn't at the top of his list for entertainment. Two or three club memberships put paid to evenings in together, and the other evenings seemed to be taken up with entertaining his friends and clients.

She was lonely. Her footsteps slowed, and she sat down on a garden wall, afraid she was going to faint. Realising this had happened a couple of times over the last week, she gave a rueful grin. It was obviously a part of early pregnancy, her body changing, but when you don't know you're pregnant, it's standing up too quickly, or eating too much chocolate, or trying to believe the backhanded blow to the head hadn't caused it...

The journey home seemed to take a lot longer than the earlier journey to the doctor's surgery. She had set out with a definite jauntiness in her stride, happy that she was taking control of her life, her destiny, possibly even thinking of Nell's words in her first letter, *hook up with me.*

Wendy wouldn't be hooking up with anyone now, that option had disappeared in some test tube somewhere. And was she truly ready for the pain of childbirth? She shivered as she put her key in the lock of the front door. No, she bloody wasn't ready for giving birth, and she certainly wasn't ready for the nine months of waiting for it.

'They'll give you a due date at the hospital,' Dr Charlesworth had said. A due date? Suddenly it was real, and in her brain was the true probability that her birthday money would be spent on maternity clothes, and not the short skirts and dresses she had set out that morning to buy.

She sat at the kitchen table and dropped her head onto her arms.

Five minutes later, her shoulders aching, she lifted her head, gave a deep sigh and stood. Acceptance of the situation was written into her features, and she moved across to switch on the kettle. A cup of coffee would help.

She made the drink, lifted it to her mouth and as the smell hit her, she retched. She threw it down the sink, and started again with tea. Another big change for this momentous day – coffee was no longer for her.

Taking her cup of tea through to the lounge, she sat at the bureau and took out her stationery set. It seemed ironic that this was to have been her hiding place for her contraceptive pills. Sliding out a sheet and picking up the pen she had bought specially for writing to Nell, she wrote her address at the top of the page.

Tuesday 5th June 1979

My lovely Nell,

I have such exciting news to tell you. I have arrived home from the doctor's, and I am expecting a baby. It will be born February, although I don't have a proper date yet. They will give me that at the hospital when I start my antenatal appointments.

This is so overwhelming; I can say that with a lot of confidence! A child, growing inside me! And you will be the baby's Aunty Nell, and its godmother, of course, so don't plan on being in far-flung places next spring, because I will need you to be here.

I actually would have loved you to be here for the whole of the time, because while it is exciting, it's also bloody scary. I think I need to go and see Beryl, ask her a few questions, because I can't really talk to Mum about stuff like this. Don't get me wrong, you know I love her, but everything I know is from you and from school, not from her. I'm also going to get a book from the library about it, I know nothing about children.

Mum and Dad gave me money for my birthday – Mum said she was sick and tired of seeing me in the same clothes, and wanted me to go and buy lots of new stuff. I've decided to save it and get some maternity clothes when I need them. I'm sure Mike will go with me for the baby stuff we will need.

I have so much to learn.

Did you have a good birthday? I sent a card but it's difficult never knowing if you're still in the same place. I know you've only recently arrived at this address, so you should get this letter.

Fancy us both reaching twenty-one! Soon be middle-aged, then in our fifties. Depressed now? Sorry, you know I love you.

Write back quickly, won't you? I need to know how you feel about my wonderful news. The doctor says I can go on the pill as soon as I've had the baby. And soon I'll have boobs as big as yours!

Love you, Nell,
Wendy

PS I'm going to break the news to Mike tonight. Wish me luck x
PPS I forgot! I passed my driving test! First time! Mike has bought me a cheap little Mini and I love it. She's called Wendell and she's red with a white stripe down the side. See what I did there? Combined our names. Miss you, best friend ever.

Wendy walked slowly to the postbox, and slipped the flowery envelope through the slit. She felt better because it was on its way, and her step was a little lighter as she returned home.

Shepherd's pie, she decided, *we'll have something we can't normally have when we have guests.*

It didn't take long to make, and she sat for an hour reading.

By the time Mike walked into the lounge, she had put the book under a cushion and stood to greet him.

'Smells good,' he said.

'Me, or the meal?' She attempted a joke but he didn't smile.

'The meal. What are we having?'

'Shepherd's pie.'

'What? Minced meat?'

'I've used lamb...'

'Oh, for God's sake, let's get it over with.' He poured a whisky, and headed into the dining room.

There had been silence for too long.

'Mike, I have something to tell you.'

He glanced up from the rice pudding. 'It's tinned. You're going to tell me it's tinned rice pudding, aren't you?' He threw the spoon down into the dish.

'No, of course I'm not.' *Not this one anyway. However, the last one...*

'You made it?'

'I did. With cream.'

'Good.' He picked up the spoon. 'So what is this thing you have to tell me? She's coming back, isn't she?'

'No, she isn't.' Wendy knew he meant Nell.

'So what then?'

'I'm pregnant.' Not the violins and flowers sort of declaration she had envisaged, but it was out there. She waited for the fallout.

There was a prolonged silence. Eventually he smiled. 'Pregnant? We're having a baby?'

'We are. I don't have a due date yet, but it's early days, and will be due sometime in February.'

Mike stood and walked around the table to kiss the top of her head. 'That is wonderful. You found out today?'

She nodded. 'I went to the doctor last week because I felt queasy all the time, so he did a pregnancy test. I got the result today.'

'And you didn't bother to tell me for a week?'

'I didn't want you to be disappointed if it was negative. It's been lovely telling you the good news. It would have been awful if I'd had to say there's no baby.'

He thought it through. 'Okay. But anything else from here on, I want to know before you do. Is that understood?'

Again her head almost dipped. 'Of course. You'll come with me to the hospital?'

'Certainly. This is my son.'

'It may be a daughter.'

He didn't bother her with a response.

6

It was almost sunset and after a long day serving cold beer to rowdy tourists, Nell was winding down with her friends, listening to the swish of the Mediterranean as it lapped against the shores of the seaside town of Torrevieja. She had read Wendy's letter twice, a huge smile spreading across Nell's face with each word. Wendy sounded so happy about having a baby. The thought alone terrified Nell and not for the first time did she thank God for the little packet of pills she kept by her bedside table.

After the third read through, Nell felt a tinge of regret that she wouldn't be there for such an exciting time in Wendy's life and had the grace to feel guilty, as if she'd abandoned her best friend. Not that Nell would be of any use because she knew zilch about babies and had no desire to either. Still, Wendy had her mum to help out and... come to think of it, apart from creepy Mike, she never actually mentioned anyone else, other friends.

Nell tried to remember the content of previous letters and apart from Beryl, it seemed as though Wendy's factory mates had dropped off. The dinner party guests she talked about were simply that; nameless people who ate the lovely meals Wendy prepared. Perhaps the guests were a bit snooty and dreary. What about the Conservative Club? Wendy and Mike went there for social events so surely some of the women had kids. They would be able to pass on bits of useful poo and nappy-related information, or invite Wendy and her nipper to their house where they could coo and swap mumsy stories. Nell decided to mention it in her letter and give Wendy a nudge because she could be a bit too shy sometimes. It would make her feel better if she knew Wendy had some support.

There was something else. Why was Wendy wearing the same old clothes? She was always so smart and had amazing fashion sense. Nell couldn't remember her ever looking unkempt, even Wendy's hair was always styled and her make-up perfectly applied. Everyone said you got complacent when you got wed. Men went podgy from the home cooking and women let themselves go once they bagged a bloke. That's what happened when you married an old fart like Mike.

Nell would never fall into that trap or turn into a frump – not that she wore the latest trends or anything but she did her best with second-hand clothes, and the stuff she swapped with Molly and the other girls.

Nell's heart immediately sank when she thought of Molly, who only the day before had broken the news that she'd be heading home at the end of August. Her parents had called time on her gap year and insisted she went back to university and buckled down. That meant that Nell would have to carry on with her adventures alone or maybe hook up with some of the other travellers and seasonaires.

She thought back to Wendy's letter and her twenty-first present. It would be Nell's birthday soon but there'd be no big bash, or wedge of cash, she'd be lucky if she got a card from Aunty Sue. The only letter of congratulations Nell was assured of was from Wendy. Nell hadn't even told the gang that her milestone birthday was coming up; it was simply another year. The words of the traditional song that she'd heard everyone chorus at the community centre when she was little – some friend of Aunty Sue had come of age – 'she's got the key to the door, never been twenty-one before.' A huge lump formed in Nell's throat as the prick of tears forced her to suck in air and suppress the unexpected wave of homesickness.

What on earth could she possibly miss about Sheffield? She had one useless family member and one real friend whose husband despised her. Even if she went home when Molly did, where would Nell stay? What would she do for a living? She had meagre qualifications and no idea what she wanted to be, even if she could get into college. The thought of being stuck indoors all day, studying at a desk or trapped in a typing pool didn't appeal one bit. Okay, it wasn't as though working in a beachfront bar or cleaning chalets was the best career move in the world but it damn well beat pulling pints in some smoky inner-city dive. At least she'd breathed the Swiss air and here, she had the sun on her face and sand under her feet, not a sticky pub carpet, and best of all she had lots of friends. They weren't Wendy, nobody could ever replace her, but they were fun and wild and up for an adventure.

It looked like Nell and Molly were going to have to go their separate ways although she had invited Nell to stay in Hampshire at the family home, or at her uni digs should she ever turn up in the UK. That was another thing about her travelling friends, they were like a nomadic community who offered the hand of friendship, sharing what they had, making room for one more. Their doors were always open, like families should be.

Nell took a few moments to watch the sunset and admire the orange glow that set the clouds on fire, turning the horizon pinky-red. Wendy would have loved this, and Nell wished they had seen the Alps and the apple fields and the nodding sunflowers together. That they had drank too much red wine and schnapps, danced on bar-tops and skied down slopes, screeching with fear. Even a damp caravan would have been more fun with Wendy to share it with. Nell missed her so much.

Taking out her journal that was full of names, telephone numbers and addresses, and her depleted pack of daisy paper, Nell pulled out a fresh sheet then rummaged in her bag for a pen. She'd had an idea that might solve two problems in one go. Maybe a trip home was what she needed, to get things into perspective and take a look at Sheffield with fresh and more mature eyes, even for a twenty-one-year-old. It might not be as bad as she remembered, and she did miss the Pennines and the sight of the craggy peaks, but not the rain and the litter. The thing was, until she went back she'd never know if she could make a go of it, or give up her life of freedom. It would make Wendy happy too because Nell sensed she needed her, something wasn't right, call it intuition.

Placing her journal on her knees and using the campfire to see, Nell wrote.

Apartamento Maya
Calle Gravina, 9
03002 Alicante Spain

14th June 1979

Dear Mummy-to-be Wendy,

I cannot believe that you are going to have an actual baby!!

I had to read the line twice before I believed it was real but when it sunk in I felt so happy for you, I still am, grinning like an idiot.

Is Mike chuffed? You didn't really say in the letter. At least we know he's not past it and firing blanks.

Before I forget and start rambling, I want to remind you not to be shy. You never mention that you have any fun or visitors. Or are you saving my feelings so I won't get jealous? I'm not, I promise, and I hope you're not jealous of mine. Nobody is as special as you. Try to make friends at the Con Club and with the wives who come to dinner. Surely they can't all be as ancient as Mike! I bet you'll meet lots of other mums at the clinic – remember Beryl told us they get you to do breathing classes and teach you how to bath a doll, so I'm sure you will manage without me taking the mickey out of your HUGE belly.

I expect you to tell me what every single stage is like – I intend to experience the whole thing through you, then I'll be an expert without actually having to do any of the gory bits. Even have it off with Mike! Kidding.

Do you realise that now you're in the pudding club, your mum and dad know for sure you have sex, how embarrassing is that? I bet they think it's the second Immaculate Conception rather than admit their little princess has been a naughty girl. Ignore me – you know I like to tease.

Nothing much to report from here, it's the same old thing really. Working shifts, sunbathing, drinking too much Sangria and eating not a lot. My wages cover my rent but the boss feeds us when we are in work so I'm surviving. I have a fab tan, and wait for it... I've had my nose pierced. Hurt like bloody hell but I love it. I might do my belly button next but I'm a bit scared because a girl I know had it done and it went septic. I swear it was gross.

We have cockroaches in the apartments that are as big as bloody crabs. They are the most disgusting things I've ever seen. I hate them and they make this awful clicking noise when they come out at night so we are sleeping on the beach. We just store our stuff in the apartment and go back to get a shower and changed.

Big news from Molly – she's going home which means I have to head off up to Andorra for the snow alone unless I can tag along with someone.

Now don't get your hopes up but I'm thinking that if I can save up over winter, I might come back for a break when your baby is born. There's no point in coming before Christmas as I'll be in the way if I stay at yours, it's family time after all, and no way am I kipping at Aunty Sue's, but maybe after New Year. That means it's only six months to wait – what do you think? I might be able to afford a cheap B & B or something.

I'll post this in the morning and wait eagerly for your reply. I do miss you a lot and feel bad that I'm not there to help you – although what good I'll be is anyone's guess.

Right, I'll sign off. Guitar Nigel has turned up and we are going to have a sing-song – everyone laughs at me cos I'm tone deaf. Do you remember the hymns in assembly and the time when Miss Earnshaw made me stand at the back because I put everyone off – how rude! The cheeky cow.

You take care of yourself and my godchild. I'm picking the names, by the way – hippy ones, of course. Ziggy for a boy and Rebel for a girl. Mike would love that!

Adios for now my chubby friend,

Lots of love,

Nell xxxxxx

P.S. Forgot to say congratulations on passing your test – I like that you can ferry me around everywhere when I visit. I love Minis and yours sounds cool, you trendy thing! And that's a belting name – Wendell.

Do you remember that skipping song we used to sing in the yard? 'I had a little bubble car number forty-eight, I took it round the corneeeeer... and forgot to pull the brake!'

I'm not going to be able to get that out of my head now or the picture of you zooming around Sheffield. I wonder if Nigel can play the tune on his guitar.

So proud of you, mate. xxx

7

Wendy wiped away the tears as she read the letter from Nell; the ache inside her was worse with each bundle of news that arrived, she missed her friend so much. She put it back in the envelope, then took it out again to reread it.

She scanned through it once more, this time slowly, pleased that Nell was planning on being here for the baby's birth, but she also recognised how flighty Nell could be. Saying she was coming home didn't mean she was coming home, it meant *I'll try hard to do it, but don't be surprised if I end up in Cape Town.*

Rubbing her stomach seemed to be the thing Wendy did almost constantly, although it didn't help her moods or her discomfort. She was beyond the six months stage and had finally had to give in and buy maternity wear.

Since finding out she was pregnant, Mike hadn't touched her in bed, or anywhere else for that matter. He said he didn't want to harm the baby.

Does he think his dick is the size of Mount Everest? she mused. *He's bloody wrong.*

With his birthday rapidly approaching, she knew she had to make the effort to go shopping. She thought she might get him a new dressing gown, and she really must remember to get a card, even if it was only to rub it in that he hadn't got her one for her twenty-first. He'd managed to be mildly annoyed with himself for that faux pas, because his in-laws had spotted there wasn't a card with *wife* on the front.

Wendy went to have a shower, and stared at herself in the mirror. Her breasts had become truly magnificent, but unfortunately were starting to rest on the lump that was her baby. No wonder Mike wanted nothing to do with her, she was huge.

A small voice inside her pointed out that she hadn't been huge until about a month earlier, but she dismissed the thought and stepped under the shower. It seemed to take forever to get the shampoo and conditioner out of her long dark hair, and she added a trip to the hairdressers to her list of jobs.

Finally ready to drive into Sheffield city centre, she paused at the bottom of the stairs to select which coat to wear. Which coat would actually fasten was more the issue, she realised with a smile.

Mike had decided it was colder today, and had taken his heavier coat, leaving the lightweight one from the day before hanging on the coat stand. She removed her green jacket, and saw the exposed inside pocket of Mike's coat, complete with a white envelope almost concealed by the pocket front. Almost concealed.

She carefully pulled it out, and looked at it. A birthday card, she surmised, but he had obviously opened it early, and hadn't added it to the three or four cards on the mantelpiece waiting to be opened in two days.

Carefully noting which way round it was in the envelope, she pulled it out. A small red heart fluttered out and onto the rug. It was handmade, coloured on both sides with felt tip pen, and Wendy eased herself down to pick it up.

I love you.

She stared at the words handwritten on the heart, and retched. She turned and ran for the downstairs toilet, and stayed there until she had emptied everything from her stomach, including what she felt must be the lining.

After splashing water on her face, Wendy returned to where she had dropped the card in her haste to get to the toilet. She picked up the card, the envelope and the heart and carried them through to the lounge.

I love you.

The words were repeated inside the card, written by the person who thought she loved Mike. On the front of the card, in a more professional font by some designer at Hallmark Cards, it said, To The One I Love.

Paula. Bloody Paula Newcombe, Mike's precious secretary who could do no wrong. She'd fucking done something wrong now. No wonder Mike didn't need to screw Wendy, he was getting it away with his damn secretary.

Wendy cancelled thoughts of going into town, and sat on the sofa and seethed. She couldn't ignore it, she had a baby to think of, who unfortunately was going to be blessed with a lying, cheating, conniving bastard for a father. Screwing Paula would have been so simple; she lived in the back of beyond on the Derbyshire border in a tiny cottage, her closest neighbours some considerable distance away. So easy, nobody would have seen his car visiting whenever he felt like it.

Wendy's brain went into overdrive. She began by putting the card back exactly where it had been, complete with the little heart inside it. He wouldn't be able to tell she had seen it.

She removed two steaks from their stock in the freezer, and began to prepare a meal he would never forget. She chose the best wine, a beautiful deep red Châteauneuf-du-Pape, and left it out to rest. She settled on Hasselback potatoes, with petit pois tossed in butter, and for dessert they would have his favourite; homemade rice pudding made with cream. She briefly wondered if Paula fed him rice pudding out of a tin. Wendy would prepare a small starter of half a slice of toast with a small piece of pâté. She wanted to make sure he had room in his stomach for his extra-large portion of rice pudding.

She rang him at work. She could hear the surprise in his voice, but explained that as they were going out for a meal on his birthday, she had decided to cook specially for him that evening, just the two of them, because next year there would be three.

'That sounds lovely, Wendy,' he said. 'Let me check my diary–'

'I've already checked the one you keep here,' she interrupted. 'You're free tonight, out at a function tomorrow night, and then it's your birthday meal the evening following. Tonight is the only night, my darling. Please don't disappoint me, I've already started preparing the rice pudding, and the steaks are defrosting nicely.'

He sighed. Paula would be none too pleased when he told her he couldn't get out tonight, but she'd get over it. He was seeing her at the function, when Wendy wouldn't be there...

'Okay, my love,' he said to his wife. 'That will be lovely. You need me to pick anything up?'

'Nothing. I've got the Châteauneuf-du-Pape breathing, and everything else is under control. Everything,' she emphasised.

'Then I'll look forward to it. I have to go, there's another call coming in.'

She replaced the receiver and smiled. The preparations weren't quite done, but would be shortly.

Wendy took the sleeping tablets out of the bedside drawer. The doctor had stressed that she mustn't take more than one, but as she wasn't sleeping...

She took them down to the kitchen and emptied four out of the small brown container, thought about it for a moment, then added a further two. One had acted pretty quickly with her, but she didn't like how sluggish it made her feel the next day so hadn't taken anymore.

She put the six tablets into the mortar and picked up the pestle. She ground them until they became a fine white powder which she tipped into the measured rice. She stirred vigorously until it was dispersed evenly, then put it to one side until it was time to add the rest of the ingredients. She also made a smaller one for herself, and if Mike noticed she would tell him she had omitted the cream in hers, she couldn't eat such rich food while still feeling queasy.

She looked around, pleased with what she had done. Everything was ready, and she had a few hours before she needed to start the actual cooking.

Mike arrived home feeling a little disgruntled. Paula hadn't reacted well to his news that he was having an early birthday meal with his wife, and she made damn sure he got an eyeful of her breasts before he headed home.

'Think about these,' she said, 'while you're eating your swish meal and canoodling with Wendy afterwards. Will she do the things for you that I do? Or will I see you later when you've had enough domesticity and you want to fuck me silly?'

'Unless Wendy falls asleep straight after the meal, I've no chance of getting out.' He smiled. Paula had a massive enthusiasm for sex, one he shared, he simply didn't like her that much.

'I'll wait up until midnight. After that, forget it.'

The dining table looked lovely. He sat down, and Wendy kissed the top of his head. 'Happy advance birthday, Mike,' she whispered.

'Thank you, Wendy, and I must say, this looks beautiful.'

'I've really tried to make it special for you, because in future we'll have to consider our baby first. So, we'll begin with pâté. Can you pour the wine, please. A tiny amount for me, don't forget.'

She headed into the kitchen, and removed the pâté from the fridge. The toaster had popped the slice out, and she cut it into triangles, two each.

Wendy walked through, a small plate in each hand.

'I thought pregnant ladies weren't supposed to eat pâté?'

'I have a really tiny piece. You know how much I like it; I couldn't sit and watch you have it and me not.' She smiled at him. 'Shall we say grace?'

He shook his head. 'No, that's only for when we have guests who go to church. Between us we can be simply us, heathens.'

It was a perfect evening. They chatted like an almost normal couple for the first two courses, with Mike complimenting her on her Hasselbacks, saying she had really perfected the technique. She wanted to smash one down on the top of his head, but refrained.

The rice pudding was a triumph, and he didn't spot at any

point that hers came from a separate dish. He drank three quarters of the bottle of red wine, and about a quarter of the white, so by the time he manoeuvred his way through to the lounge where Wendy had promised him brandy and coffee, he was feeling a little woozy.

Within five minutes he was laid on the sofa fast asleep. The brandy bottle, with some poured into his glass, and both bottles of wine were placed strategically on the coffee table, along with a cup of coffee which Wendy guessed would be cold by the time she returned.

She picked up her car keys, slipped on a dark zip-up jacket that wouldn't zip up, and headed out of the door towards her car.

Ten minutes later she was parked outside Paula's house, trembling, still unsure of what would happen if she saw Paula. Wendy needed to tell her to stay away from Mike, that she knew about them, and she would, if necessary, go to the board and tell them what was happening.

Her baby was her priority, and her baby needed its daddy at his home, not at somebody else's. She had pulled the little car as far onto the grass verge as she could and knew it would be hidden from the house by the height of the privet hedge.

She got out of the car, leaving the door slightly open, and the engine running. She searched the rockery inside the front gate until she found a rock big enough for her requirements, headed towards the front window which showed no lights, and threw the rock.

The glass shattered; Wendy had been afraid it wouldn't have enough impact, but it worked as she had imagined and hoped.

Holding onto her stomach, she ran back to the car and quietly closed the door.

Paula yanked open her front door. 'Who the fuck's done that?' she yelled, and came outside to inspect the damage.

She looked around, and walked towards the garden gate, clearly intending to look for anybody running away from the scene. Immediately she saw the car, and ran towards it, incensed.

Wendy momentarily froze. In her mind she had imagined Paula coming towards the car, intent on talking to the person in the driving seat; she hadn't envisaged a screaming banshee running towards her at full pelt. The baby kicked, galvanising Wendy into action.

She jammed her foot hard down on the accelerator in utter panic and the little red car travelled at some speed towards the shocked woman, who stared straight at Wendy behind the steering wheel.

'N-o-o-o-o!' Paula screamed out, as the car hit her. Her body flew over the top of the Mini and landed in the road. Wendy hit the brakes and turned to look through the rear window. She saw Paula move, heard her screech of agony.

Paula was almost rigid with pain. She knew her leg had snapped; knew she couldn't move. She had to hope somebody would be around and help her.

She couldn't be dead. She couldn't be dead. The mantra chugged over and over through Wendy's brain as she drove back home. She remembered nothing of the journey, had no idea what traffic light violations she had caused – she needed to get back to be sick, and to make sure Mike hadn't woken.

Paula lay, unable to move, and then she heard an engine fire into life. She lifted an arm, but even that caused intense pain in her shoulder. Hoping to attract the attention of whoever the car driver was, she listened as it began to move. There was a sudden increase of speed, and Paula's life disappeared beneath the wheels of the blue Toyota. She wasn't dead with the first pass over her body, but the reverse travel finished her. The car drove away, a self-satisfied smirk flitting across the driver's face. An opportunity grabbed, most definitely with both hands, or all four wheels as the case may be.

Mike had never felt so ill. He took the two tablets his wife was holding out to him, and swallowed them, washing them down with water.

'How much did I drink?' He moaned, and Wendy pointed to the coffee table. 'I've put the brandy bottle away, I didn't want you to wake up and drink anymore, I knew you wouldn't be well this morning. I tried to get you to bed, but I couldn't do it. I didn't want to risk hurting the baby...'

He looked with disgust at her stomach. 'Oh yeah, the baby.'

'Are you going to work?' Wendy asked quietly.

'I am, but you'll have to take me. I'm too ill to drive.'

'I have a doctor's appointment at nine...'

'For fuck's sake,' Mike roared. 'Order me a cab for nine then. I can't rely on you for anything, can I?'

'Can I suggest you shower first?' Wendy indicated the front of his shirt where she had poured half a glass of red wine the previous night. 'It looks as though you spilt some.'

. . .

She watched him get into the taxi and breathed a sigh of relief. She could get out to the Mini, and give it a good clean. She wanted no blood on the paintwork or the tyres. Her fear had settled overnight and she hoped somebody had walked by and helped Paula. And she also hoped Paula didn't know she had a Mini, but Mike had never had to use it for work, so Wendy was pretty sure she was in the clear.

She cleaned the car as thoroughly as her burgeoning stomach would allow, and then for good measure, she drove it to the automatic wash. It would be the cleanest Mini in Sheffield, without a doubt. She was driving home when she heard the news on the radio.

By the time she reached home, the passenger seat was full of vomit, the rose fragrance the valets had infused, replaced by a sourness it would be impossible to disguise, and her bowels were at the point of exploding as she pushed open the front door to her home.

Paula was dead. But what made Wendy feel so bad wasn't that she had killed someone, it was the sense of relief that an issue had been removed.

8

For several days, Wendy was glued to Radio Sheffield; she hardly moved from the house, listened to each item of news and waited. She expected every person walking down the road to be a policeman, and her brain went wild with images of giving birth in a prison cell, and the baby immediately being taken from her.

Everything was wrong. She hadn't gone to kill Paula, Wendy just wanted her in the car where she could explain how much she needed Mike to be at home with her, and Paula had to stop the affair.

Stupid Paula had ruined everything by racing towards her, and now Wendy couldn't breathe for the oppressive feeling of guilt that was overwhelming her almost every minute of the day. She had killed another human being, and she would have to pay for it.

And where the bloody hell was Nell when she needed her? Wendy needed to tell her what had happened, to try to get everything into perspective.

. . .

My dear Nell,

It was sheer pleasure to receive your last letter, but I am afraid this one is going to be really short. I am tired all the time; the baby is quite big, so the hospital tells me.

It is Mike's birthday today, but he is ignoring it, I fear. His secretary has been killed in a hit-and-run accident, and it's knocked him for six. They were close, working together every day, and I think she carried him at work, doing a lot of what he should have done.

Her name was Paula, and it's a big police investigation, but they don't seem to have found any evidence of anything. They've talked to all their colleagues, but nobody knows who she was seeing, or anything about her, really.

I think it will be wonderful if you can come for the baby's birth, but if that isn't possible, you must be here for the christening. I definitely want you to be the godmother.

I'll write more next time, I promise. Please book your travel tickets and a hotel nearby – I'll send you the money. Let me know how much.

Love you,
Wendy and bump

9

29th September 1979

Dear Wendy,

Would you really pay for me to come back? Maybe you could loan me the money and I could repay it bit by bit. Once I'm settled in my next place, I'll make some enquiries about flights. That's the quickest option, although I'm happy to come by coach – it depends on what you can afford. I don't mind roughing it. Lots of my friends have used Dan Dare (Dan-Air) as they are cheap, and they fly to Manchester too. I'd only book one way though. Then I can stay as long as I want or until you get fed up of me. Remember that B & B down from the town hall, the Tudor-looking one with the black and white wood, maybe I could go there. Or somewhere cheaper, I'm not bothered about breakfast, a room will do. Will you ring them and find out how much it is? I will save like mad from now on, I promise.

From what I've heard, babies don't always arrive on time so it might be more sensible to wait until Ziggy or Rebel is here. And I would LOVE to be a godmother as long as Mike won't object. He probably thinks I'll be a bad influence. I swear I won't.

I have my christening certificate here with me. Will you need it to prove I'm part of the flock? It's amongst my other worldly possessions like my birth certificate. I couldn't risk leaving anything important with Aunty Sue. Can you believe everything I own fits into a giant rucksack? It's nearly as big as me and weighs a ton but I can squash my entire life inside.

That's a bit of a shocker about Mike's secretary – are you sure she didn't top herself out of boredom? It can't be much fun working with Mike so maybe she threw herself under the car in desperation. Sorry, that's a bit crass, poor woman. Are you going to the funeral?

I'm going to hang on here until the work dries up but I'll try to ring you before I head to the Pyrenees. I worry that I'll miss one of your letters. Once I have a contact number I'll let you know.

Please take care of yourself, Wendy. I am a bit worried about you being so tired. Is it awful being preggers? I bet the thought of having a gorgeous baby keeps you going but I imagine being the size of an elephant isn't fun, and you've still got to actually give birth. Ouch.

It's probably best I'm not there – for a start you'd have slapped me by now for being sarky and then I'd faint if I saw anything gory. I remember those books in the library we used to look at – the ones with the photographs. You were fascinated but they made me feel queasy. I'm sure you will be fine though. Get lots of rest, and I hope Mike is taking good care of you, or else!

Sending you and the bump lots of love and a kiss.

I'm counting the days till I see you again.

Lots of love,

Your Nell xxx

Sealing the envelope, Nell allowed herself a smile. It made her feel giddy inside thinking of seeing Wendy again and there had been moments when Nell contemplated heading home there and then. The only thing that stopped her was the glorious sunshine and holiday atmosphere, and a rather delicious life-guard who was keeping her occupied in between shifts and the sheets. It would be stupid to give up her job and fun lifestyle and go back right now. Wendy would be fine and it wasn't as though she was on her own.

No, Nell was going to stick to the plan; get autumn and Christmas over with and wait patiently for Wendy to ring and say the baby had arrived. It was best to save any big decision-making until Nell was back in Sheffield, once she had gauged the reaction from Mike and worked out if, after all this time, he would accept her as part of Wendy's life and give her a chance. She was no threat to him. Nell had kept quiet about what happened that night in the beer garden so she really couldn't understand why he had made things so awkward and tried to force a wedge between her and Wendy. Maybe he was incredibly insecure but hopefully, a happy marriage and being a father had mellowed him. After all, Wendy said Mike had asked after her, so surely that was a good sign.

All she could do was wait and see. Fingers crossed, returning to Sheffield would be a fresh start, the chance to put down roots at last. Glancing over to her rucksack that was hooked on the back of the door – no way could she leave it on the floor to be infested by cockroaches – Nell sighed. She was definitely getting tired of her nomadic life. In the meantime, she resolved to enjoy her summer fling, sangria, sun, sea and beach, maybe even have a wintry affair in the Pyrenees with some unsuspecting fit-bit, then she was going home, to Wendy.

10

Wendy rubbed her ever-expanding stomach, in a vague attempt at conveying to her baby that the kicks were a bit naughty, and Mummy could do without them at the moment.

Tenth of December, Christmas almost here, and after that would begin the proper countdown to the birth. She glanced at the other expectant mums sitting around the room in the large antenatal clinic, and smiled. Several of them had to be nearing term, they looked like great leviathans as they adjusted their gait to accommodate the huge lumps they carried in front of them.

Some of the women hardly appeared to be pregnant at all, and she guessed they were the ones here for their inaugural visits, and they wouldn't visit again for several weeks.

Wendy took out her crochet work, and settled down to do a couple of rounds. She had found a beautiful circular shawl pattern in an antique book incongruously displayed on their shelves at home, and had immediately bought the three-ply wool it needed.

She did a few stitches and then checked back to make sure she'd remembered the pattern correctly. She felt somebody sit down in the seat beside her, and counted aloud. 'Four, five, six, seven...' she muttered.

'Sorry,' the woman said with a smile, 'did I disturb you?'

'Not at all, I was checking I was on track. It's a complicated design, and while I love crocheting, I don't enjoy pulling it back and having to redo it. But I'm good, I'm where I need to be.'

'It's beautiful. A shawl?'

Wendy held it up. 'Yes, a circular one. I thought it was so different, and baby isn't due until February so I should get it finished. The pattern's from a really old book I found on our shelf.'

'I'm doing a square one, but it didn't occur to me to bring it here. That's an hour of crocheting time wasted,' she said with a laugh. 'You been here long?'

Wendy glanced at her watch. 'About half an hour. Should be my turn soon, the last name called was a woman I followed in.'

She wrapped the wool around the hook and inserted it into the correct stitch. She had only done three stitches when she heard her name.

'Wendy Summers.'

She quickly slid the hook at random into the work, and dropped the shawl into her bag.

'At last,' she said. 'Good luck with yours.'

The woman stared at her.

The nurse was waiting for her, but Wendy paused for a moment and turned back to the woman, whose face was drained of colour. 'Are you okay?'

'What's your husband's name?' she croaked.

'Mike. Do you know him?' She turned to the nurse. 'Sorry, I'll only be a minute, this lady isn't well.'

'No, I'm fine. You go. When you come out, if I've been called in, will you wait for me?'

Wendy nodded in agreement, touched the woman's shoulder and followed the nurse through to the examination room.

After her appointment, Wendy took out the shawl, and continued to work her way around the circle. It felt so beautiful, so soft, and she could imagine her tiny baby swaddled in it. It was a peaceful five minutes, and then suddenly the woman from earlier was sitting down next to her once again.

'Thank you for waiting. I was so worried you wouldn't have...'

Wendy popped the shawl into her bag and stood.

'Shall we go for a cup of tea? You looked as though you needed one. Is everything okay?'

'With the baby? Everything's fine.'

They left the antenatal unit, and walked to the WRVS, where Wendy ordered two cups of tea. As she carried them across to the table where the woman sat, quietly waiting, and looking so serious, Wendy felt her heart go out to her.

She put the teas on the table, and held out her hand. 'Hello, my name's Wendy.'

'Hello.' The woman hesitated for a moment, then took Wendy's hand in hers. 'My name is Margaret. It used to be Margaret Summers, and the book you're making the shawl from used to be my book, in the days when I thought I might have a baby with Mike.'

Wendy sat with a thud. The room seemed to be spinning around her, and she lowered her head. Margaret stood and moved to stand by her. 'Do you need a doctor?'

Wendy shook her head, unable to speak. Slowly the whirling vortex that was the WRVS coffee shop ground to a halt and she lifted her head once more. 'You're... Margaret?'

'I am, although no longer Margaret Summers, I'm using my

maiden name of Margaret Cassidy now. I do have a partner, but despite this' – she pointed to her stomach – 'I won't marry him. Never again will I be so stupid.'

Wendy sat quietly, not because she wanted to, but because she had no idea what to say to this heavily pregnant woman.

Margaret reached across and clasped Wendy's hand. 'You have to get out. You're not safe living there. Does he hit you?'

Wendy shook her head. 'Not too often.'

'Wendy.' Margaret frowned. 'The correct answer should have been *never*. Think of your baby. If he can hit you, a grown woman, what could he do to a tiny baby who is totally defence-less and doesn't know the constant crying is making Daddy extremely angry?'

'But he threw you out because you'd had an affair!'

'No, he didn't. I left. I ran. I ran with bruises covering almost every part of my body because I had caught him with someone else, and it was the third woman. I forgave him twice. The third time was a step too far. I took one suitcase and left everything else. I couldn't go to my parents because he would have followed me there, although in all fairness, when he did turn up there demanding he see me immediately, my dad hit him. Knocked him out cold. Apparently, Dad knew about Mike screwing around with all and sundry, but hadn't told me and hadn't told Mum. I promise you, Wendy, apart from my present partner, the only man I have ever slept with is Mike Summers. There was never any affair on my part, never even any thought of sex with someone else. The biggest problem between us was I wanted a family, he didn't. Not ever. Which is why I was so shocked when they called out your name, and you said your husband was Mike. It made sense when you spoke about the old crochet book – I bought that to make some clothes for whenever I had my baby with Mike.' Margaret gave a short, bitter laugh. 'Didn't work out though, did it?'

Wendy pulled her cup of tea towards her. She needed some sort of comfort. 'What if he's changed?'

'Has he? Have you never felt there was something not right, that he was going out too much, that you hadn't seen him properly for a couple of days? Be honest, Wendy.'

'He's had an affair recently. His secretary.'

Margaret gave a sympathetic smile. 'Ever the secretary. Two out of the three were secretaries of his. The first one was Carol Weston, and I threw such a strop he sacked her. The second one was Paula Newcombe. I didn't have to throw a strop, he sacked her as well. The third one was some tart at the golf club called Frances. I didn't stay long enough to find out her surname.'

'Paula Newcombe?' Wendy gulped as she said the name.

'Yeah, she was on the news a few weeks ago because she died in a hit-and-run accident. Do you remember it?'

Wendy nodded. The guilt she thought had subsided to an itch suddenly overwhelmed her once more. 'He might have sacked her, but he set her on again. She was his secretary when she died.' Wendy could feel herself trembling. She'd tried so hard to bury the memories of that night, that grief-filled night when she had discovered her husband had a floozy on the side. The woman would still be alive if she'd stayed away from Mike, and not gone back to work for him.

Margaret leaned back in her chair. 'You know, Wendy, I adored that man. It began to die when I mentioned having a family. He wouldn't, and made it clear it was a lifetime decision. He wouldn't change his mind. I hung on and hung on, thinking he would mellow as he got older, but he didn't. The third affair, if I'm brutally honest, was a relief. I'm in a stable relationship currently, but one I wouldn't be afraid to walk from, if things deteriorated. Really and truly, it's me and my baby, and that's what Mike did for me, turned me into a proper selfish cow.'

Wendy put down her cup. 'I don't want any more of that. I feel sick. I'm going home. When's your baby due?'

'Beginning of January, so about a month from now. Yours?'

'Tenth of February. My next appointment is two weeks today.'

Margaret looked at the younger woman. 'You want to meet again?'

Wendy smiled. 'Do you mind?'

'Of course not. I'm here weekly now, because the date is so close, so that means next week and then the week after, which coincides with yours.' She took out her appointment card. 'Does three o'clock fit in with your time? We'll meet in here?'

'That's perfect. I have to go, Margaret. I need some thinking time. I presume you know my phone number if you go into early labour, or anything happens to stop you being here.'

'I do if you're still in the same house.'

'We are. I wanted to move but he said no. He seems to say no to most of my suggestions.'

Margaret stood and hugged Wendy. Margaret rummaged in her bag for a piece of paper and wrote down her own phone number. 'Keep it safe. Ring if you need me. And don't do anything to anger him, not while you're carrying this baby.'

My darling Nell,

Today is the 11th of December and I feel so happy. It's almost Christmas, everything is festive and we're going out to pick our Christmas tree this weekend.

I can't wait for the time when you arrive here. I can't book anything yet until we know the date of the baby's christening, but as soon as that happens I will book you into the bed and breakfast you mentioned. I'll pay for everything; I have my own money. It will be worth a million pounds to see you again.

Everything was really good yesterday at the hospital. I had an antenatal visit, and I was soon in and out. Took my crocheting with me, and it's beautiful. A circular shawl from a really old pattern. You'll love it when you're carrying the baby to the font wrapped in it.

I hope you have a wonderful Christmas, try not to get too drunk, and keep yourself safe. I've sent you a little gift, so I hope it arrives in one piece.

Love you,
Wendy

PS Don't worry about me with this impending birth, everything is as it should be, and I'm not afraid. Not a lot, anyway. This baby will be so welcomed into this world. It's what Mike has always wanted, and he talks about it all the time. He asked after you again last week, and I think he's really looking forward to your visit, and to meeting his son. He even has me convinced it's a boy!

11

26th December 1979Hotel Bonavista
   Meritxell
   Canillo – AD100
   Andorra
   Telephone number – do not lose this!
   Andorra 564 996 997

Hello my dearest hippo friend,

   Are you completely huge now?

   I hope you received your Christmas pressie and postcard – they don't really have proper cards over here so I had to make do. I know a snow globe is a bit naff but I thought it would remind you of me. I love them. Did you like your musicature? I love that they make things out of natural stuff so chose a wooden necklace for you. It will look fab in summer.

   Thank you, thank you, for my lovely charm bracelet. This is the only proper piece of jewellery I own. I will treasure it forever.

   I'm counting down the days until I get the phone call. The lady who runs the hotel here is lovely and she's promised to come and find *me as soon as you ring. It shouldn't cost you too much if you tell her if it's a girl or a boy and that you are okay. You will have to find out what the code for Andorra is, I have no idea.*

You haven't mentioned any baby names. Have you got a list of favourites? I take it my choices aren't suitable – can't think why.

I meant to ask you about the christening and the other godparents. Who have you picked? I hope they are good, God-fearing people like me (ha ha). Did Mike not kick up a fuss when you said you wanted your floozy friend? Are the godfathers dishy? Will I need to dress up, because I haven't got any fancy clothes? Where is the reception being held and are some of the girls from the factory going to be there? Is that enough questions?

How clever are you, doing this crocheting. I suppose you have lots of time on your hands now. I still have my lovely hat, by the way.

It sounds like you are being unusually brave about this childbirth malarkey. Will Mike be in the hospital room with you or is he going to pace the corridors like in the films?

I can't wait to push the pram, I'll pretend I'm the nanny and swan about the park while you get some rest, but I'm not changing nappies, no way, José!

Talking of José, there's a gorgeous one who delivers the laundry but at the moment I am snuggling up to Martí – it's essential, it's freezing here at night!

I hope you looked up Andorra, like I said. We're squashed in between France and Spain. Did you find me? The nearest and most easily accessible airport is Barcelona. I'll get the coach from here. I'm really looking forward to going on a plane – it will be my first time. You need to get Mike to book you a holiday to the Costa del Sol in the summer as a reward for giving him a little baby. I bet he thought he was running out of time before his bus pass came.

I'm only teasing you know, about Mike. I can't help it sometimes. I do hope me and him can bury the hatchet and put the past behind us, more so because I want you to be happy and for us all to be friends. It does sound like he's mellowed a bit, so fingers crossed.

Please don't worry if you can't reply to this or wobble down to the postbox. I will sit tight and wait for your phone call but if you do write, bloody answer my questions. Sometimes you are truly cagey, Mrs Summers, unless being preggers has completely fried your brain.

I am counting sleeps until I'm back in Olde Sheffield Towne and thinking of you every minute.

Your faraway friend, but not for long,

Nell xxx

12

December 23rd had been quiet up to the point when the telephone rang. Mike had left for work, and Wendy was busy stringing some pine cones together she had collected in the woods. She had given them a quick burst of silver spray, and thought they looked so cute.

She hoped it wasn't Mike ringing to say he would be home late; it had happened so many times over the past two weeks and her overactive imagination was leading her down different alleyways.

'Hello?'

'Wendy? Is that you?'

'Yes. Margaret?'

'It is. I didn't want to say my name and get you into trouble. I'm about to set off for hospital. I haven't felt the baby move for two days...'

There was a sob, and Wendy clutched the receiver, unsure what to say.

'God no, Margaret,' she finally managed. 'Do you need me to come and pick you up?'

'No, I'll get a taxi. It's... I'm on my own, and I'm scared. I'm sorry I've rung you, but I don't have many friends. I'll call you later from the hospital.'

'No, you won't. I'll come to get you. Tell me your address.'

Wendy quickly wrote it down on the pad, taking care not to press hard and leave an indentation. She didn't want Mike knowing anything about this relationship. 'I'll be there in a quarter of an hour. They're expecting you?'

'Yes, and as soon as I said I hadn't felt it move, they said to come in immediately.'

'I'm on my way.'

The tension in the car was palpable. Margaret was fishing a tissue from her coat pocket every minute or so to dab at her eyes, and Wendy kept reaching across and squeezing her hand.

'I know it's hard, but everything I've read says that once the baby reaches birth weight, there's little movement anyway because there simply isn't room.'

'Wendy, there's nothing at all.'

'Your partner... I'm sorry, you didn't mention his name, does he know what's happening?'

Margaret shook her head and stared out of the window. 'He's gone. He left last week. We had a massive argument and I told him to get out. I've no idea where he is, and don't want to know.' She rubbed her stomach. 'Come on, little one,' she whispered, 'give Mummy a little kick.'

Wendy didn't leave Margaret's side. She watched as the midwife helped her lay on her back on the examination table, and then Wendy waited with bated breath as the trumpet was held against Margaret's stomach, time and time again.

'I need to get a doctor,' the midwife said, 'and I'm going to get an electronic heartbeat monitor.'

'Please,' Margaret implored. 'Can you hear anything?'

'Let's wait and see what the doctor says.'

Wendy clung onto Margaret's hand, hardly able to comprehend the enormity of what was happening. Surely they could do something.

The door swung open. 'Hi, I'm Dr Khan. I'm going to listen to this baby, and see what's going on.'

Once again the trumpet was used in different areas of Margaret's abdomen, and then he asked for the electronic monitor.

He moved it around the stomach. Absolute silence, and Margaret couldn't hold it in any longer. 'There's no heartbeat,' she wailed.

'Ssh,' the doctor said. 'Listen. This machine will pick up the faintest sound. Let's listen.'

He was about to give up when he heard it. 'There,' he said triumphantly. 'Very faint and slow, but let's get this baby out now. I want theatre made ready immediately.' He took hold of Margaret's hand. 'I promise I will do my best to save this little one, but the heartbeat is only just there. You'll be in theatre in five minutes.'

He left the room, and Margaret was wheeled out. Wendy followed until they reached the theatre doors, and then she sat in the waiting area.

It was an hour before someone arrived to take Wendy through to Margaret. She was propped up in bed, holding a pink wrapped baby.

Wendy felt confused. The nurse had explained the baby had only lived for five minutes, and yet...

Margaret lifted a hand in acknowledgement of Wendy's presence, but couldn't smile.

'Natalie didn't make it,' she whispered. 'So beautiful, but she wasn't meant to be in this world.' Margaret pulled back the edge of the shawl, and Wendy felt the tears running down her cheeks.

'Oh Margaret, she's lovely. Have they given any reason...?'

'They think her lungs didn't develop properly. I called her Natalie because it means "born on Christmas Day", but I think the 23rd is close enough. My Christmas baby.' The sobs began deep inside her, and Wendy placed her arms around Margaret's heaving shoulders.

They sat for a long time holding each other, with Margaret cradling her baby, determined not to put her down until someone came to take her away.

When they did, Margaret collapsed. Sedatives were given, and Wendy left her in the compassionate care of the nurses.

Wendy's mind was in a whirl. She was home four hours after leaving to take Margaret to the hospital, and yet so much had happened in those four hours, it actually felt like a week.

She made a massive cup of tea, and sat at the kitchen table, deeply sucked down into the darkest of thoughts. What if... no, surely it was a rare thing, the death of a baby that had almost reached full term... Wendy picked up the receiver and dialled her midwife, talking through tears and telling her the activities of the day. There was little Rosa Yelland could do to comfort Wendy, but she did keep stressing that there must be calm, she didn't want complications because of high blood pressure.

· · ·

Wendy was asleep on the sofa when Mike walked in. 'What the...?' he said, as he saw his wife curled up with a blanket over her. There was no food smell, and he walked through to the kitchen to see what preparations there had been. None.

He stormed back into the lounge and shook her shoulder roughly. 'Hey, Wendy! There's no food.'

Wendy felt drained. She struggled to remember what she should be doing, and looked at Mike.

'What?'

'Food! I'm hungry, and there doesn't seem to be anything happening on that front.'

'I'm tired, Mike,' she said quietly. 'I'm not far off eight months pregnant, and I'm tired.'

'I'll have to go out then,' he said, his voice getting ever louder. 'And see if you can make yourself a bit more presentable before I get back.'

He left the room and she heard the front door slam, followed by the sound of his car engine starting.

Christmas Eve and Christmas Day were non-happenings in Wendy's head. She kept remembering the tiny baby who had only lived for five minutes, and the woman who had carried her and lost her. Wendy could tell no one; there was nobody to tell.

She was in bed by nine on the evening of Boxing Day, feeling grateful that the festive season was at an end. New Year's Eve to get through and Mike would be back at work, and she could get on with life.

The crocheted shawl was almost finished, with a couple more rounds to go, and yet she had no feelings towards it. What if the baby didn't survive? What if it happened as Margaret's had happened? How would she cope? Wendy had managed to ring Margaret once, but it was obvious she was deeply depressed, and she promised she would drive over to visit as soon as Christmas was out of the way.

New Year's Day, Mike hit her. The shirt he wanted to wear was creased from being hung in the wardrobe incorrectly.

She landed awkwardly on the bed, and pain shot up her back. Curling her arms around her stomach, she protected her child and stared at him. She said nothing, and he slammed out of the bedroom and down the stairs, carrying the shirt that had offended his sensibilities.

'Get down here and get this fucking ironed,' he called from the bottom of the stairs. She crawled off the bed and stood upright, testing each joint carefully.

Going downstairs was an effort, but she made it to the bottom without further problems, and went into the kitchen. He had taken the iron out of the pantry, but there was no sign of the ironing board. It dawned on her that he didn't know where she kept it.

She went and got it, still without speaking, plugged in the iron and ironed the shirt. She handed it to him and he looked at her.

'Sorry.'

She said nothing in response.

'I said sorry.'

'I heard you.'

He shrugged on the shirt, put on his jacket and went down the hall.

He stopped at the front door. 'I'll be back before midnight.'

She said nothing, so he slammed the door with a huge crash as he left the house. She knew he was going to see a woman; she didn't yet know who, but she would. It briefly occurred to her that she no longer had the desire to confront any more of his floozies, no desire to want them dead, only him.

2 January 1980

My darling Nell,

What a welcome surprise your letter was. And yes, I am a huge hippo. I know you would laugh at me. What a lot of questions you've asked!

Thank you so much for everything you sent in the parcel, and I truly love my snow globe. I will look at it and think of you.

I have put your telephone number on the pad by the phone, you will know almost as soon as I do what my baby is! It may be Mike who rings you, we will see. I had to ring Directory Enquiries for the code for Andorra.

I've tried coming up with a name that's a bit different for the baby, but so far nothing is standing out. I may have to revert to your choices!

So far, we haven't picked any other godparents, because until the baby is born we won't know whether we need two men and one woman, or two women and one man. Either way, you're in the mix no matter what. I think Mike is considering his brother, so sorry, I can't fulfil your dishy man request. And he's married!

You do need to look smart, but I'm sure you'll have something that will do. Don't go to any expense, I'm sure our baby won't care what you're wearing.

Mike put his foot down when I suggested inviting the girls from the factory, so no, nobody will be there. It's family and his friends only – oh, and you, my lovely best friend.

I haven't asked Mike if he wants to be there at the birth. He's so busy at work, and seems to be out such a lot in the evenings; I rarely have a full conversation with him. I think I'd rather be on my own anyway, where I can swear without getting black looks.

Mike is looking forward to seeing you, and I'm not being cagey! I tell you all sorts of things that happen in my life. Nothing much has happened over Christmas though, and the truth of it is we had a quiet one because I can't move around so much now.

See you soon, my best friend,
Wendy hippo

13

Something wasn't right, Nell could sense it. She'd read Wendy's letter over and over, and it was as though some strange vibration was coming through in the words, across the miles and getting under her skin. Nell's cosmic musings had nothing to do with spending too much time lying on beaches gazing at the stars with her hippy friends, or the joint that she'd shared with Martí earlier that evening.

Despite her denial, Wendy *was* being cagey and no, she certainly *didn't* tell Nell all sorts of things about her life because reading between the meagre lines in her letters, Wendy didn't sodding well have one.

Nell was watching the blizzard from her bedroom window. Huge fluffy flakes had been falling throughout the day, getting heavier by the hour, sending even the most experienced skiers indoors. Now, a sheet of white obscured Nell's normally unbroken view of the skiing village so that the golden glow from the restaurants and chalets was barely visible.

Shivering, Nell pulled the curtains shut and grabbed a blanket from the back of the chair before wrapping it around her shoulders. Her room was heated but the system was old and inadequate, although the rustic furnishings made it feel warmer than it was, homely even. In fact, it was one of the nicest places she'd ever stayed and the owner, Alba, a jolly woman, was the kindest boss she'd worked for. Surprisingly, Nell did feel rather settled there, which was a first. The work was repetitive, cleaning rooms and waiting on in the restaurant, but she preferred it to being a chalet maid, at the beck and call of demanding toffs who more often than not needed to learn some manners and humility. Here, Alba was the boss and Nell only answered to her.

Nell flopped onto the bed and rested against her pillows before returning to thoughts of Wendy. As she touched the tiny silver charms on her bracelet one by one, the 21st key, the wishing well, the bell, the house, and finally the heart, crazy as it seemed, Nell was sure they were trying to tell her something. To prove her point, she jumped off the bed and unhooked her rucksack from the door and rummaged to the bottom, pulling out the carrier bag that rested there. It contained every letter she had received from Wendy, along with postcards and correspondence from her growing army of long-distance seasonaires.

Going back to the bed, Nell went through them one by one, looking for clues.

She remembered suggesting to Wendy that she should make friends at antenatal classes but she hadn't even mentioned going there or what they did, let alone the names of other women at the clinic.

And Nell was sure she'd asked what Wendy did all day, apart from bloody crocheting baby clothes; again, nothing. No talk of days out, weekend trips, visiting the in-laws, going to the cinema, romantic meals in fancy restaurants. It wasn't like they were skint so why weren't they having fun before their lives were turned upside down by a baby?

Nell's eyes skimmed over the pages, flicking each sheet onto the bed when she drew a blank. Baby names – that was another thing that puzzled her. One minute Wendy said Mike talked about the baby all the time and it was all he'd ever wanted but in the latest letter, she said they hadn't picked names or godparents, or even discussed if he was going to be at the birth. That really was weird. What on earth did they talk about over dinner, when they were cuddled up in bed at night or while they watched telly, sitting in their lounge on their posh sofas? Surely these things were important.

Then there was that woman, what was she called... Paula, Mike's secretary who was killed. Not a peep about her, or if they'd gone to the funeral, or caught the driver. That was odd because if Wendy's life was truly as boring as Nell suspected, surely a bit of grave gossip would liven things up. Wendy didn't gossip anymore, about anything.

What had really set Nell's mind ticking were Wendy's final comments about Mike being out a lot in the evenings. Why? Where did he go? Wendy didn't say he was doing anything specific, like a hobby, and Nell didn't think trainspotters went out at night. But what sent shivers down Nell's spine were the final remarks, that Wendy would rather be on her own, and why would she be swearing? She said Mike gave her black looks, that wasn't good, not good at all. Nell reread the sentence again, focusing on the part about being on her own – did Wendy mean in the evenings or generally, permanently even?

Nell pulled the blanket around her shoulders and stood. She was restless and wished she'd asked Martí for another joint but instead of oblivion, Nell paced the room trying to piece everything together.

Had she sensed defensiveness in Wendy's denial about being cagey? Yes, she had. But the facts spoke for themselves. They were right there in black and white, or the lack of it. Wendy was unhappy, Nell knew.

What confused her most was why Wendy hadn't confided in her if something was wrong. They had shared so many secrets, albeit silly childhood ones, and when it came to talking through their fears or worries, their hopes and crazy dreams, there had been no holds barred... until Mike. That's when everything changed. It had seemed like overnight; Wendy grew up and moved a step away from Nell. Mike was like a huge wedge, widening the gap, causing problems at every turn.

Nell knew he was wrong for Wendy, for a zillion reasons, and she had been honest enough to tell her best friend how she felt. The messenger had almost been shot but they weathered the storm and in the end, Wendy's stubborn nature actually saved their friendship.

Nell smiled, remembering her quietly determined friend who always got her way, eventually. Wendy was the complete opposite to flighty, eager Nell who barged into situations head on, getting into scrapes then looking to Wendy for help. And she was always there to make it right. Wendy wasn't one to make a fuss or draw attention to herself. She didn't overreact in arguments and instead thought things through; she bided her time, never shouted or stormed off, never made mistakes... until Mike.

That was it! Nell realised why Wendy was keeping things to herself. Pride, pure and simple. It was so obvious now.

Wendy had told Nell she was getting the pill but left it too late and fell pregnant. Whatever her feelings for Mike at the time, where the baby was concerned she had no option but to get on with it.

If Nell knew one thing about her friend it was that she wasn't a quitter and would hold her head up, facing the world and the consequences in her own steely way. How awful must it be to admit you'd made a mistake, especially with something huge like marriage? Nell immediately saw the irony in her own question because she too was guilty of exactly the same.

How many times had she wanted to tell Wendy she was fed up, desperately homesick? Nell had spent hours crying into her pillow, wishing she'd done things differently, bloody listened to her best friend and stayed in Sheffield. But instead of telling the truth, pride had got in the way and Nell had painted a fake but fabulous picture of a life on the road. So was Wendy also painting a fake and fabulous picture of married life? Were they both liars?

But what could Nell do? Glancing at her rucksack, she was tempted to pack up there and then and race back to Sheffield. The baby was due any time so at least Nell would be around, in case her fears were unfounded.

Sitting down on the bed, Nell gathered the sheets of daisy paper and her thoughts. She had to be sensible and think this through. Wendy would wire the money or the ticket straight away if Nell asked but once she got to Sheffield, she had nowhere to stay apart from the guest house. Delving into her rucksack again, Nell pulled out a battered map of Europe and from between the folds, extracted an envelope that contained her savings. Would this be enough to tide her over until she could get a job? Nell could look for pub work as soon as she arrived, anything would do. It was worth taking the chance, for Wendy, and if push came to shove, Nell would swallow her pride and go to her Aunty Sue's.

Looking at her watch, Nell saw it was far too late to ring Wendy and anyway, he would be there. Crawling into bed and covering herself with the blankets, Nell turned off the bedside lamp and decided to wait until morning, then start to make arrangements. Even though her mind was buzzing, she tried to switch off, her body was tired and she had an early start. Soon her eyes drooped and sleep arrived to ease her worries for a while.

. . .

Outside, the snow continued to fall, layer upon layer, like lies upon lies. Roads around the town gradually disappeared from view, becoming impassable as they merged into the surrounding fields and slopes. Trees sagged and boughs strained while the mighty Pyrenees shouldered the burden of dense frozen ice that was topped by virgin snow, until it became too much to bear.

In the early hours of the morning, as Nell dreamt of Wendy and home, dark craggy peaks and grey city rooftops, she didn't hear the whoomph as powdery snow compressed, then slid across layers of ice. Nor did the thunderous sound of the avalanche as it tumbled down the mountain, watched only by the moon and stars from an inky black sky, disturb her or the residents of the hotel.

But when Nell was woken early the next morning by Alba, asking her to hurry downstairs as she was needed in the kitchen, she found the hotel abuzz with news of an avalanche. The town was cut off and it would take days to clear the roads of rocks, ice and debris that had been hurled from the mountainside.

While Nell helped to prepare food and drinks for the volunteers and emergency services, she prayed nobody had lost their lives during the night. She also prayed for her friend who was so many miles away and out of reach. Nell was trapped and her precious Wendy was going to have to manage for a bit longer, alone.

14

City Road Cemetery, with its imposing stone-built entrance, was eerily quiet as the hearse and funeral car passed under the archway and turned left, heading towards the children's section. So many tiny graves, so much colour from toys and flowers, so much love.

Both drivers exited their vehicles, and Margaret and Wendy were helped from the Daimler. The other driver moved to the back of his hearse and lifted the tailgate. Inside was the tiniest of coffins, topped with a heart-shaped wreath of pink and white carnations.

Two further cars pulled up behind, and Wendy looked back at the occupants. She recognised Margaret's neighbour, and presumed the occupant of the second car was a friend. Both women moved towards Margaret, and hugged her.

The funeral directors waited patiently, until it was the right time to move towards the newly dug grave.

The vicar walked towards Margaret and took hold of her hand. 'We're ready whenever you are, Margaret. Take your time.'

Margaret gave a slight nod and looked towards Wendy.

'Are you ready?' Wendy asked, not prepared to allow anybody to bully her new-found friend into anything.

'I am,' she said, and took Wendy's hand as they moved to stand behind the man lifting the coffin from the back of the hearse.

The four women formed a small procession, led by the vicar and the man carrying the coffin. They arrived at the edge of what seemed to be such a deep hole for such a tiny occupant, and gathered around.

Tears were flowing freely down Margaret's face, and she clung to Wendy. Margaret knew she had made the right decision to have a graveside service; she doubted she would have been able to live through a service in church, or even at the crematorium, then have to bury her baby at the end of it. This way felt right; this way was what she wanted.

In the end, Margaret heard nothing of the service. The words hovered in the air, but she was in such a traumatised state all eyes were on her. Finally, the coffin was lowered, their roses were dropped in, and that small act finished Margaret off.

She stumbled back to the car, unable to take any more, and climbed into the Daimler. The hearse had disappeared, and that in itself caused more tears. It almost felt to her that while the hearse was still there, so was Natalie.

Wendy thanked the vicar, who smiled gently and told her to follow her friend. 'Tell her I'll pop round and see her later in the week,' the vicar said. 'But she needs you today.'

Wendy nodded, and went to join Margaret. The other two

ladies stayed a couple of minutes at the graveside, then went to their own cars.

Within ten minutes the grave was being filled in, with the pretty wreath placed carefully on top, along with three smaller sprays of white flowers from the other attendees. Snowflakes gently fell, and by mid-afternoon the new grave looked exactly the same as the others in the special area, a pristine white mound.

Wendy stayed with a distraught Margaret, afraid to leave her. They used many teabags that afternoon, talked about inconsequential rubbish because they were afraid to touch on the one thing that mattered above all else: Natalie.

Wendy tried not to stroke her own baby bump when the baby moved; the sense of guilt for being pregnant when Margaret had lost everything was overwhelming. They watched as the snow grew deeper and deeper, and eventually Wendy gave in.

'Margaret, I think I'd better make a move, or I'll never get home.'

'You can stay. Please don't risk an accident.'

'I can't. How would I explain this to Mike? He doesn't even know I've gone out, and our friendship has to remain secret. You know what he'd be like if he found out anything about today.'

She stood and went to get her coat. 'When I get home I'll ring you and let you know I'm safe. Can I do anything for you before I go?'

Margaret shook her head. 'No, I'll be fine, honestly. Let the phone ring twice, then I'll know you're home. I'll not answer it, because it will show on your bill. Let's not give him any ammunition. Do the same again if he goes out and I'll ring you.'

They walked to the door together, and Wendy kissed her. 'Take care, Margaret. I'll come and see you as soon as the roads clear.'

Margaret gave a small smile, the first of the day. 'Let's hope you don't go into labour until they clear. You've only got about three weeks, so really it could happen anytime.'

They hugged, and Wendy walked carefully out to her car. She cleared the snow as much as she could, then waved at Margaret, who was standing in the lounge window watching her. Wendy negotiated the side road with difficulty, but the main roads had been gritted and she made good time getting home.

Her home was on a small side road, on an incline, and she cursed out loud as the car slipped backwards. 'Bloody Sheffield hills,' she muttered, and breathed a sigh of relief as the car came to a halt.

She could see that a little higher up the road there was another struggling car, so she decided to abandon hers. It had come to rest at the kerb, so she picked up her bag and got out of the car. She locked it and trudged up the middle of the road, following the tyre marks she had made. The other car had been abandoned, and she shook her hair to get rid of the snowflakes that were accumulating. She had had the thought *only another twenty-five yards or so* when she felt her foot go from under her, and she went down with a thud.

She sat for a moment, feeling as though there was no breath left in her body. She knew she had no chance of getting back onto her feet with any semblance of elegance, so she slowly rolled over until she was on her knees. She crawled to where she knew the kerb was, and levered herself upright, then went down with another crash as pain shot through her body. She couldn't support her weight on her right ankle.

'Shit,' she said, and stayed where she was, waiting for the agony to subside. She looked around and there was no one. The snow was, if anything, increasing in volume and she knew she had no choice. She would have to crawl.

It took half an hour and by the time she reached the driveway she was soaking, shivering and her knees felt raw. Mike's car was there.

She stared in horror, frantically trying to come up with a reason for her being out. The door opened and he stood there, staring at her on her hands and knees.

'Get up, you stupid woman. It's not that bad.'

'Please, Mike, help me up. I can't put my weight on my right ankle. I left my car at the bottom of the road because I couldn't drive it up, but I fell. I need help.'

'Do it yourself,' he said, and turned to walk back into the house.

Wendy crawled towards the steps, and levered herself up and into the hall. She managed to get herself onto the hall chair, and sat there feeling mind-numbingly exhausted.

Mike came from the kitchen and threw her a towel. 'Dry your hair, woman, you're dripping all over the carpet. And where the fuck have you been? I've been home hours; it was obvious it was going to come down heavily.'

'I went to Mothercare,' she lied.

'And bought what? Do I need to go out in this and bring it from your car?'

'No,' she said quietly, trying to calm him down. 'I didn't get anything. The snow was getting really bad, so I came back home. It's taken forever, there's hold-ups everywhere. I've been an hour getting from where I left my car at the bottom of the road. I've had to crawl all the way.'

She hoped she was covering enough hours in her explanation. The last thing she wanted him knowing about was Natalie's funeral.

'Mike, I think I need to go to A & E. I really can't put my foot to the floor.'

'Then get a taxi,' he said. 'I'm not going out in this.'

He left her sitting there and walked into the kitchen. 'And don't be long before you start putting a meal together. I'm hungry.' He slammed the door, and she leaned her head against the console table to her right. She pulled on the cable, and the telephone moved towards her.

From memory, because she daren't write it down, she dialled Margaret's number, let it ring twice then replaced the receiver. The kitchen door flew open and he stared at her.

'Who the fuck are you ringing?'

She wrapped her arms around her stomach. 'A taxi,' she whispered, 'but I couldn't remember the number. I need to look it up.'

'They'll not come out in this, silly cow. I'll go and get a bowl of water; you can soak the ankle for a bit. I'll see if we've got a bandage, and if we haven't I'll cut up that woolly thing you've been making and wrap it up in that.'

Wendy said nothing, and a couple of minutes later, Mike returned with a bowl of hot water. She put her foot in it and screamed. Not only was her ankle resembling a melon, the entire foot was bright red.

He laughed, and once more headed for the kitchen. 'I'd leave it to cool for a bit,' he called.

Wendy reflected in mild shock that it seemed Mike had relented somewhat. He opened two tins of soup for their evening meal, not knowing how to do anything else, and eventually found a bandage. He strapped the ankle up for her, and then went out to the shed, returning a minute later with a cobweb-shrouded walking stick.

He cleaned it and handed it to her. 'I think it was Dad's. It might help you hobble around.'

'Thank you,' she said, expecting some nastiness to follow. It didn't.

Her thoughts drifted to Margaret, and Wendy's eyes prickled with tears. Under normal circumstances, Mike would have gone out for some reason or another, and Wendy would have been able to speak to Margaret. Her ringing twice a second time that night to indicate he had gone out had meant Margaret could ring her and they could talk, but tonight there had been no second double ring. Margaret was alone on the day she had buried her daughter.

Wendy pulled a cushion towards her and stuffed it around her back. Backache had settled in, and she assumed it was from the falls. She tried to massage herself, but it didn't help. Should she ask Mike for a hot water bottle? She decided against it. He was comfily settled on the sofa, and his mood had mellowed; best leave him alone.

She was starting to doze, and decided she would be better in bed. She still had the stairs to negotiate, but the pain had settled in her ankle and she hoped the climb wouldn't be too difficult.

'I'm going to bed, Mike.'

'Okay.' He was reading a book, and his voice was muffled.

She stood, and leaned on the walking stick. Hobbling carefully, she moved into the kitchen to get a drink to take up with her. Her back was becoming more painful by the minute, and she rubbed it as she leaned over the sink.

She gasped as fluid gushed out of her and onto the kitchen floor.

'Mike! Mike! We have a problem!'

She heard him mutter, and he came through the kitchen door.

'What now?'

'My waters have broken.'

He stared at her. 'No, Wendy, we don't have a problem. You do.'

15

Alba had taken the call from the hospital early that morning and after thanking the nice nurse for the message, bounded up the stairs to tell Nell that her friend in England had had a baby girl.

Even though she'd been expecting the call, picturing Wendy all those miles away in a hospital, with a babe in her arms, having gone through whatever women went through giving birth, brought on more than tears. Nell was overcome with homesickness and wanted to be close to Wendy, which was why she broke the news to Alba that when she headed home for the christening, she wouldn't be coming back.

Used to the comings and goings of her seasonaires, Alba didn't seem to take the news too badly and being of a kindly nature, even allowed Nell to use the office phone to make a quick call to the hospital. Unfortunately, Wendy was sleeping when she rang and it would be four more days until Nell heard the weepy voice of her dearest friend.

· · ·

When Alba came rushing into the dining room and told Nell to hurry, there was a call from England, serving breakfast was forgotten.

'Wendy, I'm so glad you called. I've been thinking of you constantly. How are you? How's Jessica?' Nell was bubbling with excitement but when she heard the voice at the other end, the fizz went flat.

'I'm fine, and so is Jessica.' There was a long silence apart from the sobbing and sniffing sounds at the other end of the phone.

'Wendy, what on earth's the matter? Please don't cry... tell me what's wrong? You should be happy, has something happened?' Nell was slightly panicked and those miles seemed to be stretching further with each second.

Nell listened to Wendy blow her nose and when she eventually spoke, she sounded slightly calmer and managed to squeal out a sentence.

'No, nothing's happened, but I want you to come home, Nell. Please use the money I sent and book the tickets as soon as you can. I'm so lonely and I don't think I can manage on my own. It's nothing like I imagined, I need you and I miss you so much.'

Nell had gleaned from snippets here and there that it could be a shock going home with a baby, especially the first time around, or maybe Wendy had those baby blues everyone talked about. Nell's head was in a spin.

'Of course I will. I'll do it right away and let you know when I'll arrive. But I don't understand, what isn't like you imagined... having a baby?' When Nell got her answer it wasn't quite what she'd expected.

'Everything, absolutely everything.'

The day Nell flew into Manchester she was a bag of nerves, so much so they had ruined her first time on an aeroplane, something she had been so looking forward to. With each air mile, her confidence dribbled away and by the time she'd collected her almost bursting rucksack and set off towards passport control, Nell was completely overwhelmed and self-conscious. Her jeans had seen better days, as had her walking boots and winter coat and she felt like a scruff compared to some of the other travellers.

Nell had planned to get the National Express coach up to Sheffield but apparently Mike had insisted he drive to Manchester Airport to collect her. She suspected that Wendy was really behind it. The mere thought of spending over an hour in a car with a man Nell detested was not the start to her homecoming she had wanted, but what could she do? Wendy had sounded pleased he'd offered and a lot more cheery when they'd made final arrangements over the phone. So while Nell remained dubious, she went along with it, to keep the peace.

Literally dreading what was to come, seeing Mike's miserable face for a start, Nell took her passport from the stern official and followed the other passengers. Summoning her courage, she stepped through the automatic sliding door and searched the crowd, a sea of strangers standing behind the barriers on either side. When she heard someone call her name, Nell turned her head towards the sound and was met by Mike's smiling face, waving enthusiastically and trying to grab her attention. If this didn't nonplus Nell, the helpful man who insisted on taking her rucksack which he heaved onto his shoulders, and then asked if she wanted a warm drink in the café before they headed off, certainly did.

As he led her to his car, chatting most of the way about the clear road conditions and asking if she'd enjoyed the flight, Nell suspected someone had bodysnatched Mike and replaced him with a rather nice bloke. By the time she was belted up and heading towards the motorway, Nell was convinced of it.

'Look, Nell, I'm glad we've got this chance to talk alone because I wanted to clear the air between us. We got off to a bad start and I really would like to make amends and give it another go, that's if you can forgive me for being such a grumpy so-and-so before you left?'

Nell was taken aback by Mike's direct approach and also his admission, so really, what could she say?

'Of course I want to start over and I'm sorry too. I didn't help matters by acting like a jealous friend so let's wipe the slate clean and move on. The least said the better.' It was a bit cringeworthy, more so because they were trapped inside a car therefore Nell wanted to close the conversation down.

'That's great, I'm relieved, I can tell you and I'm sure Wendy will be too. The poor thing's had a tough time lately, what with the baby coming early and this touch of what the midwife calls baby blues. Wendy really isn't coping but I'm sure seeing you will be just the thing to cheer her up.'

Nell twisted in her seat slightly, and noticed the concerned look on Mike's face when he glanced over, before he smiled warmly.

'Oh no, what's wrong, why isn't she coping? She was a bit weepy during one of our conversations but I put that down to tiredness. She seemed fine last time we spoke.'

'Wendy is good at hiding her feelings, Nell, and likes to put on a front, you know, with our friends and her parents but once we are alone, I see a different side and I have to admit it's been a bit of a trial since we brought Jessica home. Sometimes I can't do right for wrong and I'm at my wits end.'

'Why? I don't understand.' Nell was really rather shocked at Mike's tone because he sounded somewhat sad and a bit defeated.

'Oh you know, mood swings, bouts of tearfulness and terrible fatigue. Sometimes she has to drag herself out of bed after a bad night. Jessica isn't sleeping too well and keeps us both awake. I try to do my bit but I have to go to work.'

'Yes, I'm sure it's hard if you're both up all night, but doesn't Wendy's mum help out? Surely she's lending a hand.'

'That's the thing, Wendy insists she can cope by herself and has been a bit snippy with her parents, and me most of all, but the fact of the matter is she's struggling with running the house and looking after a baby.'

Nell tried to lift his spirits. 'I'm here now so I can muck in and give Wendy some time off, whether she likes it or not. Then you can concentrate on work and hopefully, things will settle down.'

'I'd appreciate that, I really would, because she's so up and down and can say the most awful things when she's angry. I'm public enemy number one most of the time... I don't know whether I'm coming or going and I'm getting worried about her.'

'Fingers crossed we can sort it out. I'm so looking forward to seeing her again and I'm glad I came back early.'

'Me too. And thanks for listening to me going on with myself but I really haven't had anyone to talk to about this. It's not something I'd discuss with another man and anyway, I don't think Wendy would be too pleased if she knew I'd been disloyal.'

'Don't worry, this is between the two of us. I promise I won't say a word.'

By the time they pulled onto the drive, Nell was itching to see Wendy and give her the biggest hug in the world. When Mike opened the front door, Nell heard the sound of Jessica crying upstairs, then his voice calling out to Wendy.

'Darling, look who's here, the wanderer has returned.'

Within seconds, Wendy appeared at the top of the stairs which she took at speed, almost skimming each one in her haste to hug Nell. It felt so good to hold Wendy again, and even though her bones felt jagged and her body trembled through the tears, Nell felt such comfort, being there with her best friend. As if she'd come home.

In the days that followed, Mike had been a pleasure to be around. Not only was he attentive to Wendy who hadn't shown any of the traits he'd described, he simply adored Jessica. It was plain to see. Maybe the 'Nell effect' had calmed things down because Wendy accepted help and while she napped, the house was cleaned and the ironing done, and Mike had a cooked meal waiting for him.

When it was suggested, Nell turned down the offer of the spare room, insisting to Mike that they were a little family of three and needed space. Instead, every night after dinner he drove Nell back to the B & B, thanking her profusely for bringing calm and order to their lives. She'd even managed to persuade him to invite a couple of Wendy's old work friends along to the christening, insisting that it would be fun and a great surprise. He'd agreed almost instantly and left Nell to sort it.

Still conscious of how worried she had been about Wendy after her tearful phone call, and bearing Mike's concerns in mind, over tea and crumpets in the local café, Nell had tentatively broached the subject.

'I wanted to say that even though I had my doubts, you and Mike seem really happy and I'm so pleased for you both. I have to admit you did have me worried when you rang me at the hotel. I suspected he was being an arse and unsupportive but I can see I was wrong. So what was the matter, were you having a bad day?'

Wendy sighed. 'Of course I was having a bad day. This new Mike is exactly that, a new Mike. I have no idea why, and I'm not confident it'll continue, but I'm taking each day as it comes. Accept him for how he is with you, Nell, but for heaven's sake don't be taken in by him. For the moment he is being wonderful, and I am happy with that, but I'm not complacent.'

Placated by Wendy's assurances but hearing the impatience in her voice, Nell decided against delving further. Mike had insinuated that Wendy was prone to anger and the last thing Nell wanted was for her to take the huff, so instead Nell chose to get another pot of tea. While she waited at the counter, Nell watched Wendy as she rocked Jessica to and fro.

There was a faraway look in Wendy's eyes, one Nell had noticed a few times, and it made her wonder if she was putting up a front, like Mike said she did. On the outside, apart from being skinnier and a bit frumpy, Wendy hadn't changed too much; on the inside, maybe she had. It was probably to do with living in the real world and not one where you flitted across Europe on a whim. Come to think of it, now and then, Nell thought she sensed a kind of detachment, a switching off perhaps, and the faintest hint of sadness in Wendy's eyes.

Aware of her propensity for delving too deeply into the human psyche, something Nell conveniently blamed on weed and her hippy friends, she forced her mind to the positive and obvious.

Wendy looked much perkier than she had when Nell arrived. She had a spring in her step and colour in her cheeks, probably due to the walks in the park they took together where they chatted about the good old days and Nell's adventures.

They'd agreed not to talk of the future, to enjoy being together and then once the christening was over, Nell would decide whether to stay, or head off into the world. She knew Wendy desperately wanted her to remain in Sheffield, so Nell kept her secret plans to herself. It would be a post-christening surprise.

Nell had been searching the newspaper for suitable work and there were plenty of menial jobs she could turn her hand to, but it was accommodation that proved a sticking point. She desperately wanted a place to call her own, but rents were too high in decent areas for a single girl on a low wage. Then she'd spotted a vacancy for a caretaker in a newly built block of city apartments, and it came with a small self-contained flat.

It was perfect and Nell was well equipped for the role. The lady who interviewed her had been most impressed and promised to ring early the following week to let her know. Nell had everything crossed but didn't want to get her own or Wendy's hopes up. All being well though, she would soon have a job and a place to stay but best of all, she'd be close to Wendy and thanks to Mike's transformation, be welcome in their home and lives.

Nell scrutinised her appearance in the mirror, smoothing down the soft fabric of the olive-green jumpsuit, then turning sideways, making sure she looked presentable from every angle. The charm bracelet Wendy had bought her for Christmas jangled at Nell's wrist, a classy embellishment, the only seriously decent thing she owned.

Yes, she would do, even though in normal circumstances she wouldn't be seen dead in such a get-up. Nell loathed the padded shoulders and long sleeves that puffed out at the cuff, not to mention the black high heels she'd been forced to buy because she had sod all to match. The jumpsuit was no problem and would be going straight back to C&A as soon as it opened the next morning. Nell had left the tag on and tucked it inside the collar so nobody would see. It was a bit scratchy but she'd have to grin and bear it. The shoes were another matter because there was no way she could get through the day without the soles getting scuffed and she'd had to remove the sticky white price labels as they stood out a mile.

Wendy had offered to pay for a new outfit but Nell refused, not after she'd shelled out for her flight and lodgings, so there was no other option than to use some of her savings to buy a respectable outfit for the christening. The last thing she wanted was to embarrass Wendy, or Mike for that matter. Nell thought back to the events of the past few weeks and apart from the arrival of beautiful baby Jessica, albeit earlier than expected, the other surprise had been Mike's personality transplant.

Satisfied she looked okay, Nell tottered over to the bedside table where her card and christening present lay next to the C&A receipt. Tucking the receipt under the base of the lamp, Nell picked up the clutch bag she'd borrowed from Wendy and headed towards the door. She would have to manage without a coat as she didn't have a smart one, and Wendy's were too short in the sleeve so Nell would have to shiver her way through the service.

Making her way carefully downstairs in case she tripped, Nell shouted goodbye to Mrs White, the owner of the B & B, then waited by the door, watching out for Mike's car. He and Wendy were picking her up on the way to the church.

Spotting Mike's car as it turned the corner, Nell took a quick look in the hall mirror and opened the front door. As she approached the car, she saw Wendy wave and give her the thumbs up, clearly impressed by how Nell had scrubbed up. Not only that, as she passed the driver's door, she felt rather chuffed by Mike's appreciative smile.

Forcing the thought from her mind, Nell climbed into the back seat and after fastening the safety belt, fussed over Jessica who looked adorable in her silk and lace christening gown. The cooing baby provided a welcome distraction, that and Wendy's chatter about the caterers, and hoping it wouldn't rain and spoil the photos. It also helped Nell avoid Mike's gaze, who seemed to be watching her the whole time, and that rather odd fluttery feeling it gave her whenever their eyes met.

16

'Margaret? It's so good to hear your voice. Did you enjoy your holiday?'

Margaret paused before answering. 'It was good. But are you okay? You're picking up a bit? So it's Monday, the day after Jessica's big day.' She laughed. 'Was it good?'

Wendy bit her lip. 'The christening itself was good, and Jess was well behaved. It's... Mike. I can't forgive him. He left me to crawl around having contractions and did nothing to help. He didn't even go and look for the ambulance. I had to go and let the medical people in, he did nothing.'

'Wendy, your time will come with that apology for a man. Your friend is looking after you?'

'Yes, she's not been in touch this morning, but it was a late night last night so I'm assuming she's sleeping it off. Mike's at work so I jumped at the chance to ring you. I've popped Jessica in the pram, and we've come out for a walk so I could use the phone box. He goes through that damn phone bill with a toothcomb, but he'll not see your number on it. And you know what is making me uneasy at the moment? I think he's fancying his chances with Nell.' Wendy gave a short bark of laughter. 'If he only knew what she really thinks about him. I know she's being nice to him, but she's like me, really, constantly keeping the peace. You know, Margaret, I love Jessica to pieces, but I think I was wrong to have her.'

There was a prolonged period of silence from the other end of the line, and then Wendy thought about what she'd said. 'Oh God, Margaret, I'm so sorry. I shouldn't have said that, not when–'

'Don't worry about it, Wendy. I realise your head is all over the place. And there'll be no more babies for me. It's why the holiday was a spur-of-the-moment thing, I had to get away. It seems I have a condition called Lupus Anticoagulant. It used to be called sticky blood. Put simply, it means my blood couldn't get through to feed Natalie, and that's why she died.

'If I do decide to have another baby, I can have some injections, but I couldn't take the risk of ever going through that again. And that's apart from there being no man in the offing. So please don't apologise for saying random things that might upset me, that's not how friends work. I'm here for you now, as you supported me. For God's sake, Wendy, don't trust Mike. If he's changed, it's for a reason. A selfish reason. Probably Nell. You'll warn her? Or maybe it might be better if she went back to France. Is she returning the flattery and stuff?'

'I have already warned her. She laughed and said as if. She's been so good to me, really helped me through this baby blues thing and I'm feeling much better, but then I look at Mike–'

'Look. Wendy, if it ever gets too much, you bring Jessica and you come to me. Mike doesn't know where I live, doesn't even know we've met, so at least you'd have safety here. Nell won't be there forever, she'll be heading off back to Europe soon, I guess, abandoning you again, so always know I'm here.'

'You think this niceness towards Nell is an act?'

'I'm sure of it. I had a friend called Christine. We'd been

friends for years, but he seduced her and she fell for it. She's dead now.'

'Dead?' There was horror mixed with fear in Wendy's voice.

'Yes. I hadn't guessed, but I think the guilt was hitting her hard and she told me about it. I had a massive bust-up with Mike, and within a week she was dead. She overdosed on painkillers and vodka, lots of both. I didn't walk away from Mike, we patched things up, but Christine was only the first of his conquests. They said suicide, but... I never really felt it was right. If somebody had asked me if she was the type of person to even contemplate that, I would have laughed. But even more than that, she was pregnant. Three months, they said. The Chris I knew wasn't the Chris who supposedly took her own life.'

'Margaret, I'm so sorry. I had no idea...'

'He'll not tell you, will he. I hope your Nell can see through him, because he's got a track record with your relationship, and it sounds to me as if he's following a pattern with Nell. You say he's changed? He did that with Chris. Watch him, Wendy, watch him, and run for your life, yours and Jessica's, if you need to, but run towards me not Nell; he can track her down.'

Margaret replaced the receiver and smiled. She had often wondered if she would have given Chris the vodka with the crushed-up pills disguised by the Coca-Cola if she had known she was pregnant, but by the time that did become public news, it was too late for poor Chris.

Chris hadn't wanted the alcohol, but didn't want to confess to a baby fathered by Margaret's husband, and so had accepted it, feeling comforted by her long-term friendship with Mike's wife.

And Margaret had delivered another crushing blow to Mike.

How she hoped that baby had been a boy. She did miss Chris a little though, they had been friends for a long time.

Wendy walked around the park, deep in thought. It was drizzling, and she secured the rain shield on the pram and headed for the café.

She knew, somewhere in the recesses of her brain, that if there had been no Jessica, Wendy would be heading back to France with Nell. But Wendy also knew that if there had been no Jessica, there would also have been no Nell, she wouldn't have returned to England.

Wendy sipped at the coffee, checked in the pram to make sure there were no waving arms indicating it was feed time, and took out her book. She loved having Nell with her, but she also loved her quiet times when she could read and leave her dubious world behind.

A little boy ran up to her table, and she heard his mother shout, 'Leave the baby alone,' before dashing across and rescuing her errant son. 'I'm sorry,' she said. 'We've told him he's going to have a new baby brother or sister, and he's taken to checking every pram or pushchair in sight.'

Wendy smiled. 'Don't worry about it. I'm really only sitting here waiting for her to wake for her next feed, so it won't matter if she comes round.' Wendy turned to the blond-haired little boy. 'So what's your name?'

'Timerffy.'

'Timothy! That's a lovely name. And do you want a baby boy or a baby girl?'

'A boy.' He grinned, and shot off across the café to check out another pram he had spotted.

His mother said, 'Sorry!' and sprinted after him.

And then Jessica's arm really did wave, so Wendy took out

the still-warm bottle from her bag, and lifted her daughter from the pram. She hoped 'Timerffy' would be anchored to his mother's side and not feel the need to check out the baby that had been relocated to her mother's lap. Wendy enjoyed the peace of feeding time, and settled down as she watched her daughter's tiny face pucker in anticipation of food.

Her mind wandered to home, to the banter she had unexpectedly witnessed between her husband and her best friend, and she knew that Nell was being taken in by him. Should Wendy say something? Would it spoil her and Nell's relationship? Or would it cement it?

She checked the bottle, sat Jessica in an upright position, and waited for the inevitable burp. With the baby once more snuggled into her arms, Wendy's mind returned to her home and she knew something had to be done. It wasn't Mike's infidelity that caused her angst; she accepted that as part of her life for the moment. It was the fact that she knew it would destroy Nell if anything ever did happen between them.

Nell was her gentle friend, always there with a smile or creating laughter, something that had been missing from her own life for so long. But she wasn't convinced that Nell could resist sex, and it would be the aftermath that would destroy her. And destroy their friendship forever.

With Jessica fed and back in her pram, Wendy began the walk home, slowly. She hoped the house would be empty, nicely clean and tidy thanks to Nell, and Wendy could go in, pop Jessica into her cot if she was asleep, and sit down with a cup of tea and her book.

But she felt restless. The rain was a little heavier, the sky much greyer, and as she turned the corner to go up the incline to her home, she saw there was only darkness.

Despite what she'd hoped for, Wendy felt surprised. She had half expected Nell to be there, probably looking a little sheepish after the impromptu dance exhibitions and the singing of the previous night, but maybe the hangover was a little more serious than that.

Wendy unlocked the door, and struggled inside with the pushchair, crossing her fingers that the baby wouldn't wake. She left the pushchair in the hall, debating whether to take Jess out and carry her upstairs.

In the end, Wendy decided she should, leaving her free to vacuum the lounge carpet without waking her daughter.

Wendy picked up the phone and rang Nell's boarding house but Mrs White explained Nell hadn't yet surfaced. 'It must have been a good night,' the landlady remarked. 'I'd try again in an hour or so, love.'

And so Wendy followed instructions. She tried an hour later, and then half an hour after that. 'Okay,' she said to the some-what-irate Mrs White, 'I'll leave it. She clearly needs to sleep it off. If she does get out of bed, can you tell her I rang, please, and hopefully I'll see her tomorrow?'

'Of course I will. She'll maybe ring you later, because if she doesn't get up soon I'm going to go in and check she's okay. This isn't like her. Don't worry, she'll contact you at some point today.'

Wendy felt strangely alone. No Mike, no Nell and Jess upstairs in her cot. Wendy wandered into the lounge and sat on the sofa, thinking about the day before and how she had longed to be like Nell, able to enjoy herself, to have a laugh with friends, to have a bloody drink, for heaven's sake.

It had been a strange Monday; the day after the day before was how she thought of it, and she couldn't wait for it to be over and become Tuesday.

17

Nell felt the roll of her stomach before she managed to open her eyes and gulp down the swell of nausea that surged upwards. What was that smell? As she lifted her head and looked downwards, Nell focused on her soggy pillow that was covered in vomit and clung to her hair and lips. Slowly, while the stench worked its way up her nostrils, alcohol-infused blood pumped through her pounding brain, allowing it to compute.

Clasp hands to mouth, fling back blankets, engage legs, you are naked, grab dressing gown, now run.

By the time she staggered back to her chilly bedroom, stepping over her shoes and jumpsuit that lay scrunched in a heap, Nell was shivering. Not only from the arctic conditions of the shared bathroom but the after-effects of whatever the hell she'd drunk the night before. Flopping back onto the mattress then dragging the blankets over her body, Nell rubbed her arms in an attempt to warm up, keeping her eyes closed, trying to block out the drumming pain in her head and grey-blue light of dawn.

It was as the throbbing ebbed slightly, Nell noticed something else was rather tender and had stung when she'd had a wee. Her ribs felt bruised too. That was odd, why did... oh God, no, no, no, she didn't, she hadn't, please let it not be true.

Opening her eyes, Nell looked again at the pile of clothes on the floor. Her underwear was lying discarded by her mud-splattered shoes, one of which had a snapped heel, and the sight of it, that dirty broken piece of shiny plastic, was the catalyst that dislodged the shameful images from the night before. Nell knew what she had done, what they had done, and what it meant.

She had broken something precious, cracked and ruined the one thing that was true and solid in her life, sullied it with lust and betrayal. An angry sob erupted as Nell closed her eyes that leaked tears onto her pillow, but they weren't for her, they were for Wendy.

The previous day, after shivering through the dreary service where five screeching babies were christened and welcomed into the house of God, Nell couldn't wait to get to the Conservative Club. They were words she never ever thought she'd hear herself thinking.

Wendy had been so thrilled to see Beryl and her husband waiting at the church, accompanied by one of the secretaries from the typing pool at the factory. Nell had awarded herself brownie points for arranging it and gave Mike a secret wink, silently thanking him for agreeing, which was returned by a courteous nod.

The reception was attended by all the churchgoers and some latecomers, the majority of which were friends and colleagues of Mike's, stiff and formal. The afternoon got off to a bit of a slow start in a stilted conversation type of way, but once the guests had enjoyed a complimentary drink and tucked into the cold buffet, things warmed up.

Mike and Wendy had remained with their respective parents, seated on a table near the front of the room whereas Nell and her old factory friends found a nice table close to the bar and next to the jukebox. Two or three times, Wendy had managed to sneak off, briefly chatting to the other guests before making her way over to Nell where she lingered for longer, clearly enjoying the banter and jovial company. The drink flowed, someone suggested some music, the jukebox came alive and so did the Conservative Club.

Some of the previously buttoned-up guests gravitated towards Nell's lively group where after a few more gin and oranges, she regaled them with her tales – The Life and Times of Sheffield Nell, Seasonaire and Femme Fatale.

When Beryl said she fancied a dance, Nell followed suit and while Irene Cara sang about fame, poor Wendy remained in the corner. She spent the rest of the afternoon nursing baby Jessica, and glued to the side of Mike who looked on, his expression unreadable.

It was the bar manager who called time and while she'd been tempted by Beryl's offer of a few more drinks down the pub, Nell was having trouble standing, let alone walking, and her lips didn't seem to be working in time with her voice. Drunk as the proverbial skunk, she allowed herself to be guided to Mike's car by James and his wandering hands. He was one of Mike's golf buddies whose rather pissed-off wife gave Nell the evil eye as they passed by.

Once everyone was loaded into the car, Mike announced he was dropping Wendy and Jessica off on the way as it was getting late and time for a feed. Nell heard Wendy tell Mike to hurry back, but make sure Miss Jelly Legs was safely inside the B & B.

Nell had no recollection of getting out of the car or up the stairs, but she did remember going to the loo and splashing cold water on her face, then looking in the mirror at her runny mascara and smudged eyeshadow which she removed with some toilet roll. When she got back to her room, she was startled to find Mike sitting on her bed, the room lit by the low-watt bulb from the bedside lamp.

'Bloody hell, Mike, what're you doing here? I thought you'd gone.' Nell held onto the door frame as she entered the room, swaying slightly as she closed the door.

'I wanted to make sure you were okay and not sick or anything. I did promise Wendy I'd get you inside safely. Do you think you should drink some coffee and sober up? You are steaming drunk, you know.'

Nell shook her head, some shred of sense telling her that Mrs White wouldn't be too pleased about her clattering around in the kitchen in this state.

'No, no, it's fine. I think I'll sleep it off. Thanks for bringing me home, Mike, but you can go now.' Without really thinking what she was doing, swaying and trying to keep her balance, Nell began to unbutton her jumpsuit and kick off her shoes and as she did, noticed they were covered in mud.

'Bugger. Look at my shoes, did I step in a puddle or a bloody bog... and who sewed these stupid buttons on? Fuck, I hope I haven't got mud on the trousers... I need to take this back to the shop and get a refund.'

Mike smiled, his voice kind. 'I think it might have been when you lost your footing outside and stood in your landlady's flower beds. Don't worry, I'll smooth them over on the way out. Here, let me help you with that.'

When Mike stood and began helping her with the buttons on the front of her outfit, slowly undoing them, one by one, Nell was not only aware of how close his body was to hers but the rush of heat that had set her body alight. When she looked up and into his eyes, seeing immediately the desire that matched her own, Nell stepped back, quickly pushing his fingers away.

'I think you should go, Mike. I'll be fine and Wendy will be waiting.'

Mike reached out and stroked the side of Nell's cheek. 'God, you are so beautiful. Do you know how jealous I was this afternoon when I saw those men gathered around you? I wanted to come over and fight them all off.' He stepped closer as he spoke.

'What do you mean? Mike, you really shouldn't be saying this, really you need to...'

'Shush, don't spoil the moment. I've been wanting to say this ever since you arrived, from the moment I saw you at the airport.'

Nell swallowed, her head felt fuzzy and she was so sleepy. 'Say what? I don't understand.'

Although she'd heard his words, her gin-sodden brain was finding it difficult to make sense of them and her lips still weren't working properly because her voice was slurred, of that she was sure. She wanted to sleep, close her drooping eyelids and rest her dancing feet.

'That I think I'm falling for you, Nell, in fact I know it. I can't get you out of my mind, it's like you've put a spell on me.'

Nell was truly astonished. 'I don't know what to say...'

'Then don't say anything, let me kiss you, just once so I can remember it always.'

Their faces touched; the side of his cheek brushed hers.

'No, please stop this, we have to think of Wendy...' Nell was confused, her brain wasn't working properly and she knew she sounded sleepy; she was so tired yet mesmerised by him.

Mike traced Nell's lips with his finger, gently silencing her while with his other hand he pulled her closer, waiting, watching. When she didn't move away, her legs disobeying her brain, but at least they stayed upright, Mike kissed her gently. Through the haze of jumbled thoughts, Nell responded, their every touch becoming more urgent. Was she pulling him close or was he holding her to him? When Mike continued to slowly undress her, Nell didn't resist. Maybe it was a dream, a soft fuzzy dream, not really happening at all.

Nell swayed as she watched Mike silently place her clothes on the wooden chair and then held his hand as he guided her towards the bed. Flopping down on the mattress, Nell gratefully floated on the blissful precipice of sleep, only to be dragged back to reality by desire, its flame burning her skin with every caress. She allowed herself to be seduced, to be accepted and loved, and when a whispered voice told her to stop, she pushed any thought of friendship or betrayal from her mind. Flattered and consumed by passion, Nell floated.

The kisses along her neck and throat lulled her to sleep but then the hands that grappled with her bra and pinched her skin jolted her into lucidity, allowing her to savour the thrill of Mike. Running her fingers through his hair, Nell heard Mike's moans of passion, while her charm bracelet lay against his silver-streaked hair. Key, wishing well, bell, house and heart. The sight of the silver symbols of friendship, hers and Wendy's, made Nell's heart lurch.

What was she doing? Oh God, this was so wrong. Pushing Mike's shoulders with all her might, Nell cried out. 'Mike, no! We can't, stop it, get off. Mike, stop.'

But when Mike carried on, tugging at her pants, Nell grabbed his hand, her voice more forceful this time. 'Mike, stop!' This time he obeyed and pushed himself upright. What she saw in his eyes made her blood freeze.

'Stop. Why? You want this, you know you do. You've always wanted it.' Mike held her gaze and without flinching, his face a mask of stone, hardened by the shadows of the dimly lit room, reached downwards and tore her pants from her body. Nell only had time to gasp. The force he used came as a shock and the graze of cotton slicing against her skin made her wince, before he turned his attention back to her bra. This time he ignored fiddly hooks and instead ripped it undone before groping her breasts while further down her body, no matter how hard she clenched her thighs, he forced his way inside.

Nell struggled but he was too heavy and strong so as his weight bore down on her ribs, compressing the air from her lungs, she scrunched her eyes shut and gave in. It was the easiest way, less painful, and maybe, once she could look herself in the mirror again, Nell could tell eyes that knew the truth a great big lie.

Of all her reckless moments of abandon she'd enjoyed with men she would never think of again, the stupid, irresponsible things that she had done – and there had been many – this one, Nell would regret forever.

She had been such a fool; taken it all in, Mike's play-acting. Even with her head stuck down the loo, or lying staring at the ceiling rose, Nell had struggled with the notion that he really was infatuated with her. It wasn't something she was pleased or proud about, in fact it would have made the whole situation even harder to deal with. Having one-off meaningless sex with your best friend's husband was reprehensible, but Nell knew that if Mike was actually in love with her, that was a double insult to Wendy, two stab wounds to the back.

It was as Nell rolled on her side, then stared at her forlorn scrunched jumpsuit and broken shoe that the light dawned and the truth was confirmed by the absence of the receipt Nell had left lodged under the lamp. After searching the room and then examining her clothing that had lain on the chair, but somehow ended up on the floor with a ripped sleeve, Nell knew she'd been had, in more ways than one.

Nell stood at the end of Wendy's avenue from where she could see the detached suburban home of her best friend. It was dusk and while she still felt dreadful, Nell had been forced from her bed after Mrs White had knocked on her door for the third time to say her friend had rung, *again*. Mrs White was also bloody sick of traipsing up the stairs and told Nell to get off her lazy arse and ring Wendy back.

Mike's car wasn't on the drive, yet the absence of him didn't make what Nell was about to do any easier. She was going to have to face Wendy sometime and pray that shame hadn't actually stained her face, like it had her soul. Mike wasn't due home for another hour so there was time to speak to Wendy alone, and then say goodbye.

Nell had it planned, her script and escape route. Sucking in the chill February evening then exhaling a puff of frozen air, Nell gathered courage and strode along the pavement towards Wendy's. There was a light on in the front bedroom as Nell made her way up the neat path, then raised her hand to lift the door knocker. The sound of a car engine and then the glare of headlights beaming on the driveway halted her, and as she turned, Nell shielded her eyes from the glare.

Once the lights and engine had been switched off, Nell watched impassively as Mike almost leapt from his car and paced towards her at speed, his face etched with anger.

18

'What the hell are you doing here? I want you to go at once. I can't believe you have the nerve to show your face around here after your behaviour yesterday.'

Nell gasped, before her shock was replaced by anger. '*My* behaviour... are you serious?' Lowering her voice, she stepped closer to Mike and pointed her finger as she spoke. 'It takes two, you know, so don't you dare come the innocent with me, you sly bastard. But for the record, I was pissed. What's your excuse, Mr Stone Cold Fucking Sober?'

Mike shook his head and snorted sarcastically. 'Yes, we know how paralytic you were, Nell, which I suppose you'll use as an excuse for your slobbering advances last night. You should be ashamed. If poor Wendy knew how you'd behaved, I think it would destroy her and your friendship, don't you?' Mike was smirking.

'You sick, evil bastard... I know what you are now, and I'm not standing here listening to this shit. I want to speak to Wendy, not you.' Without giving Mike time to react, Nell spun round and was about to hammer on the door when it was flung open.

'I heard voices and saw the car... Why are you both standing out here in the cold?' Wendy was framed in an aura of yellow light from the hall lamp, enveloped in the aroma of cooking that wafted down the corridor and with it came a gust of warm centrally heated air.

Amidst such panic, as they all stood on the brink of Armageddon, the strangest thought occurred to Nell, that it was the scent of home, the glow of warmth, and a complete sham.

Back in the real world, as Wendy looked from one to the other, clearly waiting for an answer, Nell saw immediately the suspicion in her friend's eyes, so sought to reassure her.

'Mike and I were discussing yesterday, weren't we, Mike?' Nell turned and waited for him to respond, feeling smug that she was calling his bluff, not for one second expecting his response that came like a slap in the face.

'Yes, we were, and for that reason I was making it clear to Nell that she is no longer welcome in our home, in fact I was asking her to leave.'

Mike held Nell's gaze for a moment, his eyes like bullets boring into her, striking her heart that was beyond wounded by his words. It was Mike's turn to look smug as he ignored Nell and turned to Wendy who still had hold of the door, her free hand on her chest, mouth wide with shock.

'Mike, what's going on? Why isn't Nell welcome? I don't understand.' Wendy's voice wasn't angry, she sounded scared if anything.

'Why... are you simple, woman? Did you not see the way she behaved yesterday in front of our friends and family, getting inebriated, dancing like a tart and telling her sordid little stories? My parents were utterly disgusted and thank God the vicar was too busy to attend. And how dare Nell invite those common women from the factory? Who gave her the right to bring people like that to the christening of our daughter?' Mike was visibly enraged, stepping forward to shout in the face of his wife who shrank away in fear, diminished further by his harsh vitriol.

Nell reeled then gasped before lunging forward, getting between Mike and Wendy, jabbing her finger into his chest.

'You lying bastard! I asked you if they could come.' Turning to Wendy, Nell looked straight into her eyes. 'I swear, Wendy, I asked him and he said it was okay, it was supposed to be a surprise. He's a lying *git* and the whole Mr Nice Guy thing has been an act since the moment I arrived. He's a fake and a weirdo, and I was right about him all along.'

'Right about me, that's rich coming from you. Do you know who rang me at work today and told me exactly where you touched him as he helped you into the car? James was horrified and wanted to warn me, in fact he couldn't believe I even counted you as a friend, let alone allowed you near Jessica. To think that I gave you a chance, I forgave and forgot, dear God I even asked you to stay in my home and this is how you repay me.' Mike was holding his head, like an angst-ridden amateur dramatic.

'You fucking liar! I didn't touch what's-his-bloody-name... if anything it was him that copped a feel, like you did all those years ago. Thought I'd forgotten, did you? Not a chance, mate!' Spittle escaped from Nell's mouth and her hands trembled with sheer rage and injustice.

At this, Mike gasped and grabbed Nell's arm then dragged her away from the door. 'Right, that's it. I'm not having you speak to my wife like this, or me, for that matter. Come on, off my property immediately or I'll ring the police.'

'Please stop, please, will both of you calm down, I can't bear it.' Wendy was chasing them down the path, pulling at Mike's coat.

'Wendy, go inside right now. I mean it,' Mike bawled at Wendy, stopping at the end of the drive, pointing towards the door, like he was commanding the family dog.

Wendy was sobbing, still holding Mike's coat, tears cascading down her cheeks. 'But Mike, Nell is my friend. You can't banish her so please can we go inside and talk about this civilly. I'm sure Nell's sorry for getting drunk yesterday and there was no harm done, so can we not start again? We were getting along so well.'

Wendy swiped away her tears and then looked towards Nell, as if willing her to apologise, but Mike had other ideas.

'No, Wendy. She will not set foot in our home ever again, do you hear me? I don't want her anywhere near my daughter or you. Is that clear? Now go inside.'

Nell watched in horror as she listened to Mike speak to Wendy as if she was his property, and watched in stunned silence as her best friend struggled with what to do. It was then, during a moment of much-needed clarity, cutting through the panic and sheer confusion, Nell saw exactly what Mike was, what he had so cleverly engineered, and how it was going to go.

He would have hated the fact she was back on the scene, maybe he was worried she might stay this time; Mike wanted to make sure he got rid of her for good, and he'd played a blinder. She'd fallen for the nice guy act, and was flattered that someone older, slightly refined, and who she thought despised her, could actually be a friend, accept her into his home and family. What a fool she had been.

And he was testing her. He was probably enjoying it, like the previous night, where, after he'd taken the last bit of dignity she had before she passed out, Mike tore her clothes, snapped her shoe and took the receipt. It was a subliminal message and she'd received it loud and clear.

All Nell had to do was tell Wendy, right there and then on

the street, in front of whatever nosey neighbours were peering through their net curtains and straining at half-open windows, exactly what they had done the night before. Nell could kill Wendy's marriage in one sentence, but at the same time she would snuff out their friendship with the cruellest betrayal of all. No matter how she told it, Nell was as bad as him.

Would Wendy forgive Mike, or did she have the strength to leave him and walk away with Jessica? Nell looked at the sobbing mess that was being manhandled up the driveway, turning then pulling away before being dragged onwards, Mike hissing for her to do as she was told. Wendy was going nowhere and Nell wasn't going to ruin her life in front of the witches of suburbia.

Shouting, her voice firm and clear, Nell tried to take control of the situation for Wendy's sake. 'Mike, stop. I'll go. Let me say goodbye to Wendy. I promise I won't cause any trouble.'

Mike paused and turned, giving Wendy a chance to break free yet still she remained by his side, a sight that painted a thousand words for Nell.

'Look, I'd just called to say goodbye. My friend Molly is sick and I'm heading to London. I didn't come here for a row and I'm sorry I caused any offence yesterday. Give me two minutes with Wendy then I'll be gone.' Nell would have told him anything because the only thing she wanted was a moment alone with Wendy.

'Please, Mike, she's said she's sorry. I won't be a minute, I promise.'

Wendy shivered in the cold, or was she shaking with fear, her nerves shot? It was then that Nell noticed she was wearing her slippers, soggy and ruined, and Nell's heart literally lurched, full of pity for the rather pathetic figure in her twin set and sensible pleated skirt. Where had her Wendy gone?

A neighbour walking his dog seemed to bring Mike to his

senses. As the man approached and the poodle sniffed the kerb and cocked its leg against a tree, Mike hissed at Wendy, keen to avoid further embarrassment.

'Two minutes and I'll be at the door and then I want her gone. I mean it, Wendy.'

With that, he glared at Nell and strode off, taking up a sentry-like position in the hallway, keeping out of the rain that was pattering softly, turning the avenue murky and grey.

Mike knew he'd won. Nell was no threat to him, she accepted that now. All that was left was the inevitable, something she'd decided on before she even knocked on the door. It was time to leave. There would be no settling in Sheffield, no new job, no place to call her own. No cosy friendship. No Wendy.

Stepping forward, Nell reached out for Wendy then grabbed her shoulders and held on tight. Keeping one eye on Dog Man and the other on a pathetic excuse for one, she whispered, 'Please, please leave him. You have to get away. You can come with me. We can go anywhere, somewhere far away from here. He's bad, you know that, don't you?' Nell felt Wendy nod into her shoulder.

'I was going to stay. I want you to know that. I'd had enough of roaming and I missed you and this shitty bloody city so much. But I can't now, Wendy, there's no point if I can't see you and he'd make it too hard for us.'

When Wendy found her voice it was broken and weary. 'Please don't go. Let's try to work it out.'

Nell shook her head. 'I can't. Too much has happened and been said.'

Wendy clung on tighter, almost choking on her tears. 'I'm sorry, I want to choose you, I really do but it's too much, do you understand?'

'Yes I do and I know you haven't got the strength to come

right now but you might, and when you're ready I'll be waiting. I'm going to ring you with my new address because I don't trust him not to destroy my letters, not anymore. He's played me for a fool this time, Wendy, but I'm not, and neither are you.'

Mike's voice calling from the step startled Wendy who pulled away from Nell's embrace.

'I have to go. It'll make things worse if I don't.'

Nell saw the fear in Wendy's eyes and couldn't bear for her to walk back to that man but she had to let her go.

'You should have told me, you should've been honest and told me what he's like. I could kill him, knowing what he's done and I'm starting to wonder how he really treats you.'

Wendy remained silent. Her eyes cast downwards so Nell continued. 'I feel such a fool, he conned me, made me think he'd changed and now look at us. I've ruined everything and that makes me the worst friend in the world. I've let you down so badly.' Nell could hardly get the words out.

Wendy almost shouted her reply. 'No, no you're not. You're my Nell and I love you and I always will. Promise me you'll stay in touch. Don't ever desert me, Nell. As long as I know you're somewhere out there, I'll be okay.'

Nell squeaked her answer, unable to speak properly. 'I promise.'

Dog Man was almost out of earshot, his unwitting layer of protection fading fast.

The sound of Mike's booming voice broke the moment. 'Wendy. Now!'

Letting go of Nell's hands, Wendy straightened. It was like she was gathering her strength, taking control, speaking so Mike could hear.

'Thank you for coming back, Nell. It was lovely to see you. You get off otherwise you'll catch your death out here.'

Holding each other in their sights for one last second, Nell watched as Wendy dipped her head then turned away. As Nell's face crumpled, allowing angry tears to flow, she did the same; turning, walking quickly, leaving Wendy and Sheffield behind.

19

It took two days for the grief of losing Nell to really hit Wendy. Until the christening everything had been moving along smoothly, and she had finally begun to believe that Mike and Nell had settled their differences.

So what had gone so devastatingly wrong that had made Mike push her best friend away, effectively banning Nell from their home and their lives? But it was more than that, he had made it clear she wasn't to have anything to do with Nell in any way – no letters, no phone calls, no clandestine meetings while he was at work, because the consequences of any such activities would be bad. Too bad for her to think about, he had said.

Wendy watched as he got into his car to drive to work, and she turned away from the window, clutching Jessica to her. In that moment she felt that the tiny baby was the only thing in the world she had to give her any comfort.

She had no idea where Nell was, and no way of finding anything out. Still holding tightly onto Jessica, Wendy moved towards the bureau, and reached down to the bottom drawer where Nell's letters were stored. She pulled out the box of flowered notepaper and turned to carry it across to the coffee table.

Mike was standing in the lounge doorway, watching her every move.

Wendy gasped, and stared at her husband.

'Didn't expect me back?' he said.

She didn't reply; didn't know what or how to reply.

He moved further into the room and took the pretty box from her. 'Saved them all? Let's have a look, shall we?'

He tipped the contents onto the coffee table and systematically ripped every piece of paper lying on the surface.

'No,' she said, at first quietly, but then more insistent. 'No, they're all I have of her now.' She moved towards him, still clutching Jessica, and he stood. He lifted his arm and hit Wendy with a backhanded swipe across her face, then followed it up with a repeat of his action across her other cheek. She teetered, and felt herself fall.

Jessica seemed to take her actions from her mummy and began to cry as Wendy collapsed backwards. Wendy instinctively tried to protect her baby by letting her roll as they both landed on the carpet, and the baby's wails grew louder.

'Shut the fuck up, kid!' Mike roared, then he picked up the destroyed letters and threw them onto the log burner. It took less than a minute for them to burn, but Wendy didn't see them going up in smoke. She was cradling Jessica in her arms, trying to soothe her; at the same time she was trying to suppress her own tears. Her face felt as hot as the flames emanating from the fire, and she knew it would be some time before she could venture out. Usually the bruises were hidden, but these would be obvious.

Mike walked to the open lounge doorway and looked back at the devastation he was leaving behind.

'Tidy it up,' he said, and left the room to return to his car.

. . .

Wendy made a bottle of milk for Jessica and sat on the settee, trying to soothe her daughter. 'I'm so sorry, baby,' Wendy whispered, even now afraid that Mike was lurking somewhere, that he had doubled back after taking the car down the road.

A nappy change and another cuddle finally settled Jessica, and Wendy carried her up to her nursery, afraid to have her anywhere near Mike if he should choose to come home early – Wendy knew he would use any means to keep her on her toes, not letting her rest, making sure fear ruled her life.

She went into the bathroom and ran some cold water into the washbasin. Her face looked a mess, and she dabbed at the bruising that was already appearing. There was even a small cut under her right eye where presumably his ring had caused some damage.

She finally stepped back and looked at her face from about five feet away. It looked no better than up close. Her sigh seemed to start in her toes, and she had no idea what she would say to anyone who happened to catch a glimpse of her battered and bruised features.

She lay on the bed, and drifted off to sleep.

Jessica's cries woke her, and Wendy spent the next half hour feeding and changing her before laying her on a blanket with the baby gym tantalisingly close to Jessica's grasping hands.

Taking out her small make-up bag, Wendy opened the compact and looked in the tiny mirror. She tried masking the bruises with foundation cream, then powdered over it; it didn't help.

That was when she realised she still had something to

connect her with Nell – the pretty box in which the letters, fresh paper and envelopes had been stored. She hugged it to her then headed upstairs with it to tuck it into the airing cupboard, underneath the pile of sheets. She knew he would never see it there; he'd never made up a bed in his life.

As she reached the bottom of the stairs, the telephone shrilled. She answered it, aware of the ache in her thigh after her journey to the bedroom, caused by her striking the floor as she fell over. She guessed it would be an extra bruise to add to the facial ones.

'Wendy?'

She felt sick.

'Yes.'

'I'll be home late tonight. I have a meeting.'

'Okay.'

'You're okay?'

'I am.'

There was a moment of silence. 'You're sure?'

'Yes.'

'Jessica okay? She's very quiet.'

'She's fine. Playing with her gym.'

'Okay. I'll see you later, probably around ten. I'll have eaten, so do something for yourself.'

'I will.' She replaced the receiver without further words, and knew he had been checking to make sure she was still there, and hadn't repeated Margaret's actions of walking out on him.

But there was a difference. Margaret hadn't had a child; Wendy had Jessica. Wendy hesitated for a moment. Margaret.

Wendy felt she had neglected Margaret a little, while Nell had been staying with them, and she knew she needed to talk to her. With Mike not coming home till later...

And then she knew. He would be home any time. And this

would be the pattern of her life for the foreseeable future: the insecurity, the threats, the physical violence.

She made a promise to herself that the next time he hit her would be the last time.

He arrived home shortly after five, saying the meeting had been cancelled and so she would need to organise a meal for them both.

She nodded in agreement and walked into the kitchen, taking Jessica in her car seat with her. The baby was placed on the kitchen side, and she watched wide-eyed as her mummy peeled potatoes, chopped onions, marinated chicken breasts – all of it with a half-smile on her face that felt almost like a victory grin. Wendy had been right about Mike, and if she could be right this time, she would be able to second-guess him again in the future.

He never once mentioned the state of her face that night, but the next day made some joke about being careful not to walk into any more wardrobe doors.

An hour after his departure for work, she rang his secretary.

'Oh, hi. Can I leave a message for my husband, please, Anthea? I don't need to speak to him, but tell him I'm off to the hospital because I'm having a slight problem with the vision in my right eye, so I think I'll head to A & E and get it checked out.'

'Of course I'll tell him, Mrs Summers. Mike... Mr Summers is in a meeting with the planners until about twelve. Do you want him to meet you there?'

Wendy laughed. 'No, I'm sure I'll be back home by then. Tell him I'll see him tonight. I simply didn't want him ringing home and then being worried because I didn't answer the phone.'

She replaced the receiver, picked up her car keys, along with Jessica in her car seat and left the house.

Margaret took one look at her face, and lifted the car seat from her. 'Come in, let me make you a drink.'

'Thank you, Margaret.' Wendy followed her hostess through to the kitchen, and Margaret carefully placed the sleeping Jessica in the lounge.

'We'll hear her when she wakes,' Margaret said quietly. 'Now tell me what's happened.'

'There was a massive fall out on Monday, he banished Nell from our lives, and then yesterday he seemed to flip completely. He hit me twice across the face, knocked me down, even though I was holding Jessica...'

'She's not hurt?' Anxiety was evident in Margaret's voice.

'No, I cushioned her as we fell, but I've got a cracker of a bruise on my hip.'

'Lift up your skirt.' Margaret moved across to the sideboard and opened a cupboard. She took out a camera.

'What are you doing?'

'We need photographs. Your thigh and your face. This camera date-stamps the pictures, and you may need these pictures one day.'

Wendy lifted her skirt and she heard Margaret draw in a breath.

'This is bad. Hopefully it's only bruised and not damaged. Now, hold still.'

Wendy stayed immobile while Margaret took three photographs of her hip, then Wendy sat at the kitchen table as instructed.

'As bad as your thigh is, your face is much worse,' Margaret said. 'Somebody should do something nasty to that man, and soon.'

'You're offering?' A slight smile crossed Wendy's face.

'If only...'

Margaret steadied the camera and took pictures of several areas of Wendy's face. 'You'll be staying inside for a bit, I presume.'

'Can't really go out looking like this, can I?'

'I used to.'

'He did this to you?'

'Twice. The third time I walked. Had Nell left by the time this happened?'

Wendy looked down at her hands. 'Yes, he told her she'd to go. We managed to say goodbye, but he's burnt all her letters she sent me over the years, and he'll not allow me to see any that come now.'

'Then give her my address if she manages to get in touch. She can write to you here. Mike has no idea we've become friends, has he?'

'No. I wouldn't dream of telling him. And thank you for that offer. I'll try writing to the last address she had, and hope she goes back there. I miss her so much already, and I haven't anything of hers now.'

Margaret put away the camera, and lifted the newly boiled kettle. 'I think we need a cup of tea. What time do you have to be home?'

'Around half past eleven. He's in a meeting until twelve, and I've told his secretary I'm going to A & E to get my eye checked out. I'm safe for the moment, but after twelve I'm not so sure.'

They chatted quietly, enjoying the companionship, until they heard sounds emanating from the lounge. Jessica joined them for a short while, and then Wendy decided it was time to move.

'Thank you so much, Margaret,' she said. 'I feel a little better now, so let's hope he's calmed down.'

'Wendy, if you ever need a refuge…'

'I know. You're my first port of call, even if it's simply to get Jessica to a safe place while I sort out our lives. Is that okay with you?'

'Of course. Mike doesn't know where I am, so he'll not come looking for you. I have a spare room that you're welcome to use any time. Always remember that. He's evil, Wendy, never doubt that.'

The phone was ringing as Wendy unlocked the front door, and she tucked Jessica under one arm as she answered it.

'It's me. Is he there?'

'Nell!' Wendy felt her heart sing. 'No, but he could be due anytime. If I put the phone down it's because he's come home. Are you okay?'

'I'm fine. Write to me and let me know you're okay. Love you. I'll go in case he arrives. Make a note of it, don't risk forgetting it.'

Wendy made a note of Nell's address, reading it back to her for confirmation. 'Love you too. I have an address to send you that's a safe one – Margaret will hold on to any letters. His car's here… love you,' and she replaced the receiver, quickly writing the address on her arm before covering it with her coat sleeve.

By the time Mike walked in the door, Wendy and Jessica had moved into the kitchen.

He tilted her head and looked at her eye. 'What did they say?'

'That it's fine, it needs a couple of days and it'll be as good as new.'

'Did they ask what had happened?'

'Of course. I said I'd fallen over something on the stairs and landed on my face.'

He stared at her for a moment. 'That's okay then.'

He walked out to his car, started the engine and drove away.

Wendy gritted her teeth. If only she could get rid of him as easily as his meddling secretary...

20

Nell reached up and wiped a tear from Molly's eye. They were standing at the front door of their tenement flat on a cold January morning, grey skies overhead adding to the sombre mood. By Nell's side lay the trusty old rucksack that was ready for another adventure although this time, her heart didn't quicken at the thought, it remained leaden like it had for weeks. Rallying for the sake of her weepy friend, her saviour really, Nell fixed a smile on her face and forced some lightness into her voice.

'Hey, stop this. We've said au revoir many times and that's what it's been. I promise I'll keep in touch and a year will fly past. I'll be back in that spare room before you know it.' Nell watched as Molly nodded and took a deep breath.

Molly wrapped her fingers around Nell's. 'Yes I know but this isn't the same as saying goodbye last time, you know that, and I'm going to worry about you, and that's why I don't want you to go.'

'Molly, I have to. I can't stay. I need to go somewhere I can forget, pretend, go quietly crazy, whatever takes my fancy. We've been through this so please let me go. Don't make it harder than it needs to be.'

Molly gave a weak smile. 'Okay, for you because I love you. You know that, don't you?'

'Of course I do, Moll, and I will never ever forget how kind you've been... I swear I don't know what I'd have done if you hadn't taken me in and looked after me these past months. I'll never forget it, ever. Give me a hug, otherwise we'll both freeze to death, come here.' Nell stretched out her arms and held Molly tightly, knowing that her friend's loving words held more truth than she let on.

The feelings Molly had for her were more than friendship and this made it so much harder to leave. Nell felt like she was breaking her heart twice over.

Pulling apart, Molly seemed stronger and was smiling, just. 'Right, you get off, and ring me from the airport if you can. Leave a message if I'm not home. Who are you going to see first?'

'I'll call in at the café and say goodbye to Lou, then Mary at the launderette before I head to the station. I'll buy the cheapest ticket to Stansted and make my way there. Like I said, I don't mind waiting around. It's better than sitting here all day by myself. I'll do a bit of people-watching and I love seeing the planes take off so that'll keep me occupied.'

Nell was catching the red-eye flight shortly after midnight but couldn't bear the thought of being alone and staring at four walls. She needed to be around the hustle and bustle of nameless strangers who didn't know her past or what she had done. It was time to reinvent a new Nell.

Molly gave Nell one last hug. 'Okay, bon voyage. Take care of yourself and come straight back if you need to. Don't be proud, there's always a room here for you.'

It was Nell's turn to fill up so before she lost her nerve, she picked up her rucksack, hitched it over her shoulders, blew a kiss then turned, walking through the gate of their little balcony before taking the stone steps at a run.

Outside, she marched towards the high street, stopping as she reached the corner to wave at Molly who she knew would be there, her arm raised in goodbye.

The bus trundled through the streets of Hackney, the high-rise flats of Tower Hamlets disappearing into the distance as Nell headed towards Liverpool Street Station and the tube. The mindless chatter of other passengers provided welcome background noise, the dinging bell pulling her from her more-maudlin thoughts.

On her lap was a carrier bag courtesy of Lou who had given her a huge packed lunch and a flask of tea, shooing away her protestations that she wouldn't be able to bring it back for ages. God, she loved that cranky bugger as much as old Mary in her pinny and slippers. Mary had called her a *bleedin' 'ed case* when Nell first told her where she was going. Still, she'd stuffed a tenner into Nell's hand before she left the shop, saying she'd found it in some geezer's pocket, but Nell knew the truth. It was Mary's way of caring.

When Nell had turned up at Molly's, an emotional sobbing wreck, not only had she found a safe haven in the tiniest box room in East London, but two part-time jobs. One at the café, scrubbing pots and waitressing for Lou the Greek as everyone called him, then extra shifts next door at the launderette doing service washes under the beady eyes of Mary, a hard-as-nails taskmaster who laughed like a drain and smoked forty fags a day. Nell's employers were both East End, born and bred despite Lou's nickname, and had seen good times and bad, probably why they'd been benevolent to someone who was experiencing the latter.

And then, the bomb dropped, not from a German plane onto the streets of Hackney, but on Nell's life. Rather than shun a pregnant unmarried woman, they shrugged and said she wouldn't be the first, or the last, daft girl to get into trouble.

Molly had been an angel; by Nell's side every step of the way. She'd supported her decision to keep the baby, despite its paternal heritage and Mary's gentle and kindly meant hint that she knew a woman who knew a woman who could make mistakes go away.

Not once had Molly questioned how Nell would manage after the baby was born, and neither had she asked for a penny for keep, not that it was needed because her parents took care of most things. But Nell wanted to pay her way and this she did right up until it was no longer possible to work.

The only ripple came when Nell returned from the antenatal clinic and announced that she was having the baby adopted. It wasn't a decision she'd made lightly but after hours of soul-searching during long sleepless nights, Nell knew it was the sensible option. The midwife at the clinic had broached the subject first and once Nell agreed, wasted no time arranging a meeting with a social worker.

Nell wasn't so stupid as to believe it was in her own interests, this caring coercion, it was about the baby. She also got the distinct impression that behind her back they looked down their noses and thoroughly believed in their self-righteous mission. The thing was, as much as Nell had wanted them to offer her a viable alternative, perhaps a helping hand to grasp onto, light at the end of the tunnel, nothing could alter the baby's parentage and that reason alone sealed her baby's fate.

Even if they had suggested a different path, Nell knew that adoption was the best for her baby and the only way to keep her secret. As she'd sat in the lounge, explaining this to Molly, Nell's heart felt like it would never beat a happy rhythm ever again. The wheels had been set in motion. It was for the best. Molly disagreed.

They would cope, somehow. Molly said she would help out in between her studies and working at the hospital and once she was qualified, her doctor's wage would support the three of them. So what if it would break Wendy's heart? Molly thought it was time Nell's Sheffield friend smelt the coffee and faced up to what her husband was and did. And if she didn't accept it, then tough. Why should Nell give away her baby to protect Wendy? It wasn't fair or right. Nell had Molly so perhaps she didn't need Wendy after all. Nell couldn't give up on her baby. Molly said she had to try.

Nell, however, was resolute. The baby had no place in her life. She had nothing, and would not countenance giving a child the life she'd had, one of poverty and stigma, the kid with no dad and an unmarried mam. And yes, there was Wendy to consider, along with that thing she had married. While he deserved the worst of everything, Wendy didn't, and even if Nell could ever look her in the eye again, it would be impossible with Mike's baby on her hip.

In the end, after tears and harsh words, saying she wanted only the best for Nell, whatever that may be, Molly gave up.

And so it was that on a December evening, Molly called the ambulance that ferried Nell off to the hospital where a baby boy was delivered. He was healthy and perfect and that was all Nell cared about. She named him Darrell. Whispering in her baby's ear as she inhaled his scent, Nell told him that it meant 'beloved' and even if his new mummy and daddy changed his name, to her he would always be Darrell.

She had sobbed hysterically when they took him away, mere hours after he was born and then more tears as she wrote him a letter to be placed in his adoption file, for the future. It was one she wasn't sure she wanted him to read, because if he did it meant that eventually the truth would come out. Maybe he would never ask to see it, or feel the need to track her down. Nell told herself that would be for the best because it would mean he was happy and she'd made the right decision. But it was there, just in case.

In the days that followed, Nell could only describe the feeling that clung to her like mud, glue, fog. Giving away her baby had left her hollowed out in every way possible. She was empty and of no use to anyone apart from starving workmen who wanted their fry-ups or busy commuters who needed their laundry washed and folded by the time they hopped off the bus later that day.

Home. Nell hated that word. No matter how hard Molly insisted she had one with her, the box room was a cocoon that housed a husk whose seed had grown, and was now gone.

It had been a random meeting that sparked a hint of something in Nell when one drizzly Saturday afternoon, she returned home to find Molly had a visitor, a chap named Dai who was passing through and had been offered the couch for the night. The seasonaires spirit of camaraderie held firm and after reminiscing about shared experiences and old friends, they listened to Dai's tales of life on a kibbutz in Israel. Later, as he snored in the lounge, Nell laid awake imagining life on a farm in the desert, far away from smoky London and the memories of Mike and Darrell.

Could she escape the images that haunted her? Not of Mike, he didn't plague her at all, he was a pathetic apology of a man who had groped and grunted his way through less than a minute of uncomfortable sex. It was the face of her baby boy, wrapped in a blanket, his creamy skin, and perfect rosebud lips that twitched and searched for the milk she wasn't allowed to feed him from her breasts.

The moment the social worker took him away, to a proper family, a decent mother who could give him what he needed and deserved, had caused intense pain. Nell could actually feel it. Those were the memories that ripped out her heart and soul each and every time they came back to haunt her. This was what Nell was running from.

21

The bus ride over with, Nell made her way to the station ticket office, passing a disgruntled chap cursing at a luggage locker door that appeared to be jammed. Everyone seemed to be in a rush, too busy sometimes to say hello, smile even. The city of London and its inhabitants felt cold and unloving compared to the northern one of her birth. Pushing that thought from her mind, Nell continued towards the main concourse where she spotted huge queues for tickets. Not being in any rush, she decided to unburden herself of her rucksack and after hitching it off her already-aching shoulders, placed it by an empty bench and took a seat.

Looking up at the departure board, Nell sighed wistfully as she made her way down the list, spotting destinations that were alien to her, and even if she did spot a familiar name, or even Sheffield, would she want to go there?

So much had changed since she'd left Wendy on the pavement that night in February, even their relationship if she was honest, but that was mainly Nell's fault. It had been necessary to have Wendy at arm's length once her pregnancy was discovered and this meant keeping letters simple and phone calls to a minimum.

It had been easy really, mainly because Wendy was still terrified that Mike would find out they'd been chatting on the house phone. She had to use a public call box to ring Nell at the café, which wasn't always convenient and caused Lou to grumble. Letters went via Mike's ex-wife Margaret, a situation Nell found bizarre and quite frankly a bit creepy. Why had this woman taken such a sudden interest in Wendy? Nell thought it wasn't healthy, being friends with your psycho husband's banished ex-wife. And Nell desperately hoped Margaret wasn't making the issues between herself and Wendy any worse, by any well-placed little digs.

But there was another reason why over the past eleven months she'd only written four short letters (not including the farewell one in her bag) and spoken to Wendy twice. In truth, Nell felt let down, angry and frustrated.

The root of the problem was Mike. Nell had seen the real side of his monstrous character and she could only assume that Wendy also suffered at his hands, yet she stayed with him. Why? In her first letter, Nell had beseeched Wendy to leave, grab whatever belongings she needed for her and Jessica, take as much money as she could and come to London. Just as Molly had tried to persuade Nell that they could make it as a threesome, she had said exactly the same to Wendy. But whereas Nell felt she had valid points for refusal, Wendy came up with what seemed like feeble excuses, as though the fight and pride had been knocked out of her, either physically or psychologically.

Then, when Nell discovered she was pregnant, her panic was exacerbated by the notion that Wendy might actually turn up in London and for the life of her, Nell couldn't decide if it would be a good thing or a complete disaster. They could get everything out in the open and move on, or would Wendy be appalled and betrayed, would she even believe that Mike had forced himself on her or suspect they were having an affair?

Their friendship hung in the balance and on top of everything she had to deal with, Nell took the easy option and pushed Wendy away. Her letters became shorter, matter-of-fact and boring. After all, how exciting could you make an East End flat and two crappy part-time jobs sound? It wasn't as though Nell was living the high life in the West End and she hadn't the energy or inclination to lie.

In return, Nell suspected Wendy was once again hiding the truth or at least watering it down. Her letters were banal, literally scraping the barrel for things to say; that's what it seemed like anyway. By letter three, their correspondence was beginning to feel false. What was the point in asking Wendy if Mike was being nice to her, if things had improved, if there was any thawing in his opinion of her harlot friend? She wouldn't tell the truth and hadn't been doing so for a while. Wendy had obviously given in to her miserable existence with Mike and there was sod all Nell could do about it.

Instead of writing about reality, they merely exchanged pleasantries, both hiding behind paper, biro and words, creating a fake world. The thing was, Nell knew what Wendy was up to whereas in reverse, Wendy had no idea. No wonder Nell felt let down and frustrated. The anger, however, came from somewhere else.

Some of it she directed at Wendy and admitting that shocked Nell to the core, but it was a fact. To protect her best friend's feelings and also their friendship, Nell had given away her beautiful baby boy. Even though there were other factors involved in her decision, on the darkest of days, Nell felt the swell of bitterness towards Wendy because had she not met and married Mike, had she listened to advice and heeded warnings, history could have been rewritten. But she did, and a chain of events, none of them of Nell's making, led to that night in the boarding house and the conception of an innocent baby.

The sympathy Nell had for Wendy was rapidly evaporating and replaced by indifference. If she couldn't stand up to her husband or for her oldest friend, then maybe Molly was right and Wendy was best left to fend for herself.

Once Nell's mind took this pathway, there was no stopping it and on that bench in the middle of Liverpool Street Station, she literally trembled with anger. Here she was again, on her own with a bloody rucksack and a ticket to a kibbutz in Israel.

Later that day, Nell would be boarding a flight, flying through the dead of night and heading thousands of miles away from home and by that she didn't mean London. Hackney was just a dot on a map, another place where she'd rested her head and worked her fingers to the bone for a pittance. Sheffield was home, the place she had hoped to settle and make a life for herself until once again, Mike had ruined everything and her best friend had shown weakness.

Nell was twenty-three and what had she to show for it? No career, prospects, money. A baby, long gone, a photo of him she couldn't bear to look at, a friend she was forbidden to see, because of Mike. How she hated that man, how she wished the worst for him, even death. Yes, Nell wished he was dead. If she could take revenge she would. It would be slow and painful.

Brushing away a hot tear, Nell tried to imagine how she could hurt Mike in any way possible. And then, in the time it took for the digital clock on the departure board to click, it came to her. She knew how to do it, what would make him seethe.

He had wanted a son; Wendy had told her that but instead Jessica had arrived. Perhaps it was time that Mike found out about the baby boy who was now living with another daddy, one who would never know his natural father. And best of all there was nothing, nothing Mike could do about it. Nell had given away his son, and telling him so would be the best revenge of all.

Standing quickly, an energy coursing through her veins, Nell picked up her rucksack, shoulder bag and carrier of food. She had plenty of time before her midnight flight to get this right. Nell knew exactly what she was going to do but first, she had to buy a ticket and then, Mike was going to get his just desserts.

She took out the letter she needed to post, left her rucksack and food in a locker, and walked over to the red postbox. She kissed the envelope and dropped it into the slot, then headed for the ticket office.

Within twenty minutes she was on a train heading to Sheffield, her temper building by the second. Her brain went over and over the words she had put in the letter to Wendy and hoped it didn't mean the end. Nell had tried to get her to see sense, not to fall out with her completely. *Trust in your friendship,* her brain told her, *trust in your friendship.*

Mentally she re-read her words, the words that had taken so long to write, and what she had said was necessary. She knew it, and Wendy would know it.

5th January 1981

Dear Wendy,

As you will see there is no address on this letter because once again I am without a home and off on my travels. I'm on my way to Stansted and will post this before I fly out. I'm off to Israel where I'll be joining a kibbutz at a place called Kfar Haruv in the Golan Heights.

I will be working on the farm, dairy and agricultural, in return for my board and keep and a small wage.

I expect this news will come as a shock to you. It's much further than I have travelled before but I realise there's no point waiting for you in London. It's time to put myself first.

I have no idea what's going on with you and Mike, I suspect you hide a lot from me and I don't know why. We used to be so close but it's different somehow, like a gap has opened up that has nothing to do with miles. That's why before I leave I need to be honest and tell you some things.

I will never understand how or why you stay with a man like that, even if he is the father of your child. I truly wanted to help you, Wendy, but for some reason you can't break free but I beg you, think of Jessica and how in the future his behaviour might affect her. Only you can change things, so I pray that one day you find the strength to do so.

I feel so much bitterness towards him because I'd decided to stay in Sheffield. I even had a job lined up and a place to live. I was going to enrol at night school and get some qualifications, improve myself a bit. Mike ruined that because he erased me from your life. He made me feel worthless that night, told lies about me. I will never forgive him for that. I will despise him forever.

I was so hurt when I left and even though Molly has been an angel, I wasn't happy in London. This past year has been hard for many reasons which is why I have to get my head sorted and my life on track.

I'll keep in touch via Margaret but the fact that we have to correspond like this should tell you how wrong it is. I'm glad you've got a friend to help you out and at least she got away from him, maybe she can succeed where I failed and persuade you to leave. I hope she's giving you good advice but take care, there's something about her that gives me the creeps, don't know why but she does. Please don't let her use you to get back at Mike because he hurt her so badly. Seems to make a habit of it, doesn't he?

I doubt you'll be able to phone me anymore so we will have to keep in touch via letters. I'll write as soon as I get settled.

Stay safe, Wendy, and I hope you find a way to be happy,

Love,

Nell xxx

22

Nell waited right at the end of the chilly platform and resisted the urge to look along it or check her watch. She wanted to appear calm and in control when he saw her, like she'd sounded when she rang Mike only moments after arriving in Sheffield.

Marching towards the payphone, Nell had called the operator and asked for the number of Mike's office, memorising each digit before dialling the man himself. Even though her hands trembled slightly, Nell had forced her voice to remain firm when she heard his uppity tone at the other end.

'How dare you call me at work. What do you want?'

'I need to see you. Right now. I have something to tell you and I'd rather do it face to face. I'm at the Midland Station, platform two. I'll be sitting at the far end. Meet me there.'

Mike's voice sounded like a snarl. 'I'm not going anywhere, certainly not at the drop of a hat to meet you. Don't bother me a–'

'Don't put the phone down, Mike. You've got fifteen minutes, unless you'd prefer me to come there and tell everyone publicly what I have to say. And then I'll go and see Wendy.' Nell held her breath.

There was a moment of silence, then a terse response. 'I'll be there as soon as I can.'

'No, you'll be here in fifteen minutes, like I said. So get your finger out.' Nell slammed down the phone and sucked in air, quelling the nerves that buffered her insides.

On the opposite platform, Nell had spotted a large wall clock inside the waiting room and she knew he had only minutes left. Her feet and nose were cold, her hands she'd tucked inside the pockets of her winter coat, keeping them warm and still. By the time she was aware of a figure approaching from the right, the movement registering in the corner of her eye, Mike was at her side, his voice harsh when he spoke.

'What do you want? Why are you here?'

Mike towered above her, clearly having no intention of sitting so keeping her hands hidden, Nell stood to meet the challenge.

'I have something to tell you and I preferred to break the news face to face so I could see the look in your eyes and remember what it feels like to ruin someone's life.'

Mike huffed then smirked. 'What could you say or do that would ruin me? Oh, I get it. You're going to threaten me with Wendy, is that it? Go right ahead but I assure you that if you tell her about our little session, you'll come off worse. For a start you'll look like a mad woman after all this time, coming to stir up trouble like the proverbial bad penny. Then I'll deny it and say you threw yourself at me like the slag you are.'

Nell threw her head back and laughed, a loud derisory snort that she could see had taken him aback. 'Why would I give *you* the pleasure of destroying our friendship any more than you have already? But that's not the only thing you're wrong about because I can actually prove we had sex that night, and no matter how much you try to deny it, I know Wendy will believe me.'

Mike stepped closer and for a moment, Nell thought he was going to grab or strike her. His arm twitched slightly but then he reined it in. 'What the hell are you going on about, you mad bitch? What proof could you possibly have?'

This was it; the moment Nell had rehearsed over and over during the three-hour journey north. While the angel on her right shoulder told her it was utter madness, the one on her left egged her on.

'I'll tell you, shall I? You see, Mike, as a result of your repulsive pawing, after you forced yourself on me and I had to endure your depraved behaviour, we made a baby, yes a baby! There, is that enough proof for you?' It was Nell's turn to smirk, although holding in the rage was hard. She had so wanted to scream the words in his face but there were passengers close by. This was private, not a show for their benefit.

'Liar. You're a lying, conniving tart and I don't believe a word of it,' Mike hissed, glancing briefly at the chap reading his paper only feet away.

Nell raised her eyebrows. 'Don't you? Here you go, take a look at your baby, a boy by the way, your son.'

From her pocket, Nell pulled out the photograph, a copy, the original lay in her rucksack, in case Mike tried to snatch and destroy it. There in full colour was Darrell, wrapped in a hospital blanket, held in his mother's arms.

Nell watched carefully as Mike blanched, looked incredulously at the image of his son before swallowing. Appearing to gather his wits quickly, Mike's eyes were like slits as he spat out his next words.

'That could be anyone's baby, knowing you. Let's face it, you can't keep your legs crossed so it could belong to half the men in Sheffield.'

Nell winced at the use of 'it' but had also expected this response and didn't rise to it. 'Oh no, I assure you he's yours. I'd been a good girl ever since I arrived, and did I ever mention that I was seeing anyone? Not like I'd have had the opportunity anyway because I was with Wendy every day. The only man I spent time with was you, like when you drove me to the B & B each night. No, this time you've got me wrong and nine months after you raped me, I gave birth to our beautiful baby boy.' Her voice cracked and she hated herself for it. It wasn't the time to fall apart.

'Even if I did believe you, what are you after? Money, black-mail, is that it? You won't get a penny out of me.'

Mike had pushed his face closer to Nell's and a speck of spittle landed on her cheek. She wiped it off, held his stare and stood firm, then took a breath, keeping things simple. 'No, there's no need for blackmail. I don't want your money.'

On hearing this, Mike's shoulders seemed to relax slightly and his voice softened a notch. 'But how will you afford to look after a baby? Is he here, in Sheffield? Did you bring him with you?'

'No.' Nell put the photograph back in her pocket.

'So where is he? If he is mine I have the right to see him.'

'No you don't, you have no rights, and anyway, what's the point? He will have to be your dirty little secret unless you want to confess to Wendy, but then she might divorce you and take Jessica away and sue you for half of everything. Is that what you want? Come on, let's go and tell her together shall we?'

Mike shook his head. 'Stop playing games... Look, maybe we can sort something out. I could send you money for the boy. Keep it between the two of us.'

To Nell's delight, Mike was softening. The image of the son

he'd always wanted was planted firmly in his mind and she knew there and then that her moment was about to arrive.

'Aw, how sweet. Daddykins has got a heart after all and wants to see his baby boy. But guess what, you can't, end of story.'

'What? Then why did you come back to Sheffield to tell me? I don't understand what you hoped to gain. I mean it, Nell, if I have a son then I have rights.'

'Michael, Michael, Michael, you're not listening.' Nell's voice was laced with sarcasm as she shook her head and smiled, as though addressing a naughty child.

'I've already told you; you have no rights because your baby boy is long gone and has a new daddy and a mummy, and you will never see him, ever. I made very sure of that.'

Mike's face suddenly drained, and from the look of him he was on the verge of a seizure but managed to mutter a few angry words. 'What do you mean? What the hell have you done?'

'Work it out.' Nell clicked her fingers twice, holding them in front of his face. 'Come on, quick, quick. I haven't got all day to stand here spelling it out for you.' Nell could hear the spite in her voice and the rage inside felt like a furnace, fuelling her on.'

Mike seemed at a loss and shook his head so Nell filled in the blanks.

'I gave him away, Mike. I gave your son away to strangers. I couldn't have my boy anywhere near a piece of shit like you, taking your name, seeing your image in the mirror or finding out his father was a wife-beating rapist because that's what you are, aren't you, Mike? You're the scum, not me. You sought to destroy my life, took Wendy from me so in return, I took the son you've always wanted, from you.'

Nell could feel warm tears running down her face as she poked her finger into Mike's chest yet he remained impassive, apart from his face that wore a mask of horror.

'You evil, evil bitch.' His words a mere whisper.

'Yep, that's me. And man, it feels so good.'

'That's what this is? Revenge? You sick cow, you vile nasty–'

Nell held up the palm of her hand. 'Save it, Mike, because I don't give a shit, not about you, that's for sure. My son will grow up in a happy home far away from here, that's all I care about. I hope you think about that every time you raise a fist to Wendy, every time you shag one of your bits on the side, and remember that your filthy perversions and cruelty lost you your son – you got what you deserve.' Nell stepped away, putting space between her and Mike who looked enraged.

Sure enough, once Nell's words hit home, he reached out to grab her arm which she snatched away.

'Fuck off, Mike. I'm not scared of you, so do the world a favour, go crawl under a stone and die.'

Without giving him a chance to reply, Nell turned and walked away, leaving Mike speechless and alone at the end of a grey platform.

As she headed towards the foyer and the train back to Euston, Nell allowed herself to be swallowed up by the crowd, becoming anonymous, a nobody. After showing her ticket to the guard, she waited, watching for her train. She would have to endure three more long lonely hours but it had been worth it. A taste of revenge, the look on Mike's face, and knowing it would torment him forever.

Nell felt drained and would hopefully sleep her way to Euston where she'd take the tube to Liverpool Street, collect her rucksack and then head to Stansted. The red-eye flight in the early hours of a new day signalled the next stage of her life; a new start beckoned.

Seeing the train approaching in the distance, Nell touched the photograph inside her pocket and whispered softly, a message to her baby.

'I'm sorry, little one, I'm so sorry. Please be happy, my love, then letting you go will have been worth it. And I hope you dream of me sometimes, like I will dream of you. But mostly I want you to know that your mummy loves you, and she always will.'

23

Wendy rolled over onto her side and snuggled her nakedness against the equally naked body lying beside her.

'This so works,' she said, a dreaminess in her voice that gave her a sexy undertone.

'Certainly does,' Owain Jesmond said, his Welsh accent a lilt in her ear. 'It could work forever, my love, if you'd only say yes.'

She pulled away from him slightly. 'You know I can't say yes. He's evil, Owain, and he'd come after us, Jess and me. I'm not sure I can protect us both.'

'I can protect you.'

'Not when you're at work, you can't. Let's not spoil today by arguing about this again. Mike is my husband, and that's the way it will have to stay. If you can't take that, and remember I made it clear at the start that that was the status quo, then we have to walk away from each other right now, before we get in any deeper.'

'I'm in for keeps anyway,' he said and leaned across to kiss her.

And kiss her.

It was only the small cry on the monitor that separated them, and Wendy slipped on Owain's T-shirt to go to her baby daughter. They had only been together a week when Owain had set up his spare room as a nursery for the little girl, and Wendy lifted her out of the pink cot and carried her through to Owain's bedroom.

'Sorry,' Wendy said, 'she's wide awake. I've no chance of getting her back to sleep.'

He held up his arms to the baby and she reached for him. 'Come here, sweetheart, let's have a two-minute cuddle, then we'll maybe take you for a walk.' He looked at Wendy and she nodded, blessing the day Owain had catapulted into her life.

The bag of fruit had been hanging on the handle of the pushchair in a plastic carrier bag, a bag not strong enough for the volume of fruit she had bought. The handle suddenly snapped and she had made a grab for it. The fruit cascaded out; apples, oranges, satsumas, bananas, grapes, and assorted salad foods.

Owain Jesmond had been coming out of the newsagents and saw the disaster as if in slow motion. He ran towards her and it was an apple that did the damage.

It rolled across as his left foot came down and he ended up spreadeagled on the pavement. Both he and Wendy were helpless with laughter, and he had managed to splutter out, 'I bet you're the sort of person who laughs at people slipping on banana skins, aren't you?'

She had helped him up, they had brushed each other down and stashed the undamaged fruit in the bottom of the pram. He had suggested they go for a coffee to calm his frazzled nerves.

She knew they had fallen in love over that coffee; he was her one. Margaret had once told her that she believed there was one person, one special person, for everyone on this earth, and you would know if you ever were lucky enough to meet them. Margaret had thought her special person was Mike, as had Wendy, but on both counts they were wrong. Owain was Wendy's special once-in-a-lifetime person.

They saw each other three or four times a week, and had been doing so for a few months; Wendy hadn't felt it was right to speak about it to Margaret, but she longed to tell Nell, to regain that closeness they had shared. And she knew Nell would approve. Wendy left Owain singing nursery rhymes to the smiling baby and went downstairs to make them a cup of tea.

They strolled along the high street, chatting and smiling as only two people who have recently made satisfactory love can chat and smile, then veered off to go into the park. Jessica loved to go on the swings, and as she recognised her surroundings, her tiny legs kicked in anticipation.

Wendy strapped her into the baby swing and Owain pushed her. They stood closely together, taking it in turns to push the swing, and holding hands.

The heat from the sun was strong; the air still around them, and each person in the trio was feeling completely happy and relaxed.

'Get that child, my child, out of that swing, back in its pram, and home!' The tone was glacial, freezing out the sun temporarily, and Mike's voice created a whole new atmosphere.

Owain turned around to look at the man he'd only seen from a distance in the past. There was very little distance now, maybe a mere six feet. Although his attention was fixed on Mike, he saw on the periphery of his vision that Wendy had also turned, trembling, shaking in every limb. In that instant, Owain knew she had lied; the bruises he had seen on her at odd times weren't because she was naturally clumsy, it was because this man standing in front of him was naturally clumsy with his fists.

Owain moved towards Wendy and she stepped back. 'No, leave it, Owain. Go. I'll handle this.' Even her voice was trembling and he tried to move towards her again, but she held up a hand. 'Please, Owain, just go. I'll sort this.'

He didn't attempt to touch her again, but reluctantly turned away and headed towards the pathway leading out of the park. He turned back to look several times, and saw Wendy lifting Jessica out of the swing to place her in the pushchair. How the hell had Mike seen them? He was always in the office up to about one, then any outside business was conducted in the afternoon. They had always felt safe meeting up in the morning.

Reaching the park gates, Owain glanced back once more and saw Wendy flinch as Mike moved his arm towards her. Owain stopped. He waited for a moment and then saw the pushchair move, so he ran across the road, and into the café they had left earlier. He indicated he wanted a coffee and sat down so he could see the exit from the park.

Mike and Wendy came out through the gates and turned right, walked a few paces and he unlocked the driver door, leaving Wendy to handle Jessica and the push chair on her own. Eventually, she got everything stowed and climbed into the passenger seat. He pulled away from the kerb with a screech of tyres, causing passers-by to turn and look at the man who drove like a maniac.

. . .

Owain left most of his coffee, then ran to get his own car. He drove to Wendy's house, saw Mike's car parked outside and Owain went a little higher up the road and applied his handbrake. He switched off the engine, sat back and waited. Either Mike or Wendy would have to come out; Wendy's car was at his place, and she would have to collect it at some time.

They were hardly through the door before Mike hit her. He beat her as she lay on the floor, beat her as she tried to crawl away from him, kicked her as she used the arm of the sofa to lever herself upright, sending her crashing to the floor once again.

Finally it stopped and she lay, sobbing, on the carpet. She saw his footsteps go into the hall where Jessica was screaming for attention, still strapped into her car seat, and Wendy prayed he wouldn't go to her. He turned left and into the kitchen and she said a silent thank you. The bowl of cold water hit her head and splashed down her body. She gasped at the unexpectedness of it.

'Get cleaned up, slut. Then I want chapter and verse. And shut that kid up.'

Wendy had managed to get Jessica into her cot and asleep, exhausted by the prolonged screaming, by using one arm to get her out of the car seat and upstairs, crawling up each stair one step at a time, then resting. The pain in her left arm was almost unbearable, and she knew it had to be broken. She hugged it closely to her, trying not to move it. Taking off her clothes took some time, and she stepped into the shower with a sigh of relief.

The water was pink as it drained away and she stared in dismay at the bruises that were already appearing. Everywhere.

She dried herself with one hand, then looked at her face in the mirror. Her lip was split, and already twice its size; there was a cut on her forehead, one down her right cheek and a massive bruise on her left cheek. Both eyes were already showing signs of becoming black, and she gently touched her skin. Every part hurt. She couldn't bear the thought of struggling to dress herself with only one arm, and she could see the left arm swelling around her elbow joint.

She carefully manoeuvred her left arm into her dressing gown first, then slowly eased it onto the rest of her body. Finally, she lowered herself onto the bed, and her head dropped down. There had been many beatings over the years, but nothing like this. She needed Nell; Nell would help her. Wendy stifled a sob as she realised how far away her best friend was; Wendy was on her own. Not even Owain could help her with this.

She inched her way along the landing, checking that Jessica was still sleeping, then slowly made her way downstairs.

Mike was sitting in the lounge reading his newspaper, smoking a cigarette, a glass of whisky on the side table. The large wet patch on the floor was the only indication of the murderous attack that had taken place earlier. He looked her up and down with contempt.

'He'll not want you now, will he,' Mike said, his top lip curling into a sneer. 'Look at you, you're a mess. Who is he?'

The question was delivered abruptly, and she knew she had to tell him, to survive. 'It's not what you're thinking, we've met in the park a couple of times, usually when he's walking his dog.' *Owain, go and buy a dog*, was her silent prayer. 'It's at the vet's today, and Owain was killing time until he could go get him.' The lies were coming easily. She knew she wasn't only fighting for her own life; she was fighting for Owain's. Mike was more than capable of having Owain despatched.

'You were holding hands.'

'No, we were taking it in turns to push Jessica on the swing. We were standing close, but for no other reason than that. I'm not having an affair, and I don't even know his full name.'

'Owen? I'll find him. Then we'll see if he tells the same story.' Mike folded the newspaper, finished his whisky and cigarette at the same time, and stood. 'I hope you've learned a lesson, Wendy. You don't speak to or see anyone unless I know who it is. Give me your car keys, your car will need picking up. Where is it?'

'It's a little higher up the road than the park gates. I couldn't get any closer.' Another silent prayer of thanks that although it was parked fairly close to Owain's home, that was also near the park.

Mike picked her handbag up from the coffee table and threw it at her. 'Keys,' he said. She screamed as it hit her left arm, and she hugged it close. It took a minute for the pain to subside, and she couldn't move. He snatched it back from her and rummaged around inside it until he found the small bunch of keys.

'I'll get somebody from work to go and recover it. He'll bring it back here. Don't let him see you in that disgusting state. I'll tell him to post the keys back through the letterbox. I'll be late home tonight; I have a meeting at five to plan for tomorrow.'

'Tomorrow?' Wendy looked dazed, the pain was becoming overwhelming and she needed painkillers.

'I'm on the half eleven train tomorrow morning, for Manchester. We're meeting new clients; I'll be back in three days at the most. Two days if we can get signatures on paper. Think you'll manage?' he sneered. 'And in the meantime, I'll set somebody on to track down this Owen. He might regret taking his dog for a walk.'

Mike slammed the door on his way out and she hoped with

all her heart that he hadn't woken Jessica. His car started, and she heard it drive away.

Owain slunk down into his seat as he saw the front door of Wendy's home open, then slam loudly as Mike exited. Owain saw Mike get into his car and drive away – no squeal of tyres this time – and Owain waited.

24

Owain sat for half an hour before moving, then got out of his car and walked up the road away from the house. He guessed there would be a back way to the properties, and he eventually found it. The garden gate was locked, so he checked there was nobody around and he went over the top.

He didn't stop to admire the beautifully manicured lawn, the pretty spring flowers, but he did clock the shrubs that would provide concealment should it become necessary. He reached the back door, but it didn't have glass, so he moved to the kitchen window. Wendy was leaning over the sink, being sick. He could see she was holding her arm to her side, and he tapped on the window. She lifted her head slightly and froze, then wiped her mouth carefully on some kitchen roll before moving across to unlock the door.

In an instant he was in, aghast at what stood before him. Her face was a battered mess, and she obviously couldn't move her arm.

'He might come back,' she said. 'Sometimes he does that to catch me out.'

'Then we'll leave this door open. If he does, I can be out of here in a second. You've a healthy shrubbery I can hide in. He won't know. What can I do to help?'

She shook her head. 'Nothing. Would you mind getting me a drink of water, please. I came in here to get some painkillers, but then I was sick.'

He helped her sit at the table, and then took the glass she had already looked out, filling it with water. The tablets were with it, so he carried both to her, then went back to swill down the sink.

'Don't do that,' she said. 'I'll do it in a minute.'

'It's no problem. Wendy, I love you. I'd take a damn bullet for you, so cleaning up vomit is nothing. Besides, you'd already done most of it. Take your tablets and then we'll talk. I won't jeopardise you even further by playing the hero if he comes back, I promise I'll go if we hear that door. Does he have to use a key to get in?'

She nodded. 'It's a Yale lock.'

'Then we'll have even further warning, we'll hear the key go in.'

Owain finished the sink, then sat down by her side. 'Let's talk. Injuries first. Your arm?'

'I can't really move it; it hurts too much. I think something's broken...'

'I can take you to hospital.'

She shook her head. 'No, I'll go tomorrow. He's going away for a couple of days in the morning, catching the eleven-thirty train to Manchester, so when he's gone I'll get a taxi. I'll take Jessica to crèche for a couple of hours while I get sorted. But let's not talk about that. I need to tell you exactly what I've told him in case he does come back.'

She spent the next ten minutes filling Owain in on her story-line, but stressing Mike was out to find out who Owen was. 'I deliberately mispronounced your name so he thinks you're

Owen and not Owain, so hopefully he'll not be able to track you down. Oh my love, what can we do? I'm more scared than ever to walk away. I should have listened to Nell and gone with her right at the beginning...'

Owain gave a half-smile, and took hold of Wendy's right hand. She winced. 'I'm glad you didn't. Did I hurt you?'

'Yes, he stamped on that hand.'

Owen inspected it and noticed the swellings around her knuckles. 'Let's hope it's only bruising and not broken bones. One day something nasty will happen to this man.'

'After I've dropped Jess off tomorrow, I'll ring you. At least we have a couple of days to see each other without worrying.'

'If he's not here, I can take you to the hospital. You won't need a taxi.'

She tried to smile, but her lip wouldn't let her, and she touched it gingerly. 'Ouch,' she said.

'He's made a proper mess of you, but it won't go unpunished, trust me.'

They heard the rattle of the door and Wendy waved her right hand. 'Go,' she whispered. 'Go.'

Owain kissed the top of her head and ran out of the back door. Wendy sat still, sipping at her water, waiting for whatever was to come next. Nothing did. She heard sounds from the baby monitor, and stood, knowing it was going to be a painful ten minutes of trying to get her baby out of the cot and downstairs. Nobody came through the door, and as she reached the bottom of the stairs, she saw her car keys on the mat.

'Damn you, Mike Summers, damn you,' and she began the long pain-filled climb to Jessica's nursery.

Wendy was in bed by seven. Miraculously, Jessica had gone to sleep straight after her feed and Wendy knew she had to rest.

She climbed into bed still in her dressing gown, not able to bear the pain of removing it and having to put on a nightie. She had taken some more painkillers but doubted they were strong enough to kill the pain of a potentially broken arm.

She wedged the arm onto a pillow, and eventually dropped off. She didn't hear Mike come home, but woke as he moved around the bedroom, packing his suitcase for the three-day trip to Manchester. He made no attempt to be quiet, but she kept her eyes closed.

He climbed into bed, and she felt his hand cup her breast. She wished she'd brought a knife to bed with her, but even then saw the funny side of that thought. A knife to stab the husband, but don't use the left arm, it's probably been broken by him, and don't use the right hand because he's stamped on that.

She could smell the excess of whisky he'd clearly had, and knew he would soon be asleep. Her eyes remained closed, the hand still cupping her breast, and finally she heard the small snores telling her he was asleep.

Mike left at ten o'clock, telling her he had to pick up some paperwork from the office, then he would go on to the station.

She said nothing, not wanting to talk to him. 'And don't go anywhere,' he said. 'You'll frighten little kids with a face like that.'

He didn't kiss either her or Jessica, and Wendy was on the phone letting it ring twice before replacing the receiver as he was climbing into the cab.

'Margaret?' she said, when the call was returned. 'I need to talk to you.'

They talked for half an hour, Wendy filling Margaret in on the previous day's disasters, with Margaret telling her she had guessed there was maybe someone else in Wendy's life, because she had changed. Margaret said she had to go, because she was meeting a friend in town, and said she might drop by the station to make sure he caught the train, and then Wendy would be settled in her mind that he wasn't in Sheffield. 'That's what friends are for,' Margaret finished with a little laugh.

With the phone call ended, Wendy dressed Jessica as best she could, then fashioned a sling to support her arm. Wendy took the little girl to crèche, telling them she would be back for three to collect her, and she headed to her car. Their stares as they saw her face made her feel uncomfortable, and she left as quickly as she could. It wasn't easy driving with one arm out of commission, but she wouldn't let bloody Mike defeat her.

The rain was coming down heavily, and she blessed the day she had settled for an automatic, after getting rid of the Mini. It meant she hardly needed to use her left hand at all, and she drove to a car park near the train station and parked in the corner. It was difficult pulling up the handbrake lever, but she eventually managed it, and got out of the car. She wanted to be sure her bastard husband was out of Sheffield. She needed time to think and heal.

Owain left his car at home and caught the bus. He had things to do, but would soon be on the bus heading back home.

25

Man Dies At Midland Station

A man in his thirties was killed by train at Sheffield's Midland Station yesterday. The train, the 11.30 for Manchester, arrived on time, and the man, at the front of a small group of people, appeared to fall onto the tracks as the train drew to a halt.

He has been identified as Michael Summers, and he leaves behind a wife, Wendy, and a daughter Jessica. Next of kin have been informed. The death isn't thought to be suspicious at this stage, although further enquiries are progressing.

Wendy had only been home an hour when the police arrived. The young female officer gasped when she saw Wendy's face.

'Mrs Summers? Is your husband Michael Summers?'

'It is. I haven't reported him yet, so you can't be here to arrest him.'

'Can we go inside, please, Mrs Summers?'

After being told of Michael's fate, it didn't take Wendy long to fill them in on the previous day's beating. She told them it was because she was out at lunchtime, in the park with her daughter, and he wanted her at home doing him some lunch.

'And he did this to you? Have you been to the hospital?' Sergeant Ralph Norwood could hardly believe what he was seeing.

'He did, but when I set off for the hospital this morning I had to come back because it's hard to drive with an arm in a sling. I think it's broken,' she said, knowing she sounded stupid. 'When he went to work this morning, he was really upset because of my face, and he said how sorry he was. I can't believe it. Do you think he's jumped in front of that train because of me? Because he knows the hospital will call in the police, and he knows I'm going there?'

'Mrs Summers, I think it's urgent you get to the hospital. Do you have someone you can call to take you there?'

'I'm not allowed friends. My best friend from when we were children is on a kibbutz in Israel, and there's no one else.' Though she didn't know why, Wendy thought it best not to mention Owain or Margaret. 'I have to get my baby from crèche in half an hour, so I'll have a taxi there, then go on to the hospital. I thought Mike would be taking me, he was really sorry this morning before he went, really sorry.' She put down her head and allowed the tears to flow. 'What will I do now?' she mumbled. 'Could nobody have stopped him? He's my husband, and I'll miss him always. We love him, Jessica and I, so much. He didn't mean to hurt me when he hit me, he really didn't.'

'The few people who were still there said he appeared to

stumble only seconds before the train reached him. I think he meant to do it, Mrs Summers, and we're really sorry for your loss.' Ralph Norwood turned to his colleague then back to Wendy. 'Would you like me to leave Diane with you to take you to the hospital, give you some support?'

'No, I'll be fine. I promise not to drive, and I'll ring for a taxi to go and get Jessica. Do you think you can leave me now, to think this through? I don't know what I'll do without him.'

They both stood. 'Of course. If you need to talk, please ring us. Once the shock sets in...' Ralph handed her his card. 'You will need to identify his belongings. Diane will ring later to make the arrangements.'

Wendy waited until they had gone, got into her car and drove one-handed to get Jessica, then returned home. She felt strange. She didn't need to do anything. No meal to cook, she could ring on the telephone without any Gestapo-style interrogation, and she could either grieve or not grieve.

The sergeant had said he would notify Mike's workplace, and as Wendy came through the door, the phone was ringing. It was from work, and she cried as they said what a wonderful man he was. There were three messages on the answer machine which she ignored, and she made a cup of tea to calm her somewhat frazzled nerves. Mike was dead.

She took the handset into the lounge with her, knowing she could ring Owain without fear, but as she placed the tea on the coffee table, there was a knock on the door.

She saw the figure through the glass and knew who it was. Wrenching the door open she said, 'Owain' and wrapped one arm around him. 'What are you doing here?'

'I had to come. I saw the news. I'll stay away until you're ready to see me again, but know that I love you and I want to be with you. No more pressure now, my lovely one, no more pressure. I'll be here as soon as you pick up that phone and tell me you love me just as much.'

He smiled gently at her, turned and walked down the path. At the gate, he looked back and she touched her fingers to her lips and blew on them.

For now, for Owain, it was enough.

BOOK TWO 2016-2018

1

Nell stretched her body across the crumpled bed sheet and made the shape of a star, knowing before her eyes opened that she would be alone, yet still she smiled because it wouldn't be for long.

Laurent would return soon, bringing her coffee, as he did each morning after he'd walked the dogs and made sure everything was in order on the farm. Nell wasn't an early riser. Those days were long gone, of waking before dawn to cook and skivvy. How her life had changed, not actually since she met Laurent although their crossing of paths had played a huge part. No, it was a random act of insanity; perhaps a filament of straw that really had broken the donkey's back and the catalyst that fuelled Nell's anger, one sunny morning on the Riviera, many moons ago.

Turning on her side, Nell opened her eyes and saw that behind the voile that covered the tall windows, left ajar to allow in a gentle night breeze, clear blue skies heralded another sweltering summer day. Closing her eyes once more, yawning as she drifted back into a dreamy sleep, Nell thanked whoever was listening for sending her to this place, almost thirty glorious years before.

The kibbutz years had changed Nell immeasurably and despite any misgivings she'd had when she'd first arrived at what looked like a desert army camp, thanks to the kind and open-minded nature of her fellow kibbutzniks, she settled in quickly. There were people from every walk of life and nationality; backpackers making their way around the world, students taking a break, families living off the land, lost souls like Nell, plenty of dreamers and probably the odd revolutionary. There were also young Israeli conscripts who worked side by side with volunteers; along with defence of the outpost, farming the land a common aim.

Hard work and fatigue had helped Nell through the homesickness stage although sometimes, this yearning, wanting something that had brought only bitterness and regret confused her so she learned not to dwell on it. Instead she focused on the people around her with Antipodean accents and many a tale to tell. Her own she kept to herself.

A kind of breakthrough occurred when she received the letter from Wendy, telling of Mike's death, only months after Nell had left Sheffield. They had suspected he may have taken his own life, or it was a terrible accident but whatever it was, it had occurred on the same platform where Nell had told him about his son. As Nell read the words, her body flushed cold and goosebumps covered her skin. During that initial stage of shock, she felt a tiny flicker of guilt that her revelation may have wounded him badly, but she experienced not one shred of sadness.

Shock and guilt were immediately swept away by relief, for herself mainly because her secret was safe, then her thoughts turned to Wendy who was free at last. The demon shadow that had darkened both their lives couldn't blight them anymore and now, they could rebuild their friendship from afar. This notion brought immense joy to Nell's soul. But there was something else.

No matter how hard Nell tried, if it had been suicide, she could not reconcile the Mike she knew with a desperate guilt-ridden wreck. This was not the man who had duped and forced himself on her. Nor was it the venomous man who had vilified her on the doorstep, insinuating she was a whore, who wiped her out of Wendy's life and then got on doing God knows what to her poor friend. It didn't fit.

Even though Nell had shocked him to the core with her baby revelation, he had remained in control, never cowed, not even in the face of threats or fear for his marriage. No, Mike didn't give a toss about Wendy, or Jessica for that matter, he only cared about himself. He wasn't the type to apologise, be riddled with angst over his monstrous behaviour or feel sadness at the loss of his son. So why would he kill himself?

Nell would have been more inclined to believe he had in fact tripped. It was even more likely he'd been pushed because after all, he wasn't a well-liked man. Had a train come speeding through the station during her heated conversation with Mike, then the thought may have crossed her mind to give him a quick shove. She'd have been doing the world a favour, no doubt about that.

Going by Wendy's letter, the police were inclined towards suicide, in main owing to the dreadful injuries she had sustained. Mike knew he was in deep trouble and men like him didn't fare well in prison. Lack of evidence meant it was left to the coroner to decide. So by the time Wendy's letter had reached Nell, the post-mortem and inquest were over. Mike's death was recorded as tragic and accidental, and a nice fat insurance cheque would soon be in Wendy's bank account and a funeral had been arranged. It was more or less done and dusted. Bye-bye, Mike.

While she would have loved to be there to support Wendy, wild horses wouldn't have dragged Nell back, not for Mike. No way would she even pretend to pay her respects for a man she felt nothing but disdain for, and that was putting it mildly.

Once the 'sad and shocking' news had been imparted, Wendy then magnanimously unburdened Nell of any guilt, saying she wouldn't expect her to fly home and disrupt her life, and that she had Margaret for support. As long as Nell kept in touch and they could put the past behind them and rebuild their friendship, Wendy wished her well.

It was a sentiment for which Nell felt immense gratitude and in some ways it set her free from so many things, especially her ties to Sheffield, a place she never wished to see again.

When her kibbutznik life came to an end, knowing that Wendy had finally met a lovely man, Owain, with whom she and Jessica were happy, Nell hitched up with a group of back-packers and headed off on the hippy trail. Thanks to the Iranian Revolution and the Soviet invasion of Afghanistan, the route to India was blocked so instead, their destination was Morocco.

Nell's ethos was simple; keep on going, keep on working, keep on blanking it all out. But after silently marking two anniversaries of her secret baby's birth, the frugal yet free-minded hipster life began to wear thin. Nell was sick of hitch-hiking, starving for much of the time, and just about swerving dysentery. They lived off the land and the hospitality of locals who didn't seem to mind tribes of spaced-out smelly people camping in their fields.

It was all well and good being cut off from civilisation and capitalist extremes but now and then Nell would've liked a bath, a proper bed, an aim. If she was honest, the mind-numbing cigarettes didn't always do the trick either and she soon realised it wasn't the way to erase memories, that was impossible. Freedom might have suited some but Nell became increasingly irritated by the pointlessness of her existence. It didn't do to meander aimlessly through her days. She needed focus and routine like in the kibbutz. It was time to move on.

After hitching a ride to the port of Tangier, Nell used almost the last of her money that was hidden deep inside her trusty rucksack, and took the ferry across the Strait of Gibraltar to Málaga in Spain. From there she hitched to Alicante and did what she did best. The familiarity of the bars and cockroach-infested hotels gave her comfort, which was why at the end of the season she headed north, to Andorra and her old friend Alba who welcomed her in. It was there that Nell remained for two years, working the winter and summer seasons, telling herself the mountain air and lush valleys were what she needed to heal the wound in her heart.

Correspondence was so much easier after almost a year of sporadic contact. It did Nell's heart good to receive Wendy's letters and hear her voice in their more regular phone calls, now they were uncensored.

But while she listened from afar to tales of Jessica and Wendy's happy existence, occasionally, in unguarded moments, Nell couldn't ignore that which she'd buried – the image of her baby boy. It got easier though, and she learned to cope and manage the pain. Just as she'd heard people say that losing someone through death eventually becomes bearable, so too did her own loss. In the meantime, Nell resisted any attempts by Wendy to entice her home and stood firm.

'But we'd have so much fun, Nell, and I'd love you to meet Owain and see how Jessica has grown. I want her to know her Aunty Nell properly, not just from photos or listening to me read your letters.'

'I know, I know, and I would love to see her too so maybe I'll pop back at the end of the season, or you could come and see me. We'll work something out. At least we can keep in touch properly and talk on the phone.'

Wendy sighed. 'Okay, I believe you, but promise you're not avoiding me and nothing's wrong. I could always tell when you were fibbing but only when I see the whites of your eyes, and I'm starting to forget what colour the middle bits are. That's how long you've been away. Get this wanderlust out of your system and come home. And DO NOT fall in love with a foreigner otherwise there'll be trouble.'

Nell laughed. 'I promise nothing's wrong, okay? I like my independence and want to travel while I'm young and anyway, I know you're happy and Owain is a good guy so I can relax. And as for men, I'm off them for good, especially high-as-a-kite hippies and Hooray Henrys who ponce about on the slopes, and the locals only marry good Catholic village girls so there's no need for you to worry.'

Although she'd swerved the question, Nell knew the truth. She *was* avoiding Wendy and Sheffield and anything that reminded her of the past, and until that pain went away and the gaping hole in her life was filled or healed, Nell wasn't going back. As for men, the thermostat in her heart was turned to freezing, and that's how it would stay. It was easier.

When Alba decided to retire and throw in the towel, selling her hotel to a holiday chain, Nell signed up with an upmarket agency and took a job on the Côte d'Azur working as a house-maid in a villa owned by a rich American couple.

Merv, the husband with the shady casino-empire back-ground, was okay. A red-faced constantly perspiring heart attack waiting to happen, whose focus was food and whisky, he did have the decency to acknowledge Nell's existence whereas his wife Dionne was a viper. Despite marrying down, she hailed from New York banking stock and was entitled, rude and insensitive. The only thing she appeared to tolerate was her miniature poodle, Pinot.

Nell despised Dionne but the agency paid well enough to afford a rented room with a sea view – a snapshot across and in between the rooftops. The work was easy though, as long as you had bulletproof self-esteem and the patience of all the saints combined. The view from the villa, looking out across the Mediterranean, took Nell's breath away and was probably the only thing that encouraged her to stay.

Then during August, as the relentless sun bore down, causing tempers to fray, bit by bit, Dionne's acid tongue peeled away layers of Nell's patience and soon the sound of her braying voice began to grate. It was the lack of respect, the talking down her nose and complete absence of humility that made Nell's blood boil. Those clicking fingers Dionne used on the gardener, the chef, the postman, even the bloody dog, started the tick in Nell's head. It was like a bomb ready to go off.

The fuse was lit the day before Dionne and Merv were due to fly to Paris for a socialite wedding before heading to Switzerland for a fortnight. After neatly folding and packing all of the clothes that Dionne had flung onto the bed, then listening to her whinge about not having enough shoes and deliberating on which silk scarf to take, Nell returned after dinner to find two of the suitcases empty. The contents lay in a pile on the floor, while another lay on the bed. Dionne had changed her mind and wanted everything repacking before Nell went home.

The match was struck.

2

The following morning, as they waited for the car to take them to the airport, Merv smoked one of his favourite cigars as Dionne, with Pinot tucked under her arm like an accessory, paced and cursed the driver who was taking far too long.

Nell, hot and tired, heaved the cases to the door, noting that Merv didn't offer to give her a hand but instead, decided to humour the hired help.

'Say, I bet ya can't wait to see the back of us and take it easy for a week... and we don't want to find out you've been having wild parties and dancing on the tables while we're away.' Merv winked and laughed at his own unfunniness.

'Oh I shan't be here, sir. Once I've straightened up the house I'm having a few days off too.' As Nell dragged the last case into place, she saw Dionne's head whip around; her fluff-ball companion looked equally as surprised.

'Days off. I *don't* think so. I haven't been consulted or granted permission.' Dionne looked as though someone had told her the villa would be demolished.

'I'm sorry, madame, but the agency was supposed to tell you. I asked for some time off as the house will be empty for a fortnight. They said it was fine and would send a replacement if you needed one. Have they not mentioned it?' Nell had presumed everything was arranged and seeing as they weren't on chatting terms, hadn't bothered to mention it to Dionne.

'No they have not and I forbid you to go. I want all of the bedrooms aired and stripped for when we return. We are having guests and I expect every inch of this place spotless. I've left you a list in the kitchen. You'll have to cancel your arrangements. It's as simple as that.'

'But, Madame, the agency can arrange for another girl to step in. It was only for five days, a short holiday, because I've worked non-stop all year and I didn't think you'd miss me.' Nell could feel her cheeks flush and her armpits damp with perspiration. She was also pissed off with being spoken to like crap.

Merv huffed and stood, acting like the big peacemaker. 'Hey Dionne, come on, give the gal a break. The house is fine, she can clean your silver or whatever you need when she gets back so let's move on out. I can hear the car.'

Merv opened the door and attempted to steer Dionne outside. However, she shook him off and addressed Nell.

'I do not want another help snooping around my home while I'm away so you'll have to cancel your plans and take a vacation when I'm less busy. Make sure you check the list and complete it, and don't think because I'm away you can shirk, is that clear?' With that, Dionne turned and tottered out into the courtyard, not waiting for a response.

Nell was left speechless. Who the hell did that woman think she was talking to? As if on autopilot, Nell made her way through the house and watched from the veranda as the chauffeur-driven car wound its way along the twisty road into town, heading for the airport. Once it was out of sight and mind, she turned and smiled. *Good riddance.*

Kicking off her shoes, she wandered into the kitchen,

allowing the cool marble to soothe her aching feet. The chef had buggered off already so she had the house to herself until the cleaners came, in fact, that gave Nell an idea. Pulling the small notepad from the drawer, she found the number for Cristalle, smiling as she spun the dial. Once she'd told the grateful cleaner that *Madame* had given her and Gina two days off, Nell replaced the receiver and chuckled.

Next, she opened the wine-chiller door, removing a lovely bottle of Möet before searching for something delicious to eat in the overstocked fridge. Taking her leftover lobster salad outside, Nell stripped to her bra and knickers and dived into the pool. When she came up for air, she threw her head back and laughed into the clear cobalt sky.

'Fuck you, Dionne, you stuck-up witch, and bon bloody voyage.'

When she woke the next morning in Merv and Dionne's queen-size bed that was splattered with red wine and smeared with what Nell hoped was chocolate mousse, she felt not one ounce of guilt for her evening of debauchery or, for weeing in the pool. She was sick of being someone's skivvy, of not having any fun and being a bloody nun after padlocking her heart and throwing away the key. Yawning, Nell decided to take a bath in some of those lovely Dior oils and then she fancied caviar and scrambled eggs for breakfast, after which she would make some plans.

Smelling divine after her bath, Nell was wrapped in a luxurious towel, padding around the bedroom when she spotted something peeking out from under Merv's side of the bed. Bending down, she pulled out a thick manila envelope and when she opened the flap and saw the contents, Nell gasped.

Not only was there a wallet containing traveller's cheques but a wad of cash, easily a thousand euros.

'Merv must have dropped it while he was packing. At least he managed to do something for himself apart from wipe his...' Nell thought out loud, not sure what to do next so dropped onto the bed, trying to think it through.

The fact that they hadn't called the house to ask if she'd found the envelope told her that Merv didn't know it was missing yet and even when he did, there was a good chance he'd think the airport staff had stolen it from his case or lost it en route.

Looking again at the contents, Nell knew there was no way she'd get away with using the cheques as they had Merv's name on them, but she could use the cash. It was stealing though, and Nell had never been a thief, not a proper one; because nicking a few chocolate bars from the offie or keeping coins and the odd note you'd find lying about a chalet, or inside a service-wash pocket, didn't count. This was different, it was proper pinching and she could get in serious trouble.

That's if she got caught. That's if they could prove she'd taken the money and let's face it, they couldn't and anyway, they weren't exactly skint, probably wouldn't even miss it. Looking around the swanky bedroom furnished with the best of everything, Nell imagined the luxurious surroundings that Dionne and Merv were heading to and how Nell had been forbidden to take time off. She was only going to spend a few days down at the beach reading and swimming, nothing fancy. Dionne had begrudged her even that.

Taking a deep breath, Nell stood and marched into the huge walk-in wardrobe that housed *Madame's* every whim and inside one of the cupboards, spotted her vast collection of suitcases. Taking the largest red Fendi case, Nell opened it and, perusing the rows of gorgeous outfits in the wardrobe, selected those she thought suited her best. Dionne was of a similar build and height but her shoes were slightly too big. Nell would get away with the sandals, so after matching them with the outfits and a handbag or two, she loaded them into the suitcase, leaving enough room for one more important item.

By the time Nell was ready to leave, she'd added some scarves, two pairs of sunglasses and a bottle of Diorissimo, from one of the dozen or more unopened boxes of perfume that were stashed in a drawer. When she had everything she required, Nell closed the wardrobe door and smirked, confident it would be a while before Dionne noticed some of her clothes were missing, that's how many she had.

Taking a set of car keys from the hook in the kitchen and dragging the suitcase behind her, Nell made her way to the rear of the house and the shaded courtyard where the three cars were parked. After loading the boot, she climbed inside and settled herself on the plush leather seat of the midnight-blue Citroën before firing up the engine. Nobody would think twice about the help taking the car, she was always out and about running errands for *Madame*.

Winding down her window before setting off, Nell enjoyed the breeze on her face as she drove carefully through the almost-deserted streets of the village, where everyone was too busy eating lunch to notice, never mind care.

It didn't take long to pack her rucksack with worldly posses-sions and vacate her room. After squashing it inside the huge suitcase, Nell drove to the agency and parked in a back street. Once inside, she handed in her notice and collected the last of her wages, saying it was an emergency and she needed to visit her sick old grandmother and wouldn't be back.

Behind the wheel of the car moments later, Nell's hands trembled slightly. Was she really going to do this? Then looking down at her worn plimsolls and faded jeans, Nell grinned. Yes, she damn well was. Next stop Gare de Nice-Ville.

Alighting at Gare D'Avignon, Nell felt like a new woman. After parking the car in a deserted street close to Nice station and leaving the keys in the glove compartment, she had changed clothes in the ladies toilets and emerged in a chic outfit of comfortable slacks and a cool mauve blouse, sunglasses perched on her head. She had ripped the traveller's cheques into shreds and flushed them down the loo before sauntering across the foyer and buying a first-class ticket to Provence.

The six-hour journey had been wonderful, a bit like how Nell felt dressed in her finery, drinking champagne and savouring a delicious lunch in the buffet car. She kept herself to herself and avoided eye contact, preferring to take in the scenery as the train sped through the Alpes-de-Haute-Provence, whisking her to a place she'd heard about and always dreamed of visiting.

Taking a taxi outside the station, Nell asked the driver to recommend a hotel and within minutes she was checking in to the quaint but agreeable Hotel d'Europe. It was merely somewhere to rest her head for the night because she had to keep moving and follow her nose, to the lavender fields.

The following morning, after breakfast, Nell walked to the bus station, dressed casually in a simple white linen dress and sandals. She needed to disappear in the crowd, blend in, and not leave a trail. Her eyes were shaded by large framed sunglasses, a barrier to the outside world, protecting Nell from intrusion and allowing her new persona to walk on by.

Fifteen minutes later, with her ticket in hand, Nell boarded the bus to Roussillon, a town she had never visited but had remembered its name from a misty-morning conversation as she had picked apples. She was retracing the journey of one of her seasonaire friends who had worked the lavender fields. Nell had always wanted to send Wendy some lavender and now she was going to be there for the harvest, but not to work. This time she would be on the outside looking in, and it felt so good.

Nell hadn't been paying attention when she bumped into Laurent that day outside the gift shop, forty-eight hours after she had arrived in Roussillon. Almost thirty years later she could still picture the scene, even what she was wearing – a silk dress with pale pink flowers, and his strong hands as they gripped her arms to steady her.

She had been gazing at the assortment of gifts; bottles of lavender oil, soap and dried sprigs woven into pretty arrangements so when she turned to enter, she didn't notice the tall gentleman as he exited the shop. Laurent had literally knocked the wind from Nell and after he apologised profusely for something that wasn't his fault, insisted on buying her a drink in the bistro opposite. Rather than refuse and seem churlish, Nell accepted but also, for the first time since she'd left Nice, felt the need for conversation. It was one that would change her life forever.

Once they had introduced themselves and the drinks were ordered, Laurent wasted no time in interrogating Nell. 'So, mademoiselle, what brings you to the town of Roussillon?'

Nell shrugged. 'Oh, the same thing that brings all these tourists,' Nell gestured to the people meandering along the street in the sunshine, 'the beautiful buildings and scenery and of course, the lavender. I've been promising myself that I'd visit for years and now, I'm here at last.'

Laurent grinned at her. 'I for one am glad you kept your

promise but I'm rather surprised to see you alone. Have you a travelling companion?'

'No, I travel by myself; in fact, I have been to lots of places on my own. I like it that way.' Nell knew she was being mysterious and enjoyed the quizzical expression on Laurent's face; it was an extremely handsome one that she realised was beginning to make her feel strange inside.

'I admire you, mademoiselle, and I have to admit to feeling glad that there is no Mr Nell lurking in the shadows.'

To this Nell smiled and felt overcome, ridiculous really and totally alien, yet she liked it; that feeling of expectation, or was it inevitability – either way she didn't really care, so she focused on Laurent.

It turned out that he was single, lived with his parents, owned the gift shop and a few other bits and pieces around town, along with farmland on the outskirts. He wasn't flash, quite the opposite, and rather than talk about himself, focused the conversation on Nell, her origins and securing a dinner date.

Three days later, on a sweltering August evening as they lay on the bed in Nell's hotel room, the windows flung wide to allow in the breeze, Laurent turned on his side and brushed a stray lock of hair from Nell's face.

'You know, Nell, the days I have spent with you have been the best for such a long time and I think that maybe you are stealing my heart. But I need to know if I should lock it away, or allow you to keep it forever.' Laurent held Nell's gaze.

'Whatever do you mean?' Nell's pulse raced.

'I mean that I need to know what happens next, what is going on inside this head of yours' – he tapped Nell's forehead gently – 'and why someone as beautiful as you has spent the last of her twenty-seven years wandering around the globe?' Laurent waited, Nell however, remained silent.

'And how this woman I am falling for, in her beautiful clothes with such wonderful stories has not found a love that is strong enough to keep her in one place.'

In that moment, Nell knew Laurent had seen beyond the façade and if this, whatever it was, really meant something, then now was the time for truth.

3

Nell took Laurent's hand in hers and steeled herself, determined not to mess it all up.

'But what if I told you and in an instant, everything you say you feel is ruined and then what? I will have to pack my bags and go.'

Laurent tutted. 'My darling Nell, do you not see that nothing you can say will change how I feel in here.' He touched his heart. 'I want to know the real you.'

Nell felt a lump in her throat and tears prick her eyes but she owed him honesty. 'Okay, so what if I told you that before I came here, I wasn't a tour guide in Nice, I was a maid for a rich but horrible woman, and as soon as her back was turned I stole her clothes and money, and her car, and took a train to a place I'd only ever heard about but imagined would make me feel happy?'

Nell flicked away a tear then continued while Laurent remained quite still, listening.

'And that I have been running from a memory of something that hurts so much the only way I could bear the pain was to switch off my heart, and until I met you it had worked just fine but now, I don't think I can do it anymore.'

When a sob erupted from Nell's mouth, Laurent took her in his arms and held her until the tears dried and when they did, he spoke.

'I don't care what you did, Nell, but I do care about why you did it so please, explain. I want to know, and I want to help.' Laurent dried Nell's eyes and cheeks with his fingers.

Without speaking, Nell pushed back the sheets and walked naked to where the red suitcase stood by the wardrobe. Opening it, she pulled out her battered rucksack and then turned, emptying its contents onto the bed.

There was a wad of letters tied with twine, a tatty notebook, a woollen hat with a huge flower and a small slim cigar box that when she opened it, contained a charm bracelet and a selection of what looked like hippy jewellery and touristy souvenirs, and an envelope. As she removed the contents, her birth and christening certificate first, Nell kept hold of the photographs as she spoke.

'This...' Nell indicated the items on the bed, 'is all I have to show for my life. These are my only possessions, treasures really. These photos are from my past. I have many friends scattered around the world, wonderful people who are probably still walking, moving on. They replaced the family I have never had, the best friend I left behind, who means the world to me. Then a few years ago, someone came into my life who is lost forever and I've been running away from him ever since. He is my secret but I will share it with you. After I've explained it from the beginning, it's up to you if I pack up and move on, and I promise I won't blame you if you tell me to go.'

. . .

It was dark outside and the crickets clicked their messages back and forth. Strains of music and voices could be heard on the street below as tourists enjoyed the harvest moon that hovered above the church spire. Nell was wrapped in Laurent's arms, silent in contemplation, her truth settling on the night air.

When Laurent spoke, his voice sounded thick with emotion. 'Thank you for telling me and explaining what is in your heart but now, I think I must tell you what is in mine.'

Nell's heart lurched so she closed her eyes and waited for the inevitable, unable to utter a single word.

'What has happened in the past makes you who you are, the most beautiful woman I have ever seen. I never believed in love at first sight but it is real and has happened to me. I cannot imagine living one more day of my life without you in it so now, it is time for you to stop running, Nell. Let's make a life with each other, side by side. Let this be your home, let me be your family and your friend. Please don't go, Nell. I want you to stay, stay here forever with me.'

Through tears and laughter, Nell told him she would.

The next morning, after they'd popped an envelope of money into the charity box at the Convent of the Holy Sisters of Mary Magdalene, they went for a drive, out of town and towards the lavender fields. When they stopped by the side of the road, Laurent suggested they took a walk. The scenery was breathtaking; rows of purple blooms as far as the eye could see and the air was filled with fragrance, slightly medicinal, smoky wood and then a sweet floral hint. Taking her hand, he led her amongst the lavender, causing Nell to halt and protest.

'Laurent, stop. What are you doing?'

Laughing, he attempted to coax her onwards. 'You said you

wanted to send some lavender to your friend so pick some, as much as you want, and then Wendy can fill her whole house with it.'

'Laurent, I can't. Come on, let's go back to the road before we get in trouble.' Nell attempted to pull away but his arms were soon encircling her waist as he laughed, then kissed her forehead.

'Nell, my darling, it is not only you who has secrets, a truth to tell. Turn and look around you. Do you see these fields and that house on the hill? It belongs to my father and one day, it will belong to me, his only child and heir. And in the town, not only do I own the gift shop, but the bistro where we sat that day, and a large number of properties... oh, and the hotel where you are staying, so you won't have to pay the bill. Now, please stop looking so shocked, pick some lavender and then, my darling Nell, we are going to see my parents who cannot wait to meet you.' Laurent smiled as he watched Nell closely.

'So all of this, and that' – Nell pointed to the grand château, not a house, made from creamy stone that looked out across the fields of purple – 'is yours, and you *do* actually live with your parents?' Nell was truly astounded.

'Yes, my love, it is and I do. And I want to share it with you. I told you, this is your home now. My family will be yours.'

For the past twenty-nine years, Roussillon and the beautiful château on the hill had become Nell's home, one that she had shared with Laurent and his parents who were sadly gone, leaving their legacy in the safe hands of their son and his wife.

Laurent had changed her life and allowed Nell to put down roots. It also gave her pride, belonging, a focus, and slowly but surely she came to terms with her loss. The most wonderful thing was that it was a place to welcome Wendy and her family. They would come for the holidays: Christmas, Easter, and summer, whenever they wanted, and during these times, Nell and Wendy had laughed till they cried, ran barefoot through the fields, swam in the pool and dined on the terrace as they watched the sun burn orange.

In between times the women carried on with their tradition of letter writing, refusing to bow to technology, emails were forbidden. They spoke on the phone regularly and made much use of FaceTime, so much so that they could have lived around the corner, not in different countries. Jessica could not be persuaded to put pen to paper so sent regular emails and always a birthday card to her 'wonderful Aunty Nell'.

Even though she had a fractious relationship with her mother, Jessica and Nell had nurtured a strong bond. Being so far away meant Nell had managed to remain neutral in the continuing battle of the wills that still raged between Wendy and her daughter.

The rumblings of discontent began in Jessica's rebellious teenage years where Wendy sought to contain and control. Maybe she was scared of losing her only child to the spirit of wanderlust after listening with wide-eyed fascination to Aunty Nell's desert tales. Perhaps Wendy saw danger in the school disco, and the young men who paid Jessica attention and therefore Wendy kept a firm hold on the reins, and her daughter safe from harm. Safe from men like her father, like Mike.

Yet Nell suspected the thing that Wendy sought hardest to avoid was in fact the most impossible of tasks – denying Jessica her heritage, erasing genes. Whenever Wendy spotted a faint glimmer of Mike, the turn of Jessica's head, a look in her eye, an echo in her voice, they became a reminder of the past, one she sought to squash. There was no talk of Mike at home, no photos, no pilgrimages to his grave, none that included Wendy anyway. And even though Jessica understood exactly what her father had done, accepted his failings and openly despised his actions, she resented greatly the effect they had on her life.

Wendy had no right to punish her for *his* mistakes, or for looking a bit like him either. It wasn't her fault, or the boys who rang the house and were told she wasn't home, or had the front door slammed in their faces. Just because Aunty Nell had buggered off for years and never came back, didn't mean that Jess was going to book a one-way ticket to Australia, although now and then the thought might have crossed her mind.

Nell watched and listened to Jess from afar, as the memory of her dead father and ever-present fears of her mother slowly but surely began suffocating her.

Wendy's way of dealing with her own demons had been a huge mistake, and sent Jessica running in the opposite direction, towards anyone who simply let her be. Nell had tried to counsel Wendy, tactfully of course, in letters and during visits to the villa where it was clear to see the gap between mother and daughter widening with every year. But where Mike was concerned, Wendy had closed down, frozen her heart and unfortunately, by the time Jessica was old enough to leave home, no thaw was in sight.

The damage had been done so all Nell could do was conduct separate relationships between her best friend and her goddaughter and then one day, if needed, she could be the bridge that joined them together.

The only regret Nell had was that she had lost touch with Molly but this was tinged with a sense of relief, allowing those hard sad times in Hackney to be left in a box, the lid firmly closed.

Nell hoped Molly was happy though, and had found a love of her own.

The years had passed by so quickly. Nell adored being a farmer's wife and although it wasn't anywhere near the hard work she had experienced during her travels, she still got stuck in. There was no need, of course, but Nell loved working on the land and watching the dark furrowed soil spring into life, relished her evening strolls with Laurent as they walked hand in hand along the rows of shoots, checking progress right up to harvest time when the field came alive with pickers, seasonaires like her.

Her love for Laurent had also blossomed, the only blip was their inability to have children, the fault lay with him not her yet they had ironed out the crinkle in their life and afterwards, got on with enjoying what they had, not what they didn't. Some things weren't meant to be and for them, for two completely different reasons, parenthood was one of them.

In those rare dark moments that always came during her increasing tired spells, when she wasn't sure if the tightness in her chest and breathlessness was anxiety, her dratted age or her conscience, Nell wondered if Laurent's infertility was a punishment. If it was, her guilt was magnified that her penitence should include her beloved husband because that wasn't fair.

It was at these times, Nell couldn't refrain from wondering about Darrell, where he was, if he was happy, but one thing she knew for sure, he hadn't come looking for her. The day Nell silently marked his eighteenth birthday, the thought that he would have access to his records and the letter she had written filled Nell with such terror and confusion she had turned to Laurent who as always, soothed her fears. If he came they would deal with it, her friendship with Wendy was stronger than ever, it would survive, as they all would.

Nell told herself that the trail was dead, like Mike, and she was far away from Sheffield and hard to trace. Would Darrell be able to find her, would she want him to? As the years rolled by, the threat would rise and roll like a wave, then dissolve onto the shore, leaving Nell slightly stranded, with no other option than to simply move on and live her life.

Rising from the bed, Nell slipped on her gown, made her way to the window and looked down onto the courtyard below then out towards the surrounding blanket of lavender. Hearing footsteps on the stairs, she turned to see Laurent enter with her morning tray of coffee and croissants and resting against the cafetière, was an envelope, the writing instantly familiar.

'Good morning, chérie. Look, you have a letter from Wendy but don't take too long, we have to be in good time for your appointment and the car park at the hospital is always so full, so relax but hurry too, and eat your breakfast.' Laurent placed the tray on the bed, receiving a kiss and a wry look from his wife.

'I will do my best to do everything you ask, my love, but I hate hospitals and wish we didn't have to go. And I've told you, I'm perfectly fine, simply getting older, almost bloody sixty.' Nell had been trying to convince Laurent that her recent funny turns were merely age-related and nothing to worry about.

'Perhaps we should let the doctor decide that. Stop being difficult, it doesn't suit you. Now eat, I will be back soon.' Pecking the top of her head, Laurent departed, as always he had a thousand things to do.

Smiling, Nell took the letter, enjoying the familiar anticipation of reading the words of her oldest friend, the novelty still hadn't worn off and she was already wondering what news there would be from Sheffield. Had there been ructions with Jessica? Maybe more grumbles about poor Owain who was such a dear but goodness, how Wendy could sometimes boss him about. Taking a sip of her coffee, Nell decided to obey her husband; she would read the letter, eat her breakfast, go to the bloody hospital then once she was proved right, they could get on with life, and being happy ever after.

4

Wendy opened the door with the chain on. A glance through the spyhole showed that she had no idea of the identity of the person standing on her doorstep, but initial impressions were that he was a bit too well dressed to be a delivery driver.

'Yes?'

The man dropped his head to one side in order to see the face framed by the edge of the door and the door jamb. 'Oh, hello. I'm sorry to trouble you, but does a Michael Summers live here?'

Wendy felt as if the blood drained from her entire body and she began to tremble. She had spent thirty years trying to forget the brutality, the deviousness, the disrespect of the man, the man whose funeral had caused her to smile such a lot.

'Who are you?'

'My name is Andrew Grayson. I'd like a quick word with Mr Summers if he's available. If he isn't, perhaps I could make an appointment to see him.'

Wendy could hardly speak. Nobody had mentioned his name in her house for such a long time, and this man had the temerity to not only knock the stuffing out of her, but make her unable to think in words of more than one syllable.

'Not... here,' she stammered.

'I really do need to see him.' The man was persistent.

Anger suddenly took over. 'You can't bloody see him. He died thirty years ago.'

Grayson looked shocked. 'He's dead?'

'He is. Tell me who you are, or get off my doorstep.'

The man stumbled backwards, staring at her. 'I'll... I'll...' He spun round so his back was towards her, hesitated for a couple of seconds, then strode down the path and out of the garden gate.

Wendy closed the front door and ran upstairs to the front bedroom, where she stood at the window watching him walk down the street and get into the driving seat of a small red car.

She followed the car until she could no longer see it, then staggered backwards and sat on the bed. 'What the hell was that about?' she said out loud, then answered herself. 'Fuck knows.'

Margaret answered the phone after one ring, and listened patiently while Wendy told her the story of the man at the door, her words spilling out of her incoherently.

'He didn't leave a card or anything?' Margaret asked, trying to make some sense out of the story.

'Nothing. He looked really shaken when I said Mike was dead. It scared me, Margaret. He scared me.'

'Then let's hope he doesn't come back after telling him Mike's dead.'

'So what do I do?'

'Nothing. There's not a lot you can do. He didn't threaten you or anything, so try to put it from your mind. Tell Owain when he gets home, and maybe tell Jessica too. Don't let them be blind-sided by this blast-from-the-past situation...'

Wendy told Owain that night; she realised with some sadness that the reaction he gave wouldn't have been the reaction of thirty years earlier. He would have been supportive, he would have been loving, and he would have taken the reins so she had nothing to worry about. She had loved being able to rely on him, but more and more she was feeling that she couldn't, that she was alone.

'What did he look like?' Owain took a sip of his soup.

'Late twenties, early thirties maybe. Dark hair. Didn't notice his eyes, I was too scared. Smartly dressed though. He'd defi-nitely dressed to impress, but to impress Mike?'

'Have you told Jess?'

'Not yet, I thought we'd better discuss it first.' Wendy's mind drifted quickly to the figure her eyes had followed down the street, and there had been something... She shook her head to clear the picture.

'I don't know what we can discuss,' Owain responded. 'He might return, he might not. You want to take a break for a few days? Keep out of the way? Ask Jess if you can go stay with her and Dan for a couple of weeks.'

Wendy gave a shrill burst of laughter. 'I can imagine what she will say. She'll come up with every excuse she can think of to stop me going. There's a reason Jess moved hundreds of miles to Cornwall when she got married, you know.'

Owain shook his head, and returned to his cooling soup. 'She wanted affection, Wendy. You never forgave her for being Mike's daughter, but it really wasn't her fault. She was happy when we finally moved in together, but even then you didn't bend in any way. Don't blame Jess – or Dan – for this distance between us, you're the one who caused it.'

Wendy kept her mouth closed. This could so easily lead to an argument; there had been many that usually centred around Jess, with Owain taking Jess's side and not hers.

Owain always felt Jess should have been Margaret's child, and not Wendy's. Margaret adored her, and Jess had always had her own room at Margaret's house. The poor kid had simply had the wrong mother.

And the spectre of her bastard of a father had risen again.

'I suggest you don't tell Jess unless you have to. It'll only upset her, and as this chap is looking for Mike and not Jess, I don't think it will become an issue for her. What do you think?'

Wendy looked up from the bowl of soup she was stirring, making circles in the surface of it. What did she think? How long had it been since he had asked her what she thought about anything?

'I do love you,' she said unexpectedly.

His spoon was halfway to his mouth, and he replaced it in the soup bowl. 'I know,' he said gently. 'And I hope I've never done anything to make you question that love. If I have, it was unintentional. I feel you drifted away from me a bit, a lot, when Nell said she was staying with Laurent forever. And you didn't drift back, not even when you saw with your own eyes how happy she was. I love you, you daft woman, but you've become...' He paused, searching for the right word. 'Unapproachable.'

Wendy's tears dropped into her soup, and Owain pushed

back his chair and moved around the table to hold her. The tears flowed that she had held in for so long, and he waited.

'Thank you,' she said eventually, using the napkin to dry her eyes and face. 'If there's one thing that strange man has done, it's to open the floodgates.' She gave a weak smile to her husband.

'Look, I'll ring in tomorrow morning and arrange to work from home for a few days. I'll tell them I need a week off.'

'And you'll answer the door?'

He looked into her eyes. 'I promise, even if it's only the postman. But I need to know what you want me to do. If this chap does come back, do you want me to invite him in? I suggest we do. I'll be here to protect you, but I think we need to know what he wants. If we don't find out, this will always hang over us.'

'You're right. But let's hope he doesn't come back.'

Owain answered the door for the first time three days later. As Wendy had said, he was probably late twenties, dark hair and fairly tall, Owain reckoned about six feet.

'Please,' the man said before Owain could speak. 'Is the lady here?'

'She is, but can I help?'

Andrew Grayson held out a letter. 'Please read this, and then see if you can tell me anything.'

Owain skim-read it, then handed it back. 'Wait here.' He closed the door and went to find Wendy, sitting rigidly at the kitchen table. Fear was written on her face. She had started to hope, to believe, that he wouldn't return to her home.

Owain walked across and kissed the top of her head. 'You're not going to like this, my love, but I think we have to talk to him.'

Andrew introduced himself, then apologised for his behaviour of three days earlier. 'I had psyched myself up, and then had my hopes dashed. I'm not sure if you can help now, but I knew I had to come back and say sorry anyway, even if you spoke from behind a chain again. Thank you for seeing me.'

'Would you like a drink?' Wendy spoke stiffly. This man had so far given her three almost sleepless nights, and she actually wanted to stab him, but instead found herself being the hostess.

'No, I'm fine, thank you. As you know, I'm looking for Michael Summers. I had this address, but was using this as a starting point. People tend to move, and it has been thirty years.'

Wendy felt bewildered. What had been thirty years? Since Mike's death? But Andrew clearly hadn't known he was dead so he wasn't referring to that.

'Tell us what you need to know, and we'll see if we can help.' Wendy knew she sounded stilted, unwelcoming, but she felt stilted and unwelcoming. She wanted him out of her house.

Andrew took out the piece of paper he had already shown to Owain, and passed it to Wendy. 'I think you should read this. It will explain why I am here.'

She glanced at Owain, and he stood, reached into a top cupboard and took out the brandy and a small glass. He poured, and then carried it to Wendy.

'Read it,' Owain said.

She carefully opened it, then smoothed it out onto the table. She had no idea why her fingers were trembling, but it was noticeable, and Owain squeezed her hand to let her know he was with her.

To my darling boy, Darrell,
    I have no idea how old you will be when you read this letter but I

hope with all my heart that when you do, you have had a happy life with parents who love you.

I expect you are looking for answers so I will do my best to fill in the gaps. First, I want to tell you the most important thing of all, the one you must keep in your mind while you read my words.

I love you so much, Darrell, and at this moment, as I write this letter, my heart is breaking and I can hardly see the words through my tears. I have had to make the hardest decision of all, but I pray it is the right one and one day you will understand this and if need be, forgive me.

If there was another way, if I thought I could give you a happy life, one you deserve, then I would scoop you up and walk away with you right now. I have looked at every option but all I can see is hardship and struggle. While I would endure anything for you, it isn't fair to bring up a baby knowing you have nothing to give, and that his life would be one without a proper family, a mother who could provide everything her son would need. That is why I have to let you go, to give you a chance to have the things I missed out on.

I will be honest about my past, so that it will explain your roots and perhaps give you a greater understanding of my predicament. I have never known my father, apart from his name was Edward or Eddie and my mother's name was Deirdre. She had a drink problem and died when I was a teenager after drowning in the canal. I went to live with my Aunty Sue and only just avoided being placed into care. My teenage years were hard and although I got by, I couldn't wait to escape my existence and Sheffield. I wanted to see the world and make a new life for myself. I wanted to be happy.

I have one true friend in this world, Wendy Summers. She is married to a man named Michael, and at the time of writing this, they live at Hillside, 17 Langley Dell, in Sheffield. Wendy means the world to me but when she got married, our relationship changed and it was for the best that I went away. Michael was not a nice man at all. He was controlling and cruel and wanted me out of Wendy's life.

During a visit to Sheffield, on the night of his daughter's christening, he took advantage of me and against my will, you were conceived. Afterwards, I fled to London where you were born. I will keep this secret from Wendy as I know it will break her heart and I will carry the guilt with me always. You have a half-sister and her name is Jessica. If you decide to track your birth family down, there will be consequences but I will face them. I respect your right to seek them out.

So there you have it. I have told you about the past but I want to focus on the future. The only way I can survive the next few hours, days, years, is to imagine you growing up surrounded by love with a wonderful mum and dad, maybe brothers and sisters, a big family who will nurture and protect you.

I promise that I will think of you always, every day, especially on your birthday and at Christmas. I will mark time by smiling at the thought of you growing into a happy healthy little boy, a teenager and a man. Even though I will miss out on this, as long as you are happy, then saying goodbye will be worthwhile.

Finally, I gave you your name because it means 'beloved' and even if your new parents change it, that's what you will always be, my beloved son, Darrell. Please know how much I love you and that a second will never pass without me wishing things could have been different and one day, I might see your face again and hold you in my arms.

Goodbye my perfect boy,
I love you,
Mum x

Wendy's head crashed to the table, and her world turned black.

5

For three days, Wendy had been angry. Incandescent. Unable to cope with her life, her world, Owain.

And then she knew what she had to do. She had to write to Nell, and it wouldn't be on flowered paper and in a flowered envelope. What she really wanted was to send it on a solicitor's headed notepaper, signed for, but she settled for A4 computer paper.

Owain had tried to persuade his wife to go and see Nell, but she couldn't do that. It seemed that Nell had been lying by omission for thirty or so years, and probably lying for most of her life. Wendy certainly couldn't stand a face to face over this issue, the biggest betrayal of them all. Her words would be enough to destroy this particular friendship forever.

She pulled towards her the copy of the letter Andrew had allowed them to take and reread it, although she knew it virtually word for word. Putting it to one side, she picked up her pen. Letters had linked them for so long, had carried family news, had shown how much they loved each other although far apart, but this one was going to be the last.

. . .

Nell,

This letter will be our final one, and every word is written with nothing but hate in my heart for you. You have lied to me by not telling me a secret I should have been told thirty years ago.

A young man arrived on my doorstep during the past week looking for Mike. I should have guessed. He walks like Mike, he talks like Mike, his hair is the same as Mike's, he is Mike's. Isn't he!

He produced a letter once I'd explained his bastard father was dead and that letter clearly told the story of how he was conceived. You slept with Mike. No wonder you two became extremely friendly while you were over here for Jessica's christening.

"Took advantage of me and against my will" huh? I bet. You've always slept around, you tart. And so did Mike. A marriage made in heaven when he met you off that plane, wasn't it?

Were you screwing all the time you were here? I guess your precious birth control didn't work. You cooked his meals, you cleaned up after him, you nursed his daughter, for fuck's sake! You absolute bloody harlot, Nell.

Anyway, I've told this precious son of yours, the one you gave away because you couldn't have carried on sleeping around and having a fantastic time swanning around Europe, all about you. He's under no illusions what sort of a slut he has for a mother, so your sloppy lovey-dovey bits in the letter you left in his adoption file mean nothing.

You can die knowing he hates you.

I fainted when I read the letter. Fainted because of your words, because neither of you'd had the guts to tell me you'd had an affair, and there was a little side effect. So, here's what's going to happen. I'm going to keep in touch with your son, and I'm going to drip-feed him stories of your life, the people you've slept with, everything you've ever done. How I wish I still had those letters Mike burned. They would have made interesting reading for a child to see how his mother behaves, wouldn't they?

Except he's not a child. He's a man, and would understand every word.

I will tell Jessica, she needs to know what her precious Aunty Nell has been up to, and she will hate you also.

Have a good rest of your life, Nell. I will no longer feature in it.

Oh, and one more thing. His adoptive parents ditched your hope that he would be called Darrell. You'll never find out from me what he's really called, his true identity, not some fly-by-night name you'd thought he might keep. Didn't happen, Nell, didn't happen.

Wendy Jesmond (Mrs)

Wendy reread it, folded it carefully and slipped it into the plain white envelope. She carefully wrote Nell's name, the address coming so naturally to her, and knew it would be for the last time.

She took a stamp from the flowered paper box, falling apart after so many years, the edges bound with Sellotape to hold it in its original shape, and stuck it on the envelope. *No more,* she thought, *no more.*

It took five minutes to walk to the postbox and back, an hour to stop crying.

The sense of betrayal running around her head was defeating her, and Wendy knew she needed counselling. Talking things through with Owain was helping; they hadn't talked properly for years, so if something good could be said to have come out of the current situation, it was that their struggling marriage seemed to be back on track.

Andrew had asked for details of his father's death, and

Wendy had told him they had newspapers in the loft which told the full story. Andrew was coming for a meal; and Wendy didn't know how she felt about it. She hoped it would be cathartic, that she could move on, but as Owain had pointed out, Andrew was Jessica's half-brother. He would eventually want to meet her, and they would have to smooth the path towards that scenario. They had to keep in touch with him for the moment.

The newspapers were spread over the kitchen table, and Andrew scoured through them. He had enjoyed the meal with Wendy and Owain, but his politeness had been strained. He was really only there to find out what had happened to Michael Summers.

Finally, Andrew spoke. 'It seems unclear. He either killed himself or he accidentally fell. He wasn't pushed?'

'That we'll never know,' Wendy said. 'We weren't there that day.'

'Okay. Why would he commit suicide? Did he have some financial issues? Something else?'

Wendy glanced at Owain and he nodded his agreement. She walked across to the drawer in the kitchen that held everything they didn't know where else to put, and took out two photographs. She handed them to Andrew.

He looked at them, and then looked up at Wendy. 'This is you?'

She frowned. 'Pretty unrecognisable, yes? I also had a broken arm, bruises covering every part of my body, and a mental destruction that was impossible to imagine.'

'My father did this?' Andrew tapped on the picture. 'Why?'

'He did it the day before he died. He saw me talking to Owain while I was with Jessica at the swings in the park. Owain was walking his dog.' *A little white lie,* she thought, *not a Nell-sized lie.*

'Did Mike hit you a lot?'

'He did. That picture is the reason the coroner thought suicide the most likely verdict, but it could have been accidental. He could have slipped. There was no evidence he was pushed, just a large crowd around him. The train was too near for anyone to help when he went off the edge of the platform.'

'May I borrow these, please? I'd like to take them and photocopy the parts about my father. He perhaps wasn't a nice guy, but he was still my genetic dad.'

Owain handed him an envelope. 'Already done. I wouldn't have given them to you if you hadn't asked. We obviously don't want to let the newspapers go, they're part of Jessica's inheritance, but I've gone through what we have carefully, and you have copies of every article.'

'Thank you, sir. I'll leave you in peace. The meal was lovely, Mrs Jesmond, and much appreciated. Is it okay if I call you if I have questions? I really would like to keep in touch, now that I've found you. And of course, I have questions about my mother. But I'll get this entered in my book first before I start looking for her.'

Owain looked towards Wendy, willing her to read his mind. *Give him her address, give him her address.*

'At the moment, Andrew, I'm not in a position to be able to help you,' Wendy said with a smile. 'I don't know where she is, but if I ever find out, I'll tell you.' *A little white lie, this one a Wendy-sized lie.*

· · ·

Owain didn't speak much after that, and called goodnight from the doorway as he went to bed. Wendy attempted to speak, but he held up his hand, and headed upstairs. She thought back over the day; the letter, her feelings, Andrew's visit, and wondered if she should have done things differently.

Nell would probably receive the letter during the next couple of days, and she would try to ring. Thank God they had number recognition on phones; she had no intention of answering ever again.

She knew without any shadow of a doubt that Nell would want to see the son she had given away so many years earlier. Wendy knew Nell; those sentiments in the adoption pack letter were genuine. Nell was full of love; Nell would give her life for her son even after all these years of never seeing him.

Payback time, Nell, Wendy thought. *I'll keep him from you with every breath in my body.*

6

Nell picked at a thread on the buttonhole of her jacket and waited for Laurent to return with whatever he was buying in the airport shop. To anyone looking on they would probably think Nell was a nervous flyer when in fact she loved it, under normal circumstances.

Today though, she was dreading the whole journey, only because with every air mile and each fluffy white cloud they passed en route, it was taking them nearer to Sheffield and her showdown with Wendy.

Laurent's return was a welcome distraction and as he settled beside her, Nell placed a hand on his leg, glad of his presence.

'Are you all right, chérie? Here, I bought you some bonbons for the flight and a magazine, see.' Laurent opened the bag and allowed Nell to peep inside.

'Thank you, darling. That's thoughtful and the sweets will stop my ears from popping.' Nell refrained from mentioning that her heart already felt like it was going to explode but that would only set Laurent off with his worrying.

Wrapping his fingers around hers, Laurent turned his eyes towards the monitor where he studiously kept an eye on their flight's progress. Nell, on the other hand, tried to focus on the passengers who were milling about the lounge, but despite her best attempts, her mind wandered back to Wendy and the past fortnight, such a dreadful time.

Even though Nell had known there was a chance that one day her son might make contact and it would open up many wounds and maybe cause new ones too, she never dreamt things would turn out this way. Never in a million years would she have imagined that Wendy could be so vindictive, so cruel and heartless, but she had. Now, Nell had been forced to take action and somehow make amends but above all, she wanted to see her son. She wanted to explain properly, and hold Darrell in her arms again, see the face she had pictured in her dreams and never forgotten.

The morning Nell received the letter from Wendy, for a moment before she tore it open, she'd wondered why it was in such a dreary envelope. Perhaps she'd run out of her usual flowery ones. Once she'd removed the contents, Nell relaxed in her chair, sipping her coffee, and concentrated on the words inside.

Within seconds her whole world had crumbled.

When Laurent finally returned he found Nell in a heap on the bed, sobbing uncontrollably and was unable to get a word of sense out of his hysterical wife so while he held her in his arms, he read the letter.

'Chérie, chérie, please stop. Wendy does not mean these things; she is upset and in shock. My love, I beg you to stop, you will make yourself ill and I am sure we can make this right. These are angry words from a woman who also feels her world has been turned on its head.' Laurent rocked Nell to and fro, stroked her hair and made shushing noises but nothing worked, all he could do was wait until the tears subsided. It took a while.

Nell had descended into a dark pit and remained there for days, hiding from the world, almost catatonic, unable to process her thoughts. While Laurent fretted about her health and hastily rearranged the appointment with the heart consultant, Nell holed up in their bedroom.

The poisonous words that ran through her brain fell into a bubbling pot of confusion, anger, despair, desolation and panic. How could this be, how could her dearest friend turn on her this way? Why would she not have thought it through, given Nell the chance to state her side of the story? But the thing that she'd found most unbearable, amongst the name-calling and twisting of the facts, was that a mother would deny another the chance of contact with her child and worse, go out of her way to prevent it.

When Nell tried to speak to Wendy at home, she didn't answer or reply to the messages she left, and the final insult came when Nell realised her number had been blocked, meaning she couldn't even ring or send texts to Wendy's mobile.

Determined to be heard, Nell put pen to paper in an attempt at damage limitation, appealing to Wendy's conscience and also, in a separate missive, Jessica's good nature. An email had arrived immediately from her goddaughter who nailed her flag firmly to Nell's mast. Jessica, already fully aware of the situation and despairing of her mother's behaviour, swore allegiance and promised to help Nell wherever she could. Wendy's daughter, despite being hit with the news that she had a secret half-brother, had found it in her heart to listen and forgive.

Apart from the letter she had sent to Wendy two weeks before, lines of communications were cut and this left Nell with no other option. The timing could not have been worse, especially after the news they had received from the consultant following a thorough round of tests. Nell had severely narrowed arteries and would need surgical intervention, the sooner the better. She was to avoid stress and rest until the date of her surgery, an instruction both she and Laurent knew would be virtually impossible to obey. Consequently, when it became clear that Wendy meant what she said and had completely shut Nell out, a decision was made.

No way would Laurent allow Nell to go to Sheffield alone, the thought was inconceivable and he was adamant that he'd be by her side. 'Chérie, you made the hardest decision of your life so many years ago and it breaks my heart to think of you then, my sad little Nell. If we had been together, I know I would have made a difference, I would have been able to change your story, so whatever happens in the future I will be there to support you.'

Nell nodded and gripped his hand, hoping that the life force in Laurent would top up hers because it was waning by the day. Nell wasn't sure if it was a mental or physical depletion, her mind and soul versus her body, but whatever it was, one of them was losing the battle, she could feel it.

When Laurent jumped to his feet and gathered their things, Nell's stomach lurched, knowing what the flurry of activity meant.

'Come along, chérie, it is time to board. Let's hurry to avoid the fussing on the plane, you know how you hate to be pushed and shoved.'

Nell stood and placed her handbag over her arm, sucking in air and gathering her reserve of strength. 'Yes, yes, darling, lead the way.'

Following on behind Laurent, Nell told herself this was nothing new. It was one more journey, a few more miles to cross, another chapter in her life and with her precious husband by her side, instead of being a lonely nomad, she would get through. The only difference was instead of a battered rucksack, Nell carried her Louis Vuitton handbag and during the Air France flight she'd be travelling business class, not economy.

As she handed the attendant her boarding card and passport, Nell knew her self-ministering was bravado because this was nothing like the journeys of the past. Instead of running away from Sheffield, she was marching, flying, in its direction and this time she would hold her head up and look the city in the eye.

The day had arrived when she would admit her mistakes, laugh in the face of banishment and end her self-enforced exile. Today, Nell was finally going home.

7

Chateau du Champ de Foire
14 Place de l'Abbé Avon
84220 Roussillon
France

Dear Wendy,

It is clear that you are avoiding and ignoring my calls so it looks like our old-fashioned method of communication is the only way I can hope to get through to you. This is not my last resort and I thought you should know that if you do not acknowledge this letter than I will be forced to come to Sheffield and discuss the situation with you in person. The other scenario is that you don't even bother to read this and tear it into shreds, in which case my imminent arrival will come as quite a shock to you.

Since your letter, I have realised that maybe I don't know you very well after all because the Wendy I thought of as a sister, my oldest and closest friend, would never have said the things you did. Then again, the Wendy I do remember won't be able to resist reading what I have to say, so I hope that somewhere deep inside, that person still exists. In both circumstances I will have to take a chance.

I am doing my best to be magnanimous and forgiving as I know you will have had a terrible shock and perhaps did not consider your words or the impact they would have before you put pen to paper but then again, even the envelope sent out its own silent message so I fear I am mistaken.

I'm going to start at the beginning which is the night your husband forced himself on me. With hindsight I realised after the event, that he had manipulated me from the moment he collected me at the airport, but I was so relieved and grateful of his acceptance and change of heart to see beyond his fakery.

The evening after Jessica's christening when I knocked on your door, I wanted so badly to tell you what had happened but the events that followed, when Mike turned up, told me loud and clear that it would be for nothing, so I accepted my fate and left. You may have seen it as abandonment but truly, what was I supposed to do?

I was extremely unhappy in London despite Molly's kindness so when I found out I was pregnant I cannot even begin to describe how I felt, so many emotions. But one thing I knew for sure was that despite the suggestion otherwise, my baby deserved a chance because he didn't choose to be conceived, and he wasn't a mistake to be flushed down the toilet or left in a bucket. I wanted my baby to live.

Again, you will never know the agony of loving someone so much that you would do anything to keep him near, yet have to accept that to sacrifice your own feelings and give him away is the best thing, his best chance. The day I said goodbye to my son has haunted me forever and now, thirty years later, you seek to deny me that opportunity, out of spite and revenge. That's what it is, Wendy, and it is unforgivable that a mother would deny another that right.

I actually understand your malice, anger, even your jealousy, if that's what it is, which I do find somewhat curious considering the kind of life you led with a man you told me you despised. You see I accept that this will have come as terrible, life-changing news and in moments of extreme shock we can all act badly, but I hope that by now you may be regretting some of your harsh words that cut me to the core. They will be hard to forget, let alone forgive.

If you are still hell-bent on ending our friendship and continuing your course of action, I would first ask you to consider another side to the story. It's one in which I am not so much the villain but the victim in all of this.

Do you realise that at the root of this is Mike, the man who came into your life and changed it overnight, changed you too? You see, Wendy, had you listened to me and not been so determined to be different, better than us, looking down your nose at your friends, then maybe you'd have turned Mike away and found happiness elsewhere. You didn't believe me when I told you what he was like your best friend who had no reason to lie. You didn't stand by me, or fight for our friendship because a fancy home and a Kenwood mixer were far more important, weren't they?

After Mike's death you told me what he was really like, what you had endured and why you didn't make a stand, and my heart broke for you. But the more I think about it, even at the beginning, you actually lied in all those letters, back and forth between us where you painted a picture of domestic bliss and your saintly husband. And you know what the really sad part is, that because I thought you were so happy and knowing that Mike hated me so much, I left you to it.

Not only that, to make it easier for you, so you wouldn't worry about poor old Nell and you could live your Stepford wife existence guilt-free, I too concocted a fantasy life where the sun shone every day or the snow-covered mountains were straight out of Heidi. So many times I wanted to tell you I was fed up and homesick but what was there to come back for? I couldn't even be the proverbial gooseberry, he made sure of that.

The day I left London for Israel, I was literally empty. My baby had gone, I couldn't come home because the pain of seeing Mike would have been unbearable and I would have had to lie to your face day after day, that's if I'd been allowed to see you. I will tell you more about that day another time but suffice to say it was a low point, one of many that I had endured and was yet to face.

So let me ask you, was my predicament a result of you meeting Mike, was it because you were vain and stuck-up and weak? Perhaps, or maybe it was the bitch called Life, our shitty messed-up lives.

I'm so interested to know how I could have played things differently, Wendy, so if you have any ideas I'd love to know. Perhaps you can tell me how you would have reacted if I'd have turned up in sunny Sheffield one morning holding a bundle of joy in my arms and told you he was Mike's. Would you have welcomed me in? Would you have soothed my tears and told me you understood that he was a cheating evil bastard and you'd get rid of him straight away? Would you have given me safe haven and assured me that you and I would be okay, we would bring our children up together? Or would you have panicked because your pathetic fake world was about to implode, forcing you there and then to do something about it? Who would you have chosen, Wendy? Would you have thanked me for bringing it crashing down? Would you have forgiven me or hated me like you do right now?

If you don't know the answers today, then how was I supposed to thirty years ago? I was a scared, broken-hearted twenty-four-year-old, more or less alone in the world, pregnant and penniless.

Let's fast-forward to when I met Laurent, the past had been laid to rest in a six-foot grave, you and I had rekindled our friendship and moved on with our lives. Do you remember the happy times, Wendy? Those days at the château where it felt like the sad days were a million miles away, a different planet, a bad dream. I do. I welcomed you into my home, I hosted your wedding, I helped teach Jessica to swim and then scuba-dive and speak French.

I also remember the pain in my heart when I received her stick drawings in the post, the ones that included all of us with our names scrawled in crayon above our heads. It hurt because I knew someone was missing. Every year on Jessica's birthday, I smiled along but couldn't help but wonder if my own child had a cake and lots of presents on his special day.

It almost killed me not knowing, every single year, every single birthday and Christmas, but I hid it because I thought it was for the best. I hid so much and didn't tell the truth, turning my face away when you asked me if I minded not having children with Laurent, if I felt cheated. What was I supposed to say?

You hid the truth too though, didn't you, Wendy, and not only about Mike, but about Owain too. You see, he has a loose tongue when he's had a few too many glasses of wine and during one of his fishing trips with Laurent, he let slip about how and when you met. Yes, I was shocked and mildly hurt by how frugal you'd been with the truth but I let it go, telling myself that it was your business. I was also glad that you had Owain and somehow found the strength to rebel against Mike. It's such a pity you never found that strength for me.

Do you know what has been the most startling revelation of all amongst this mess? Do you know what astounds and confounds me more than anything? It's that for all this time, and maybe going right back to when we first met at school, I don't think that I really knew you, not deep down.

All those letters, the secrets I shared with you, telling you of my crazy life and loves, you even twisted those, turned them into something ugly. If you thought so badly of me then, that I was so low and debased, then why did you allow me to be Jessica's godmother? Perhaps you should have asked the devil himself because according to your judgement of the harlot Nell, Satan would have been a better role model than me.

Or was it that secretly, deep down, you envied me my life once the shine of your trinkets wore off? You were trapped, stuck in suburban Sheffield with a vile man and a child you merely tolerated, and you only had yourself to blame.

The events of the past few weeks have shown me that there is another Wendy I never knew existed and that really has rocked my world. I cannot think of one thing that would have induced me to react the way you have and use my son as a weapon. And now, when I come to think of it, I'm beginning to understand why your relationship with Jessica is the way it is.

If I were a spiteful, vindictive person like you have shown yourself to be, I would say this began with you and Mike, and place the blame at your feet. But I am prepared to take some responsibility for what has come to pass because you and I still have something in common. It's a trait that has become embedded in us and our friendship but for entirely different reasons. Do you know what that is, Wendy? It's so simple. For years and years and years, we haven't told the truth. We are liars.

There, I said it. We were incapable of laying ourselves bare and for that, I'm paying the price.

And now I have got everything off my chest, as you got it off yours, there is one more thing I have to say.

Fate may have played its hand in the past but I'm taking control of the future. The coming together of you and Mike may have been the catalyst that set things in motion but from here on, <u>nothing</u> will be left to chance. No more lies, no more tears, no sparing Wendy's feelings, no more running away.

I am coming back to find my son and tell him the truth. He is my boy, my blood, and I have waited long enough. You have been warned, Wendy. While I have breath in my body and strength in my bones I will find him, I will be reunited with Darrell.

Don't get in the way.

Nell

8

Jessica felt sickeningly nervous. She had promised to wear a red jacket for this first meeting with her brother – half-brother – so he would be able to instantly find her in the tea rooms, and she was so hot she thought it might have been a better idea to wear a bikini. To make matters worse, there was another woman wearing a red cardigan and she had to trust that this stranger would know the difference between a cardigan and a jacket.

Her hands felt clammy, her throat sore, and if he didn't come soon she would be a little puddle on the floor. She checked her watch. Still a quarter of an hour to go. It had seemed like a sensible idea to arrive early, give her time to calm down. It had the opposite effect; it gave her time to think and worry, and she felt a gibbering wreck.

She indicated to the waitress she would like a second coffee, and sat back, her eyes closed as she tried to calm her thoughts. This meeting was never going to be easy, but she had underestimated how difficult it had the potential to be. The sun's rays were fully on her face and she opened her eyes to see if she could move her chair slightly.

'I'll get this,' a deep, masculine voice said, 'and can you bring the same for me, please?'

The waitress agreed, and Andrew turned to meet his half-sister for the first time. 'I'm hoping you're Jessica,' he said with a slight laugh, 'because if you're not I've bought a complete stranger a cup of coffee.'

'I am. Can I take my jacket off before I melt?'

He helped her take it off, then placed it around the back of her chair.

He bent and kissed her cheek. 'I'm absolutely delighted to meet you. I've never met anybody with the same genes as me before. I understand from Wendy that we're close in age, I was apparently conceived on the night of your christening. She's told me very little because I know this has caused a massive parting of the ways between my birth mother and your mother, and for that I'm truly sorry.'

Jess nodded. 'They met when they were five, and have been so close, as close as sisters, ever since. I have always known your birth mother as Aunty Nell, have spent many wonderful holidays with her and her husband, and I think one day Wendy will regret losing Nell from her life.'

'You call her Wendy?'

'I do. To call someone Mum they have to merit the title. Meeting you has thrown a proper curveball into my life. I hoped I wouldn't like you, that I could get away with a quick *nice to meet you, and see you around*, but that's not going to happen.'

'That's a relief,' Andrew said with a smile. 'I would have hated it if I'd found a sister and lost her all in the same day. That would have been stupid of me. Shall I start our conversation, and let you know how I'm feeling? What I'm hoping for?'

She smiled at him as she picked up her coffee. 'That's a smart idea. I'm still a bit blown away by the whole thing.'

The waitress appeared and placed Andrew's coffee in front of him, along with a second bill. 'Shall we have a scone or something?' he said to Jess.

'That would be nice.' She raised her eyebrows in query towards the waitress.

'Two scones. Jam and cream?'

'Oh, I think so,' Andrew said, trying to keep his face straight.

She walked away, taking the two previous bills with her. 'I'll put them on one,' she said.

'Thank you,' Jess called, trying to hide a giggle. She'd only known her brother for two minutes and they'd managed to upset the waitress. Knowing him could be fun, after all.

'Okay, I'll begin. It seems I was taken from my birth mother almost as soon as I was born. They obviously had somebody already lined up for me because by the time I was three months old, the adoption was finalised. I never felt the need to know who I really was, because feelings, love, happiness were certainly knocked out of me from the beginning. My childhood memories are of rules, silence, a small black room that I saw more of than my bedroom, and a cane. That was my life until I was eleven, then they sent me to boarding school.'

Jess involuntarily put her hand to her mouth and gasped. 'That must have been a relief. Oh God, Andrew, Aunty Nell will be devastated if she let you go for this to be your future.'

He reached across the table and took Jess's hand. 'Jess, going to boarding school wasn't a relief. I was bullied incessantly because I couldn't stand up for myself, I had no confidence at all, I was way behind the others in my learning because he, the father, used the slightest excuse to lock me in that black room at night so I never read, never did any homework, it was a vicious cycle. I was in trouble at school for not doing my homework, and I was in trouble at home for being kept in at school to do the homework I hadn't handed in. And then came the cane. It's particularly painful across the buttocks.'

Jess wanted to cry. She wanted to cry for the little boy who had been so loved for all of his life by the woman who had given birth to him, and she wanted to cry for that woman because one day her son would tell her of his childhood and she would know she had made the biggest mistake of her life in giving him up.

'Did you never tell anybody?' Jess asked.

'Only myself. I debated whether to tell you or not, and if you'd been a bit snooty or unwelcoming I wouldn't have told you at all. I was prepared for both scenarios, but if our sibling relationship is to mean anything, I have to be honest, and I think it will mean something. It's been no hardship to talk to you, Jessica, but you're the first person I've ever told. Ever. I left home as soon as I got out of the blessed school, and I've never been back. I moved myself to Leeds, don't ask me why, it seemed sensible at the time and went straight into nursing. I've been at the Leeds General ever since, started at the bottom, and have worked my way up. You can repeat any of this or none of this, to my birth mother, to Nell, it doesn't matter. I would like to meet her, and it can be on her terms, of course. Is she well?'

'She is, and she's one of the loveliest people you'll ever meet. I've seen a copy of the letter she left for you in your adoption file, and she is the letter. Gentle, honest, loving, warm... nothing like Wendy, and yet they've been friends, really close friends for many years. I'm not going to pretend to you that this will be easy, because it won't, but I'm happy to facilitate a meeting between you and Aunty Nell. As you know, I live in Cornwall. I can ask Nell and Laurent to come to us and you can join us, if that suits.'

'Laurent presumably is her husband?'

'He is. He's French, a little older than her but not much, and although it was a real whirlwind romance so I understand, they are absolutely perfect together. No children unfortunately, but of course Nell has you, and I'm sure Laurent will welcome you into his family.'

'Wendy said Nell lived in France, but she's been pretty steadfast in refusing to tell me anything. She seems to blame my birth mother for me being born, but it takes two to make a baby. I learnt that during my nursing career,' he added with a grin.

'Our father raped Nell.' Jessica spoke bluntly. She had talked at length and in depth with a tearful Nell, and had been made aware of the circumstances of the evening of her christening.

Andrew looked at his half-sister, traces of the grin removed and replaced with a frown. 'That's not what Wendy says.'

'Was she there? How would she know what had happened? Aunty Nell was there, drunk as a skunk, but still saying no. And it seems our father had a definite track record with the ladies, even to the extent that one of them committed suicide once their affair came to light, and he was actually in the throes of an affair with his secretary when she died, so for goodness sake don't listen to Wendy when she tries to paint him whiter than white. He wasn't.'

'Can you remember him?'

'Only through pictures, and there aren't many of those. I was still tiny when he went in front of that train. Eventually, I expect you'll meet Margaret. She's Wendy's friend, and they apparently met at antenatal clinics. Margaret's baby died, but what's more to the point is that Margaret was our father's first wife. She left him because of one affair too many.'

Andrew leaned back in his chair. 'Phew! This is a lot to take in. Was Nell here during this carry on, or was she on her travels?'

Jess laughed. 'No, she wasn't here. Once Wendy and Mike married, Nell left for France. I've spoken to Nell because I believe Wendy is wrong to keep you away from her, so I know a bit more of the story than I did. Obviously, Nell had to keep everything a secret, but it seems she went to stay with her friend in London, within a couple of days of the christening. Our father banished her from our home, told Wendy she could have no more to do with Nell. It was while she was in London she found out she was pregnant with you. Nell is, or was, a wanderer. She's lived all over Europe at different times in her life, even on a kibbutz, and somehow ended up in France where she met Laurent. They live in a château, he farms lavender among other things, and dotes on Nell. But she gave you up to give you a better life than she could offer. She had no money, no home, no support, no real choice.'

'Can I go to this château?'

'Not yet. She is coming to you. Wendy assumed I would side with her and not give you any information about Nell, but as you can imagine, I wouldn't side with my mother for all the tea in China. We're not a partnership. If anything, I'm closer to Margaret than I am my own mother, although Margaret can have her moments. She's a bit unpredictable. I believe Laurent and Nell are flying here as we speak but nobody other than Dan, my husband, knows I'm seeing you today. I actually think Nell is hoping for the showdown of showdowns with Wendy, but who knows. You don't write off nearly sixty years of friendship like that. I'm staying in a hotel in Sheffield, not with my mother, I don't really want to be here when the explosion happens, but I promise I'll keep in touch as soon as I know anything. Are you going back to Leeds?'

'I am, but it only takes an hour or so to get here. Tell me about the château, Jessica.'

She laughed. 'It's huge. Bear in mind I live in a three-bedroomed cottage in Cornwall, and you could probably get twenty of my-size cottages in Nell and Laurent's home. Luckily, he has a fair-sized staff to take care of it, plus his farmworkers for the outside stuff, so Nell has a good life, an easy life.'

'So it seems,' Andrew said, with a touch of chill in his voice.

Jess didn't notice it; she was busy reading a text on her phone that had pinged through while she had been speaking. 'It's only Dan. He wants to know I'm okay.' She placed the phone inside her bag and stood. 'I'll nip to the ladies, watch my bag, will you?'

She disappeared through a door at the back of the room, and Andrew pulled out her phone. It took him twenty seconds to find Margaret's phone number and he scribbled it on a napkin before folding it tightly and putting it in his pocket. He tried to find Nell's but it wasn't under N, so he put the phone back in the bag before Jess returned. It wouldn't look good to be caught red-handed rifling through her handbag at their first meeting.

Jessica returned a couple of minutes later, and he looked closely at her. 'You really are a pretty sister.'

'And you're quite a handsome brother,' she said, 'but when you meet our mums I'm sure you'll see why we're so lucky. Wendy is really beautiful, always dresses in lovely clothes but unfortunately has a flaw in her character, and Nell is gorgeous. But she is gorgeous inside and out, loves wearing jeans rather than designer dresses, but I bet they're designer jeans.'

Jess zipped up her bag, and Andrew stood. 'Would you like me to help you on with your jacket?'

She laughed. 'No, I'll carry it. I must have been crazy to say I'd wear a jacket.'

She slung it over her arm and they walked outside, Andrew leaving money on the table to pay their bill.

Suddenly Jess felt shy. Andrew made their parting simple by kissing her on the cheek, and hugging her.

'It's been wonderful,' he said. 'Come on, I'll walk you to your car, then I'll head off back to Leeds. I'm on duty tonight.'

They strolled over to the car park, still chatting.

Andrew watched until he saw Jessica's car turn out of the car park and onto the road, then he walked across to his own car. He took out his phone, smoothed the napkin, and rang the number.

9

Margaret stood for a moment, staring at the phone where she had replaced the receiver. *So that was the famous Andrew,* she thought. *And how the hell did he get my number?*

She headed into the kitchen, put a few biscuits on a plate and sat down to wait.

Margaret shook Andrew's hand and stepped aside for him to pass by. 'First door on the right,' she said, and Andrew walked into the lounge.

'Thank you for seeing me,' he said. 'It's good of you.'

'No, it's not. I'm a nosy old bat who wants to see what a son of my ex-husband looks like, and to see if you've inherited any of his... charms.'

Andrew gave a slight laugh. A lesson in how to make someone feel uncomfortable within one minute of meeting them.

'Would you like a drink? Tea? Coffee?'

'I'd love a coffee, thanks.'

'Then sit down. I'll only be a minute.'

Andrew did as instructed; he felt he didn't dare disobey. The room was comfortable; a large sofa with plump cushions enveloped him, and her furniture was gleaming, highly polished, dark-brown wood. A bureau, a bookcase, end tables, a small round coffee table; everything added to the cottagey feel of the room. There were birthday cards standing on the mantelpiece, and as she came back in carrying a tray loaded with coffee and biscuits, he said, 'Should I be saying happy birthday?'

'Not at all. It was yesterday, and when you reach my age you don't really want reminding the years are passing.'

She placed the tray on the coffee table, then put a coaster on his end table. 'Don't mark my furniture,' she warned him.

'I wouldn't dare.' He smiled. 'It's a beautiful room.'

'Thank you. It's taken years...'

'Jessica says you were married to my father.'

'You've met Jess?' Margaret countered.

'I have. Earlier today.'

'She's here? In Sheffield?'

'She is, but she didn't mention which hotel she was in.'

'So how did you get my number? Jess gave it to you?'

'In a manner of speaking. She left her phone on the table when she went to the ladies.'

Margaret looked at him for a moment. She could see so much of his father in him, and it clearly extended to his sneaky ways.

'So Jess doesn't know you're here? It's best that we keep it that way, young man. Jess is an open honest woman, more like your mother than her mother, and she would be hurt by you looking in her phone.'

'I know. I took the risk because I need to know who I am. Jess knows who she is.'

'Okay. Let me tell you about Michael Summers. He was a lying, cheating, conniving, womanising son of a bitch, who didn't deserve to live.'

'Phew! Don't make it sound better for my benefit.' Andrew gasped. 'Was that your perception of him, or was he really all that and more?'

'I walked away from him when he was on his third affair. Then he moved on to Wendy, and she was gullible enough to marry the control freak. I saw the pictures in the paper of their wedding, and I felt so sorry for her. She had no idea what was to come.'

'You became friends?'

'We met at the antenatal clinic, when she was pregnant with Jess.'

'I see. I feel as if I have so much to learn. He died, didn't he, my father? I've looked up the case, and it seems it was pretty open. Was he pushed, did he jump or did he trip and go over the edge? These days it would be all over the CCTV cameras, but I guess back then that wasn't an option.' Andrew took a sip of his coffee, and declined the offer of a biscuit.

She smiled. 'It's something we'll never know – there was footage but not exactly there, so that didn't help. I don't think many people grieved.'

'And my mother? Nell?'

'Ah yes, sweet Nell. Wendy and I would have been so much closer in our friendship if it hadn't been for Nell. I could never compete. They wrote letters all the time, and if you ever get sight of Nell's, they'll tell you the story of their friendship. Not so much with Wendy, because your bastard of a father burned every letter she had received from Nell. After that, Nell used to write to Wendy using this address.'

'My mother has made a good marriage, I understand.'

'Is that why you're here, trying to find her?'

'I'm here because it's time I knew who I was, and who the woman was who gave me away so that I could have a wonderful life. I need to tell her she was wrong; she made a mistake.'

'I've seen the letter she left in your adoption file. She loved you. She thought she was giving you the best possible start in life. That wasn't the case?'

'I can't speak about it until I've met my birth mother, but no, she didn't give me the best possible start.'

'Then I'm truly sorry, Andrew. And while I may have kept Nell at arm's length over the years because she was Wendy's friend and I felt excluded, I do know she will be devastated.'

'My mother's married to a good man?'

'Oh yes. Laurent is lovely. But what you're wanting to know is how rich is he.'

Andrew waited. He felt a kindred spirit in this woman, and wondered if she had been a good or a bad friend to Wendy over the years. She certainly was insightful.

Margaret leaned back in her chair and brought her coffee up to her lips. She sipped at it, and then smiled. 'He's rich. Unfortunately, you won't inherit. You were adopted and legally you're out of the running. Shame, really.'

Andrew drove away from Margaret's home and headed towards the M1. His little flat in Leeds didn't display the comfort of Margaret's cottage, but he needed to get there. His shift at the pub started at six, and he couldn't do with losing his job.

He went in the communal door and checked his mailbox. There was one piece of junk mail, which he tore into tiny pieces and threw it into the recycling box. Running up the stairs effortlessly, he reached his door and unlocked it.

He looked around the room, utterly depressed by it. He sure as hell couldn't invite his new-found sister here, but maybe bringing Nell and Laurent to it might be a good idea...

Jess was asleep when her phone pinged. A text.

She rubbed her eyes, ran her hands wildly through her hair, and picked up the offending phone.

Thank you for meeting with me. I look forward to the next time, when hopefully Nell will be there. I feel proud to have a sister.

A smile came to Jess's face. She had enjoyed meeting him, and hoped he would be everything Nell wanted in her life. She texted back to him, then texted Nell.

I've met him. He's handsome, looking forward to meeting you. I can make arrangements to accommodate all of us at ours as soon as you give me the word, but I know you want to see Wendy first. Love you, Aunty Nell. xxx

Nell responded quickly.

We've landed. Laurent is waiting at the carousel for our cases, and then we're going to get our hire car. A couple of hours and we'll be there, but not seeing Wendy until tomorrow. I'm tired, and not up for a big argument tonight. Love you too, my darling girl, and thank you for all you're doing. xxx

Jess read the message. Life would have been so much better

if Nell had been her mother and not Wendy, but c'est la vie, as Laurent would have said, and frequently did.

Fully awake and knowing she shouldn't have slept because she would be watching television most of the night, Jess had a shower, checked the room service menu and ordered.

Eating the solitary meal with music playing on her phone, she reflected on the day's events, and hoped she would see more of Andrew. In her heart he was still Darrell but she recognised the fact of his name change to Andrew, and was grateful to Nell for keeping her informed. She recognised that more of the story would come out when they did meet up at her home in Cornwall, but as a glass half-full girl who didn't believe in the glass half-empty theory, she felt they would learn things about each other, and begin the next phase of life as a unit. Having her half-brother as Nell's son certainly gave her a much closer tie to Nell, and happiness hit her like a wave.

Yes, today had been a good day, and she took out her diary to record the best bits. Not the red jacket, that had been a mistake, but the hug from Andrew as they parted had definitely been a highlight, a promise of a future.

Margaret sat with a glass of sherry on the end table, and pondered her day. She had liked Andrew, but sensed there was a dark side to him. He wasn't what he said he was, that was for sure. He was Mike's son for a start and that didn't bode well for anybody.

She hoped the shock hadn't shown on her face as she saw Andrew for the first time. He looked so much like Mike, uncannily so. It was only as they sat talking in her lounge that she realised how much alike they were. Every word Andrew spoke was thought out and guarded. Nothing felt honest, everything felt calculated. He let her see nothing of the real Andrew, only the Andrew he wanted her to see. He wanted her on his team.

She had spent her short married life feeling that about Mike; nothing was as it seemed. She hadn't been able to handle it as a young wife, but she certainly could handle it in Mike's son. Oh yes, without doubt, she could handle it now. Those same eyes that had mesmerised her all those years earlier couldn't mesmerise her in her older years.

10

Nell waved goodbye to Laurent who returned the gesture with a simple nod. While he understood her desire to face Wendy alone, nothing could persuade him to wait at the hotel and instead, he'd insisted on sitting in the car for as long as it took. Nell knew he was nervous on her behalf and scared too, reminding her over and over not to get worked up and to leave immediately if Wendy continued to be hostile or uncooperative.

The strange thing was that Nell felt nothing. No nerves or anger. She was calm and completely focused on her mission, to find her son. If Wendy wanted to rant and rave and make accusations that was fine because there was sod all anyone could do about the past. It was done. Nell had made her feelings abundantly clear in her letter to Wendy and whether it had been a sobering indictment or not, one way or another, today they would either repair their friendship or write it off. The wreckage laid at both their feet.

Nell didn't hesitate when she reached the door and rang the bell, sensing eyes watching her from one of the windows. This was actually the greatest hurdle. Would Wendy open the door or hide inside, behind her bitter words and stubborn nature?

When the white door swung open, Nell got her answer. It was Owain.

'Hello Nell.' He remained at the doorway, blocking her path.

'Hello Owain. Is Wendy in?'

'Yes, she is but I'm afraid she doesn't want to see you.'

Raising her voice, Nell spoke over Owain's shoulder to the woman hiding somewhere inside. 'Really, then I'd like you to tell Wendy that I'm not going anywhere until I've spoken to her and will stand here all day, ringing your bell and knocking on the door until she grows a pair and speaks to me face to face. If she likes, we can chat through the letterbox but I'm sure she won't want the neighbours hearing her business so it's up to her.' Nell stood firm and felt sorry for Owain who was only doing his wife's bidding.

Owain hesitated, his outstretched arm holding open the door. At this, Nell sighed. She was exasperated and not in the mood for drama or pussyfooting about on the doorstep so, taking him by surprise, ducked her head and slipped underneath, puffing her annoyance as she did.

'Oh for God's sake, where is she?'

Nell looked from side to side, two identical doors, one closed, the other open, so she chose that and marched through, coming face to face with Wendy, standing in front of the fireplace.

Nell raised her eyebrows then spoke. 'There you are. Don't you think this is a bit pathetic, Wendy? The least you can do is talk to me, not hide behind your husband and hope this whole mess is going to go away.'

Nell watched as Wendy, groomed to perfection and clearly prepared for battle, not caught on the hop in her dressing gown and pyjamas, straightened her back and looked Nell in the eye as she spoke.

'A mess. Is that how you would refer to the man you abandoned? I'm sure he would be most unimpressed to hear how you think of him.'

Nell sighed. 'Oh, I see, so that's how you're going to play it, twisting my words so you can report back and score brownie points. Really, Wendy? Don't you think that's pathetic and rather weird, you know, latching onto my son and playing the hero. What do you hope to achieve by trying to poison him against me, revenge?'

Wendy smirked. 'I'm not poisoning him, I'm being honest. He deserves that much at least. You dumped him and buggered off on your travels, selfish to the core as always, and I'd rather him hear what you are really like than spend the rest of his life under some illusion about you, or his father for that matter.'

Nell was aware of a drumming noise in her ears and she felt slightly dizzy. She could also hear Laurent's voice, talking in hushed tones to Owain in the hallway. That was fair enough because why should Wendy have her husband around for backup while Laurent waited in the car? He had a right to be there too.

Taking a deep breath, hoping it would ease the light-headedness, Nell soldiered on. '*Do not* liken me to that thing you married. I mean it, Wendy. I was Mike's victim not a willing lover or whatever warped version you prefer to believe in. Yes, my son is a product of two people but I'd like to think he's nothing like his twisted father. I hope he's been spared that at least and let's not forget, Wendy, it was you who brought that man into our lives, it was you who messed up first.'

Wendy huffed before she spoke. 'You're no better than the other tarts who threw themselves at him. And none of us have been taken in by the sob story in your adoption letter to Andrew. It's just you making up excuses as always. I should have listened to Margaret all those years ago. She said you couldn't be trusted. Oh, and by the way, she's already met Andrew. It looks like he's left you till the last. I'd say that speaks volumes, wouldn't you?'

At the mention of her son's adoptive name, Nell felt her heart pound, uneven beats thudding in her chest and her neck began to tighten. 'What the hell's this got to do with Margaret? How dare she interfere and who's read my letter? That was for my son, not you or anybody else.'

Wendy held Nell's stare. 'You seem to forget that Margaret knew Mike long before me, and Andrew has the right to discuss whatever he wants or approach anyone he sees fit in order to get to the truth.'

Nell was incredulous. 'I've heard it all now. I always said Margaret was a creepy cow, totally bloody loopy in fact, latching onto her ex-husband's wife and now she's sniffing around his son too. And you're just like her, the bitter widow grasping onto her dead husband's child like some kind of trophy. Dear God, you're both pathetic and downright weird, and as far as I'm concerned deserve each other.'

At that comment, Wendy shrugged, her cocksure attitude riling Nell further.

'Well, I have news for you both. It doesn't matter how hard you try to keep us apart or poison his mind, I'll be meeting Andrew soon, despite your meddling.' Nell tried to ignore the pain in her jaw and instead, focused on Wendy's puce face, glad she had delivered a blow. What she'd said was true. Margaret was a nutter and if she wasn't careful, Wendy would end up the same way.

But Nell hadn't finished. 'Do you ever wonder why Jessica moved south, why she gravitates towards Laurent and I? Because of behaviour like this, and you know what, Wendy, I don't blame her. Thankfully, she's nothing like her parents and has turned out to be a lovely young woman who rather than thwart me, has gone out of her way to build a bridge between me and my son.'

Nell saw her adversary start, shoulders tensed, white knuckles over clasped hands giving her away. When Wendy spoke, Nell heard anger in every word.

'I think you should go. There's nothing to be gained from this, nothing at all. And stay away from Jessica. I don't want you using her as a weapon against me. You've done enough damage to my family already.'

Nell snorted her derision and shook her head. 'Wendy, I don't need weapons, I never did. You've turned Jessica against you, not me, how sad is that? But I will go, there's absolutely no reason to stay and you've made your feelings clear but before I do, remember that I didn't come here today to fight, I wanted to sort things out. So it's on your conscience, Wendy. We are both part of what happened in the past but you seem hell-bent on deciding your future and I hope you can live with that.'

When her voice cracked, Nell turned quickly, not giving Wendy a chance to reply or see the tears that were escaping from her eyes. Taking the hand that Laurent offered as soon as she stepped into the hallway, and feeling a wave of irritation at Owain's downcast eyes, Nell followed her husband down the garden path, sucking in air with each footstep.

Once inside the car, she scrabbled in her bag, desperate to locate her angina spray, pulling off the lid before squirting two blasts under her tongue. Laurent held her hand as she rested her head against the seat, eyes closed, waiting for the woozy effect and the pain to subside while her breathing returned to normal.

After a few minutes, Nell opened her eyes and found those of Laurent, wide and full of concern.

Smiling, she spoke, her voice weary, exactly like her body. 'It's okay, my darling, I'm fine now. Let's get back to the hotel so I can lie down and then I want to ring Jessica and arrange a meeting with Andrew as soon as possible. I need to see my boy before those two witches do any more damage.'

Laurent removed his hand from Nell's and started the car. 'Of course, chérie, but first you must rest and if necessary I will speak to Jessica. You have had enough worry for today. Close your eyes, we will be at the hotel soon.'

Nell did as she was told and felt the car pull away, and as Laurent listened to the satnav, she refused to look out at the city that had been her home. She hated it and had no desire to look upon landmarks that would only spark memories. The place dragged her down.

And there was something else.

Ever since they'd landed at Manchester Airport and started the drive north towards Sheffield, she had been aware of an ominous presence, like a dark cloud, oppressive and sinister. Nell had the dreadful feeling the consultant was right and this odd sensation was a portent, telling her to hurry because time was running out. She had to see Andrew before it was too late. Fighting back the tears, Nell prayed that she was wrong and even though she had just lost her oldest friend, soon she would find her son. Then, after waiting for so long, she would be able to hold him in her arms, like she always imagined.

Laurent sat by the window and looked out across the city skyline. He was deep in his thoughts, momentarily interrupting them to glance over to where Nell lay sleeping. He was troubled by two things: her health, which was clearly declining, reflected in her ashen face, contrasting with the shadows below her eyes that seemed to have darkened overnight. He was also bothered by the looming spectre of Andrew.

No matter how hard he tried, Laurent couldn't shake the fact that unlike so many he had heard of, this adopted child had sought out the father first, not the birth mother. Yes, maybe the trail had been easier to follow but somehow, Laurent sensed Andrew had already made up his mind whose side he would take, and who he blamed. Now, with his father dead and buried, his mother was the consolation prize.

Why had Andrew not approached Nell directly, after all, he had been willing and able to march straight up to Wendy's front door and ask about his father. It also seemed Andrew was far too willing to listen to the opinion of others, even seeking the counsel of Jessica before Nell. No, Laurent did not like the idea of this man, not one little bit, and he was going to make sure that Andrew didn't hurt his precious wife. She'd had enough of accusations and cruel jibes.

Laurent's thoughts then turned to more practical matters and whilst he would do anything to make Nell happy, he would not be fooled by a chancer who could be aware of his mother's financial situation. They had already been to see the family lawyer, settling their affairs and making provisions, and Laurent wholly approved of Nell's generous bequest to her only goddaughter. In return, Nell knew that the estate would always remain in Laurent's family as it had done for centuries. So, if this Andrew had any ideas of inheriting a fortune, he would be disappointed.

Regardless of his suspicions, Laurent hoped that Nell wouldn't be let down by her son. Maybe, they could forge a future and who knew, Andrew might come good and prove Laurent wrong. Somehow though, the niggling doubt that had been festering ever since Wendy's letter had arrived was growing by the day and like the looming grey city beyond the windows, had manifested inside Laurent's head.

Looking over at the pale face of his sleeping wife, Laurent wished he could scoop her up and whisk her home to the fields of lavender and their happy carefree life. But until the meeting had taken place and Nell's wish came true, they were stuck.

Creeping over to the bed, Laurent gently lay down by Nell's side and after pulling the blanket over her shoulders, wrapped his arms around her body. For now, it was all he could do. That and pray, for the health and happiness of the fragile heart that he could feel beating inside her chest.

11

Andrew checked his appearance in the mirror. It was important he made the right impression when he met Nell, there was a lot riding on the next few hours. His hair was freshly washed and groomed, his face shaven. Staring at his reflection, Andrew congratulated himself on his transformation from the shabby, bearded, tousled-haired man of three months earlier.

It had been so easy, following the paper trail to his father's door. There wasn't much you couldn't find out from online ancestry sites and it had been well worth the membership fee. Using the meagre information Nell had left in his adoption file, Andrew had set about finding his father first, having no interest in the woman who had abandoned him to his fate.

Discovering the death certificate of Michael Summers had been a shock but Andrew was nothing if not determined. So instead of giving up he decided to dig a little further, in case Michael's widow had been waiting all these years to hand over a bequest in his name, or maybe he could extract some guilt money, either option was worth a try.

The photo from the newspaper archive had been a bonus, the one of the smart business man who fell to his death at the train station, because it helped the barber transform Andrew into a younger mirror image of his father. He'd seen the effect his likeness to a dead man had on Wendy and Margaret so he was interested to see if the same could be said of Mother Dearest.

Andrew was looking forward to a spot of play-acting, he was good at it, even feigning shock when he knocked on Wendy's door and was told of Mike's death. It had been easy, like the show of remorse and faint horror when Wendy finally allowed him an audience and then dished the dirt on her ex-husband.

Christ, they were so eager to share but the best part was when Andrew did a bit of sharing of his own and gave Wendy his adoption letter to read, that was pure drama. Who'd have thought that revenge could be so sweet and in the space of a few minutes he'd manage to destroy a lifetime of friendship with a piece of paper, and the irony was that he hadn't even started yet.

It had been truly fascinating, peeling away the layers of Wendy's life. It was like a rancid onion and with each revelation, Andrew realised that there was much more to the past than a wife-beating husband. He was good at reading people, borne mainly out of self-preservation and living in a toxic dysfunctional family – that and working behind a bar. There, he was privy to all kinds of unguarded information, whether he was lending a friendly yet slightly bored ear or listening to the drunken ramblings of a lonely customer.

If he wasn't mistaken, he'd uncovered some bizarre love triangle between Wendy, Nell and Margaret, and at the epicentre was Mike. The only thing he hadn't fathomed yet was who had hated his father the most and more to the point, which one of the women was vulnerable and ripe for the picking. Andrew was sure that by the afternoon he'd know.

After fastening the buttons of his faded shirt that had seen better days – the collar and cuffs were well worn but not too tatty, like his jeans and trainers – Andrew pulled on his hooded jersey jacket. It wasn't quite suitable for the time of year and would mean he'd shiver slightly when he chatted with Nell on the park bench where they were meeting. Poor impoverished Andrew.

After glancing at the envelope on the kitchen table with the word 'photos' written in biro, Andrew checked his watch, grabbed his keys and headed for the door, eager and nerve-free. Nell wasn't going to know what hit her.

Nell was cold and wished she'd brought some warm boots. Actually, what she really wished for was to be at home, far away from Sheffield and everything it stood for. How could she have forgotten that October in the north of England was nothing like the mild climate of Provence and if she were there, she'd still have the sun on her face and be stress-free.

Wound up like a bobbin, Nell wanted this over with, checking her watch constantly and wiggling her feet to warm them up. She probably looked impatient and tried to curb her behaviour in case Darrell... Andrew, was watching from a hidden spot. Nell couldn't get used to referring to the baby who lived in her head, the one she'd carried around for all these years, by his adopted name.

They were meeting in the Peace Gardens in the city centre, somewhere neutral and close to pubs and restaurants. If the meeting went well they could perhaps go for a drink and a bite to eat and if not, she could scurry back to the hotel and Laurent. Bless him, he was almost as nervous and currently sitting in the foyer of the hotel, literally minutes away, in case she needed him.

Andrew was late, five minutes. So bored with people-watching and thinking that every male figure was the one she longed to see, Nell turned her attention to the gothic town hall situated right in front and she focused on the darkened leaded windows. They resembled beady eyes and Nell fancied that all the building was missing were a few gargoyles on the turrets, but this made her think of Wendy and her black-eyed face, full of threat and anger.

Nell checked her watch again and as she did, became aware of a figure approaching from the left. Nell knew it was him the moment she set eyes on the young man striding towards her, his hands buried deep in his pockets, but his face she would have known anywhere, it was like staring at Mike.

By the time he was a metre away, Andrew had slowed and there followed an awkward moment where Nell chose to be the grown-up, or the parent, the one to break the silence. Stretching out her arms, she said the first thing that came to mind. Or were they the words she'd always imagined saying in the reunion scenes her brain had tried hard to suppress, forbidding hope and fantasy. Whichever they were, they came from the heart.

'Andrew, I'm so happy to see you. I thought this day would never come.'

Nell stepped forward, one pace, shortening the gap and within seconds he had responded. Taking an identical step, Andrew allowed Nell's embrace and as she wrapped her arms around him in the exact way she had pictured, she felt his tense body respond. As they hugged tentatively, his hands resting gently on her back, Nell waited for it to happen. For that surge of love to arrive, for their bodies to squash together and hold on tight like they never wanted to let go, for that current of love to run from one to another, repairing the bond that had been broken on the day they were separated.

When Andrew pulled away first and Nell had the opportunity to look into the blue tearless eyes she recognised so well, she was overcome by a sense of nothingness. It wasn't there, she knew it immediately. Whatever love a mother and child were supposed to share, that overwhelming sense of belonging or knowing, had evaded her, them. It was as though a sheet of glass separated their bodies. She could see him clearly but even though she could touch, Nell couldn't feel him.

Gathering panicked thoughts, she spoke far too quickly, overcompensating for the awkwardness.

'Shall we sit? I'm a bit overwhelmed and nervous, so please forgive me if I rabbit on. I've been thinking about this for weeks.' When she gestured to the bench, he obeyed and soon they were seated side by side and out of desperation, Nell took his hand. It felt cold and limp, barely holding on, definitely no squeeze.

'So, have you come far? Where do you live...? There's so much I need to know. See, I'm bombarding you already, sorry.' At this, Nell elicited a smile and relaxed slightly, especially when Andrew managed to string together a sentence.

'No, not far, Leeds. It takes about forty minutes but my bus was late so I had to run most of the way from the station. You look frozen. Shall we go somewhere warmer and get a hot drink...? There's a Starbucks over there.' Andrew lifted the hand that Nell was holding, forcing her to let go when he pointed behind her.

'Yes, that's a great idea. I am cold, so lead the way.' Nell stood quickly, wanting to escape the whole scene yet felt duty-bound to soldier on, telling herself as they walked side by side yet inches apart that this was normal reunion behaviour, to be expected.

As soon as the thought left her brain, it was followed by an overwhelming sense of wanting to weep at her own pathetic lies. Who was she kidding? Right at that moment, Nell was fighting a fierce battle not to run because if she did, she'd never stop.

. . .

Andrew added sugar to his third cup of coffee and smiled inwardly at the building sense of desperation he saw in Nell, which had resulted in her making frequent trips to the counter, and then calling her husband for backup. She hadn't said as much and disguised her anxiety by suggesting it would be great for them to meet, insisting that Laurent couldn't wait to say hello. In the meantime, Andrew had ordered the most expensive sandwich and cake on the menu, paid for by Mother Dearest who watched with concern as he wolfed it down like he'd not eaten for a week. What a mug.

Still, he couldn't complain about the atmosphere because it was going according to plan, exactly how he'd envisaged. Andrew had watched television with interest as Davina McCall reunited long-lost families, he'd even read a few novels on the subject but the thing was, neither programme nor books had elicited an ounce of emotion in him, not even a single tear. What they had given him, was a valuable source of information, individual case studies of how not to be. Andrew was the antithesis, the exception to the rule.

That was why he purposely held back where shows of affection were concerned; playing the part of a shy, possibly damaged, young man who had trouble communicating. Andrew had no intention of making anything easy, for two reasons. The first was that he fucking hated Nell, his *birth mother* as they referred to them on telly. The other was that the harder Nell had to try, the more desperate she would be to make amends, and the more likely it was that she'd be willing to cough up what she owed him. And as far as he was concerned, in monetary terms it equated to a lifetime of misery.

Despite getting in his stride, Andrew was actually glad she'd eventually capitulated and rung Laurent because it was becoming excruciatingly tedious, making conversation, feigning interest in each other, listening to her regrets and apologies, blah-blah-blah.

How Andrew wished he could've taken a photo of her face as he described in detail, while apologising intermittently if it was causing her distress, the shitstorm that was his childhood.

'Oh Andrew, I am so sorry. Truly I am. You don't know how dreadful that makes me feel because it's the last thing I wanted for you. The thought that you would have a good life... well, I hung onto it for all these years. It made giving you up more bearable but now I have to face the fact that I was wrong.'

At this point, Andrew chose to be magnanimous. 'No, that's not true. I had to tell you how it was though. And I do understand why you did it. You have to remember it's not your fault I ended up with unsuitable parents because that was down to the adoption people. I blame them not you.' What a crock of shit.

Nell shook her head; seemingly unconvinced, which Andrew saw as a good thing.

'So, let's talk more about you... I believe you're a nurse... that's a noble profession. Do you enjoy it?' Nell was twisting her napkin into a paper breadstick shape.

Andrew noticed that her eyes looked hopeful as they zoomed in on him. He'd been waiting for this question so gave it everything he'd got, starting with the hangdog expression, casting his eyes downwards as if in shame about his next revelation. 'I need to make a confession and I hope you understand why I've told a bit of a fib.' He looked up and mirrored Nell's previously hopeful eyes that suddenly looked wary.

Filling the silence and keeping momentum, Andrew got on with it. 'I'm not a nurse, not anymore. I had to drop out of university because I couldn't afford it. I had no help from my parents and with hindsight I wasn't in a good place, you know, up here.' He tapped his head. 'I'd bottled so much up that I was diagnosed with depression and took loads of time off, then I fell behind with my studies and it was like the whole world was caving in. I was already working two part-time jobs and couldn't cope, so I jacked it in.'

Nell sighed. 'Oh Andrew, that's such a shame but I understand. I know what it's like to struggle for money and I suppose, to be in a bad place up here.' She tapped her head as Andrew had done.

On seeing this, he wanted to scream out, *No, you fucking don't know what it's like, you don't know anything.* He reined it in though, and answered her next question when she asked the obvious. So predictable!

'But why did you feel you had to lie?'

A quick shrug, then he answered. 'Because I was worried you'd think I was a failure if I told you I worked in a pub. There, it's as simple as that, so instead I went with a half-truth because one day I'd like to carry on with my studies and become a children's nurse. That's my dream anyway.'

Andrew fiddled with his spoon and imagined Nell handing over a nice fat cheque to pay for his fees and accommodation; that would be a result. Her next words fuelled his hopes of success.

'Oh Andrew, I want you to hold onto your dream and never give in because you don't know what the future holds, none of us do. Look at me, I was a nomad who found her way to a small village in France and met Laurent. All I wanted was to see the lavender and I ended up with fields of the stuff, which reminds me, I've brought some photos. I thought you might like to see them.'

Before Nell had time to open her bag, Andrew let out a sigh then held his forehead in mock horror. 'Oh no, I don't believe it... I've left mine at home. I had an envelope of photos for you but they're on the kitchen table. Damn, I'm sorry, Nell.'

Waving her hand, Nell dismissed his concern. 'Oh don't

worry, another time. But I would love to see some photos of you growing up. I wonder if they'll be how I imagined.'

Andrew didn't care, and he didn't like how she seemed to ease herself out of the uncomfortable moments with glib meaningless comments. While she unzipped her bag, he got ready to hit her with what he hoped would be a very uncomfortable question, one that would drag her right back down to earth, muddy and slimy, where she belonged.

12

He'd already come to the conclusion that Mike wasn't well liked, so Andrew avoided another character assassination of a dead man unable to defend himself.

'Could I ask you something? It's a question nobody has been able to answer so I'm presuming only you know.' Andrew saw her head snap upwards from her posh bag and then turn his way.

'Yes of course, ask me anything.' Nell stopped what she was doing and waited.

'Did my father know, about me?' Andrew saw Nell flush and then swallow. He could tell she was working out what to say and by this reaction, he already knew the answer.

'Yes, he knew. The day before I travelled to Israel I came up on the train from London and met him at the station, ironically it was on the same platform where he died some time later. I told him I'd had his baby.'

'And what did he say? Was he shocked, happy, angry, what?' Andrew's heart was giddy. *He knew, he bloody well knew.*

Nell sighed. 'A bit of everything really. He asked if you were there, which obviously you weren't and then, when he got over the shock, he demanded to see you because he'd always wanted a son, even before Jessica was born. He offered to come to some arrangement if I kept you a secret from Wendy, which is when I told him it wasn't necessary because you'd been adopted.'

'And what did he say, how did he react?' Andrew's heart was going mental in his chest. This was the million-dollar question.

'He was furious and reverted to the Mike I knew; threatening, verbally abusive, truly nasty, I suppose.' Nell sounded calm, matter-of-fact.

'But I don't understand... Why did you go all that way, why didn't you tell him when you found out you were pregnant, why did you wait until I was gone?'

Nell didn't answer immediately but when she did there was unapologetic firmness to her tone. As he listened to her words, Andrew hadn't expected the chill that invaded his blood, like it was freezing him solid. It was the weirdest sensation, especially when it suddenly morphed into red-hot boiling anger that thawed him instantly and forced him to clasp his hands together to prevent them from shaking or lashing out.

Nell's words when she delivered them were enunciated, clear and concise.

'Revenge, pure and simple. You have to understand, Andrew, that Mike raped me, he betrayed Wendy and then made it impossible for me to stay in Sheffield. Your natural father was not a nice man and I know it will be terribly hard for you to take this in, but he really doesn't deserve any loyalty so please, don't build him up to be a saint because he was nothing of the kind. I know from Jessica that Wendy and Margaret have given you their opinion of him so we can't all be wrong, although I'd be wary of Margaret because I've never been able to work out if she really hated Mike or was secretly besotted by him. But at the moment she's irrelevant and I'm sorry if I've upset you, but I owed you the truth.'

Andrew couldn't bear to look at Nell, such was the torrent of hate running through him so instead, he stood and pushed back his chair and excused himself before heading off to the toilets without even looking in her direction.

Once inside the cubicle, he closed the door then punched it hard, cursing under his breath. How fucking dare she send him away without even giving Mike a say in what happened to his own son who, by that bitch's own admission, had wanted more-than-perfect-baby Jessica. If Nell had given Mike the chance he would have taken him in, Andrew was convinced of it. He wouldn't have abandoned his own blood.

It was coming together, the pieces of the puzzle. Wendy *and* the newspaper reports said that Mike's death was a mystery because he'd had no reason to kill himself, so it must have been a terrible accident. Andrew knew the truth. Mike had been riddled with remorse and regret, maybe damaged mentally.

It was so glaringly obvious. It was in the genes. They shared the same problem because Andrew had also suffered bouts of depression, like his father. After hearing what Nell had done, Mike couldn't cope so he took his own life in the same spot he'd learned of his son's. It was more than a coincidence; it was tragic and cruel and the person responsible was sitting out there like she was proud of the fact.

Yanking open the door, Andrew left the cubicle and splashed cold water on his face then wiped it dry with a blue paper towel. After regaining his composure, he took a quick look at the reflection of his father's son in the mirror. He was even more determined than before to get what he deserved from a woman he'd despised ever since the day he'd worked out what the word 'adopted' meant, and then realised that *she* was responsible for the beatings, and so much more.

Andrew told himself to focus then pulled open the door to the toilets and headed back to the table. He had one more trick up his sleeve but first he would apologise for his sudden departure, blame it on shock then let predictable Nell soothe and cajole him. As soon as Saint Laurent turned up, Andrew intended to wallow in a little pity-party of his very own making.

He'd planned for two eventualities; the first would depend on his acting abilities that would hopefully secure a lift home, otherwise the loss of his return bus ticket and money – both were actually tucked in his sock – should do the trick. It wasn't a cash injection he wanted, not yet anyway, Andrew merely intended to lure them to his humble abode where he could twist the knife further by showing them just how the other half lived.

Nell's eyes flicked from the toilet doors to the main entrance, praying that Laurent would appear before Andrew. *What have I done? What have I done?* That's all Nell could think of the whole time she had listened to Andrew's story and now, after hearing of his terrible life, she had heaped even more misery on it by castigating his birth father and painting herself as a cold-hearted vengeful nutcase.

By the time Laurent breezed into the restaurant, moments before Andrew returned looking less flushed than when he left the table, Nell was on the verge of hyperventilating. But the sight of Laurent's face allowed the tension to turn down a notch and by the time the less awkward introductions were made, she was thanking heaven for her wonderful husband.

Laurent had a way about him that put everyone at ease and soon he was chatting away to Andrew about the bloody weather and football. Neither interested her in the slightest but the banal conversation allowed her to step back and observe her son, her baby boy.

How bizarre it was that he reminded her so much of a man she hadn't seen for thirty years, but had despised for every one of them. His hair could have been groomed by Mike himself, and Andrew's mannerisms could be those copied by a little boy who adored his daddy, and those eyes, they made her shudder. Nell wondered if Andrew had the same effect on Wendy and Margaret but was immediately sobered by the thought that she'd be unable to ask, she had been rejected, again.

There was another uncomfortable truth that Nell had to face up to – she felt not a glimmer of jealousy that Laurent had made Andrew laugh twice, or that her son was chatting away far more freely than he'd done since the moment of their reunion. In fact, it occurred to Nell that she wasn't even bothered if Andrew liked Wendy and Margaret more than her, she was really that detached and thankful for the piece of laminated wood separating them.

How terrible was that? After so long, so much time, her expectations and hopes were crumbling with every moment that passed, and worse, Nell wasn't sure whether she was happy or sad about it.

Her self-interrogation was interrupted by Laurent who asked if anyone would like refreshments and it was Andrew who called time on their meeting, when he looked at his watch and appeared slightly anxious.

'Seriously, mate, I'm swimming in coffee but thanks for the offer and anyway, I really need to get going otherwise I'll miss my bus and be late for my shift. My boss is a dragon and eats bad timekeepers alive.' Andrew stood and zipped his jacket against the cold.

Laurent, always happy to help, glanced at Nell and before she could prevent what she knew he was going to say, the words were out.

'Oh no, we can't allow the dragon woman to eat you so why

don't we drive you back. How far is it?' Laurent was already on his feet.

Nell remained seated and mute.

Andrew held up his hands as he refused politely. 'No, it's fine. I can't expect you to take me. You must have plans, so, honestly, if I go now and run, I should make it in time.'

Laurent persisted, oblivious to Nell's lack of enthusiasm; either that or he was ignoring it. 'No, we insist, don't we, darling? And I would like to see some more of the area so it's decided, let's go.'

Andrew sighed. 'Okay, if you insist but at least I get to show you where I live and I can give you the photos when we get there.'

For the first time in minutes, Andrew turned his attention away from Laurent and focused on Nell, who managed a smile and had already gathered her coat and bag, resigned to spending another gruelling session but this time trapped inside a car.

Even the thought of seeing the photos wasn't tempting because she knew that they would only induce another pang of regret and heartbreak. There was nothing for it though, so after helping her on with her coat, Laurent led the way and Nell followed on behind, telling herself to be brave, and to get it over with.

Andrew had told them they were heading towards the Harehills district of Leeds, one Nell knew to be one of the worst places to live. While Laurent took it upon himself to regale Andrew with the beautiful village where they lived and in total contrast, Andrew jokily pointed out one dismal landmark after another, she wanted to scream for them both to stop.

Laurent had no idea how terrible Andrew's life had been

because there had been no time to fill him in. Despite this, her son had managed to find humour in his clearly unfortunate situation. And while Nell had no maternal feelings towards her boy, not yet anyway, she did have the grace to feel desperately sorry for him, there was even a hint of admiration for his fighting spirit. Maybe he had her instinct for survival in dire circumstances. Perhaps she had passed on something of use after all.

Andrew chatted easily to Laurent as he gave directions, and asked about the lavender farm and how many employees they had, nothing too intrusive, more a skimming of the surface, yet it still made Nell's toes curl.

In return, she asked nothing and allowed Laurent to delve as far as Andrew allowed, which wasn't too deep. Thankfully, Laurent took the hint when he asked Andrew how long he'd lived in Leeds; eighteen months. Did he see his parents often; no, they had lost touch. Had he a girlfriend; not anymore, she'd dumped him for someone with better prospects. These revelations simply brought out the philanthropist in Laurent and Nell wanted to remind him that Andrew wasn't a charity case and their consciences couldn't be cleared by a donation to the village church, or the Holy Sisters of Mary Magdalene, not this time. Again, she remained mute and tried not to imagine suffocating Laurent.

'You should come to our farm and stay for a while, you would love it there, wouldn't he, chérie?'

Laurent looked in the rear-view mirror at his silent wife who merely nodded, then smiled at Andrew when he managed to glance her way.

'There is always something to do and maybe, if you like, we could find you a job, especially at harvest time. Almost all of my family work there, and you would get on well with our younger relatives, wouldn't he, chérie?' Laurent glanced again at his wife then addressed Andrew. 'Do you think you would like to come and visit, get to know us and help out?'

'I'd be a fool not to... It sounds like a brilliant place and yes, I'd love to give you a hand, anything is better than working behind a grotty bar.' Andrew directed his comments to Laurent before flashing Nell a brief smile.

When they finally reached the council estate where Andrew lived and he directed them to the front of a row of flats, Nell was already trying to think of excuses not to go inside. It was a fore-gone conclusion though, owing to Laurent's inbuilt sense of propriety.

'Would you like to come in and see my humble abode while I get the photos? I warn you it's not up to much but we have time for a cuppa seeing as you've brought me home.' Andrew had twisted in his seat and asked the question directly to Nell.

'Yes, of course we'll come inside, won't we, Laurent, and you don't have to apologise, Andrew, this is your home.' Nell gave him her kindest smile while all the time thinking, *It's me who should apologise, it's me.*

13

After trudging up the litter-strewn stairs, Andrew opened the door to his flat and that's when the smell hit them. Not a bad one, merely the tinge of damp and an unloved home that lacked a woman's touch, or a mother's. Nell ignored her sinking heart and glanced around. The flat was tiny, with a kitchen diner and small lounge, all in one room, with a bedroom and bathroom opposite.

Andrew looked uncomfortable when he asked, 'Would you like tea or coffee and please, sit down.'

Both Nell and Laurent declined. Andrew, however, opened the fridge door and extracted a carton then proceeded to pour himself a glass of milk. Nell couldn't avoid the sight of the empty shelves, bare of food apart from a tub of butter and a packet of ham. She knew instinctively that the cupboards would be the same and she prayed he didn't open them to rummage around for biscuits or tea bags.

Nell felt she was becoming an expert in avoidance because she also steadfastly diverted her eyes from the white envelope on the table. On the front was written *Photos*, presumably the ones Andrew had forgotten. But no matter how hard she tried,

Nell couldn't unsee the ones of Mike that were pinned to the noticeboard above the fridge.

'I see you already have photos of Mike. Did Wendy give them to you?' As soon as the words were out, Nell regretted them but it bugged her, Andrew's little shrine.

'Oh yes, and Margaret.'

Nell's hackles rose. 'I can't believe she still has photos of him... Wendy yes, because of Jessica but not Margaret. I told you she was odd.'

Andrew turned his gaze from the noticeboard to Nell. 'I've only met her the once and I have to say she was really helpful. She thought I'd like to have some photos of him from before he met Wendy. Apparently we're like peas in a pod. I can't see it myself though.'

The atmosphere in the room had taken a further nosedive and it was Laurent who cut through it, forcing everyone's attention to the envelope on the table.

'Ah, so these are the photographs you mentioned. May we look? I am sure Nell will enjoy seeing them, won't you, chérie?'

Nell rallied. 'Yes of course but perhaps it would be nice for Andrew to show us. You are so impatient, Laurent.'

Nell desperately wanted to look, to see something other than the image of Mike. She wanted a chubby toddler, a beaming schoolboy in his smart uniform, a cheeky teenager, sunny holiday snaps, opening his Christmas presents in pyjamas, his favourite pet.

Andrew pushed the envelope across the table. 'Of course. Here, have a look. I'm sorry there's only three but my parents weren't big on photos and marking happy events.'

Nell's fingers trembled slightly and she felt odd, like her ridiculous world of make-believe balanced precariously on this moment. Sliding out the photographs, her eyes fell upon a baby, perched on the knee of a faceless woman wearing a flowered dress. Her hands, adorned with wedding and engagement rings, held him around the waist as he grinned into the camera, two teeth on his bottom gum. His eyes were shining, laughing really, and this lifted Nell's heart.

She could feel two sets of eyes on her but was unable to speak, tears misting her vision which she wiped away before moving to the next image. This time it was a six or seven-year-old, a school photo, exactly like she'd hoped but that toothy grin and happy-eyed baby had been replaced by a pinched-faced child, his expression was of nothingness, unreadable.

The third revealed a sullen spotty teenager, arms over chest, reclining and seated at the foot of a tree, like he was raging against the world and it was then that Nell saw him: Mike.

It was too much, the silence, the expectancy, the sheer enormity of the situation and Nell couldn't take it any longer. When she sobbed, then apologised, telling them she was being silly, that she'd be fine in a minute, Laurent took over.

'No, no, chérie, it is fine. This has been a big day for both of you but perhaps we should go. I don't want you to be ill so I think we should get back to the hotel where you can rest.'

At this point, Nell heard Andrew intervene. 'Of course, it's a huge day for all of us and anyway, I should be getting going too. Would you like some water first, Nell? It's no trouble.'

Nell waved away the offer and allowed Laurent to help her to her feet as she tried valiantly to gain control. Maybe she was being washed away by a tide of tears and emotions but as Andrew stood before her, looking awkward and unsure, a surge of desperation rushed through her body and forced her arms forward. Pulling him towards her, Nell gave it another try.

'Thank you for agreeing to meet me, Andrew. I know it's been hard, everything, but please believe me when I say that I do want to make this work, to have you in my life.' Nell pulled away and then kissed him on the cheek, feeling his skin on her lips and inhaling the scent of fabric conditioner on his clothes.

When Andrew just nodded in response, Laurent spoke instead.

'We could make arrangements for you to come to France for a visit, but in the meantime perhaps dinner tomorrow, or lunch with Jessica before she goes home. And would you be available, Andrew? Would this be agreeable? I could collect you if you like.'

'I'd like that very much, Laurent, but only if Nell's up to it. Let me know what time and I'll be there, and no need to collect me, I'll make my own way.'

They had reached the door, walking and talking, and with each step, Nell felt the urge to drag Laurent away, flee. When Andrew pulled open the door and stepped aside, Nell walked onto the landing and sucked in the air while Laurent shook hands and said goodbye. With a weak smile and a barely raised arm, Andrew waved to Nell who met his eye, hoping for, yet not expecting a show of emotion. Unsurprised but rocked to the core, she turned and walked as fast as her weak legs would carry her.

Nell and Laurent proceeded down the stone steps that led away from Andrew's flat in silence, the envelope containing three photographs clasped tightly in her hand. The past forty-five minutes were replaying inside Nell's head, the whole miserable journey from the centre of Sheffield to the street where Andrew lived and then the debacle inside.

Not a word was said as they strapped themselves into the hire car before Laurent started the engine and drove away. They had only gone a few metres, turning a corner out of sight of the flat when Laurent reached over and took Nell's hand in his, before asking a simple question.

'Are you okay, chérie?'

When she burst into sobs again, verging on hysteria, Laurent swerved to the side of the road next to some wasteland, ignoring the honking horn of the driver behind. Laurent turned off the engine, unbuckled his seat belt, and took Nell in his arms and held on tight, unable to make sense of her garbled words so instead he waited, and waited, for it to stop.

Finally, he managed to soothe her and once she had blown her nose and wiped her eyes, Nell managed to speak.

'I want to go home, Laurent, tomorrow if possible, can you arrange it?' Nell's voice was a whisper, her fatigue echoed in every word.

'But darling, why?'

'Because this place is killing me. I'm suffocating and I can't bear it any longer so please, take me home.'

'Is it Andrew you are running away from?'

'Yes, no... it's everything, everybody, memories, mistakes. It's like they are piling up on me one by one and I can't take it, Laurent, I've had enough.' Nell turned to look at the concerned face of her husband and continued.

'And you know what, I'm sick of being the villain, of Wendy and Margaret looking down their noses at me. Nell the poor relation, ha, in fact I'm not even that, am I? I'm Nobody Nell, the poor kid from a shit family. And you know what else pisses me off? They see me as one of Mike's tarts. They've put me in the same category as the rest of his mistresses. How dare they, how bloody dare they?' Nell's previous desolation was replaced by anger, building with every second and she was glad Laurent remained silent because she had to get this out, vent her frustration otherwise she'd explode.

'Can you believe Andrew's been to see Margaret... What the hell has this got to do with her? I despise that woman, I really do. Always poking her nose in where it's not wanted. She's always had it in for me, trying to prise Wendy away, twisting the knife. Margaret didn't even come over for their wedding, turning her nose up like a jealous teenager. And she's always hated the fact that I'm Jessica's godmother and we are so close, the bitter old hag! Rattling around in a huge house she inherited from her maiden aunt. Christ, being a sad git must run in the family.' Nell blew her nose again then thought of something else.

'You know what? I wish she'd spend some of her Aunty Betty's fortune and piss off, and I bet she's loving the rift between me and Wendy, in fact she's probably at the root of it. Did I tell you I always suspected her of steaming open the letters I sent to Wendy, that's how creepy she is, not to mention latching onto her ex-husband's family, hovering like an avenging angel. Wendy might not be able to see it but I can.'

'Don't be bitter, darling, it doesn't suit you and neither does swearing. I want my gentle Nell back, not this screeching angry woman sitting by my side. You are rather frightening like this.' Laurent grinned.

Nell narrowed her eyes, not sure if he was attempting humour or chastising her but she let him off, he wasn't the enemy after all. 'I'm sorry, my love. It's being back here, it's turning me into someone I don't want to be. I know you hate swearing and confrontation but I think this has been building for a long while.'

Laurent sighed. 'Or are you really angry at Andrew?'

Nell turned away quickly and stared through the windscreen that was becoming blurred by tears, and that swell of hurt was rising in her chest, causing it to constrict and it felt hard to breathe so she tried to calm down. Laurent knew her so well.

For a few moments, anger had fended off what was really bothering her, like a knight brandishing his silver sword, his shield a barrier against the pain.

When she found her voice, it was a whisper but it told the

truth. 'He hates me, Laurent, couldn't you see it, surely you could?'

'It is early days, chérie, perhaps you expect too much too soon.'

'Laurent, you are too kind, too forgiving but I knew, more or less straight away, from those first few moments. There is nothing there. He oozes negativity. Even when we embrace, he is tense, his eyes are closed off, and it's not that he's on his guard either, it's more than that.'

'I don't understand.' Laurent took her hand again.

'He blames me for everything and I suspect he's built Mike up into a hero figure, after all, Andrew has photos of him in his flat and did you not realise, he still hasn't looked at the ones of me, he never even asked.' Nell's voice caught and she knew she was going to lose the fight again so she hurried on, got everything out.

'I wanted to show him the girl I used to be, to make him understand that before I became the woman he hates so much, I was a someone who he might have liked. The girl who camped in the desert and danced on a beach in Spain, who cleaned toilets and peeled vegetables, who meant no harm to anyone, and had she been given the chance, she would have loved him so much.' The tears were flowing properly and Nell couldn't stop them.

'I feel so wretched, Laurent, like I'm rotten to the core because I gave him away. All I wanted was for him to say he'd been happy, that I made the right choice because then we might have stood a chance, had a relationship or at least been friends but I feel nothing. Can you believe that? I don't even think I like him.'

Laurent folded her into his arms and stroked her hair. 'Shush, chérie, you cannot make a judgement after a few hours. Do not cry, you will make yourself ill.'

Nell pulled away, shaking her head and catching her breath before she spoke again, trying not to hiccup. 'Don't you see, don't you understand? I can't help it. It's like looking at Mike, even his mannerisms. And I don't want to be reminded of the person who caused so much damage and heartache, especially by his cold distant son, that beautiful baby boy I gave away. And that's why I want to go home... I can't stay here, I can't. If Andrew wants to visit then our door will always be open but that's up to him. So please, start the car and take me to the hotel. I don't feel well and I need to sleep, I'm so tired, my love, I really am.'

Nell saw Laurent nod before starting the car. As she rested her head and closed her eyes against the harsh inner city backdrop, Nell pictured home and the purple fields of lavender, trying to ignore the pain in her heart that was radiating across her chest. Reaching over, she found Laurent's hand and once his fingers closed around hers, she allowed herself to relax, thinking over and over, as she drifted into sleep, *Take me home, Laurent, take me home.*

14

Laurent was in the foyer of the hotel watching out for Jessica who was due to arrive before Andrew. It would give her some much-needed private time with Nell. The previous evening had been such a strain, more so because Laurent was becoming increasingly worried about Nell's health and, if he was honest, state of mind.

She had looked ashen and exhausted when they returned to their suite despite sleeping for most of their short journey. He had hoped she would go to bed for a few hours but instead Nell had insisted on packing while he booked flights, made arrangements and told lies.

Laurent was not a natural-born fibber but for his wife he would do anything, even vote for Macron, so when he rang Jessica and Andrew and told them of the email he'd received confirming her urgent hospital appointment, his fingers were firmly crossed.

Both had quickly agreed to come for lunch the following day so they could say goodbye before Nell and Laurent took the evening flight to Nice. In Andrew's case, Laurent added that they could also make plans for a visit, although every word had been spoken through gritted teeth.

The truth of the matter was that Laurent did not like Andrew, not one little bit. This was why, after observing the almost blatant cold-shouldering of Nell, and then his flagrant sucking up to Laurent, the die had been cast. Laurent prided himself on being a people person and in his role of manager of an estate that employed hundreds of workers each year, he'd become adept at spotting the shifty ones, the chancers, trouble-causers and the layabouts. Unfortunately, Andrew fitted the bill.

The saddest part was that Nell had been right and it broke Laurent's heart to see the state she was in when they left Leeds and he'd almost regretted offering to take Andrew home, but curiosity and intuition told him it was the right thing to do. Laurent had wanted to gather as much information as he could about Nell's son because knowledge was power.

He also knew it was the right thing to go home, as soon as possible. Nell looked dreadful and it was Laurent's intention to email the private consultant the second they got back. If, after she had been treated, Andrew wanted to make an appearance, Laurent would deal with him on home turf and set a few tests, like when he'd offered him a job and saw that twitch in his jaw. No, there would be no handouts to freeloaders, blood relation or not.

The waving hands and smiling face of Jessica as she emerged from the revolving doors snapped Laurent from his gloom and cheered his brooding heart. 'Jessica, you look wonderful, come along, Nell is waiting and I know it will do her good to see you.'

After Jessica accepted her traditional Gallic welcome, she tucked her arm under Laurent's as they headed to the lift.

'Is she no better, Uncle Laurent? I've been worried sick since your call last night but I'm sure between us we can jolly lunch along and don't worry, I'll keep an eye on Andrew. I can't believe he was so off with Aunty Nell, but maybe it was nerves, so fingers crossed today will be better.'

The sound of a ping heralded the arrival of the lift and once the doors swung open, Laurent and Jessica stepped inside along with the other waiting guests. As they ascended, Laurent remained silent, keeping his thoughts to himself because where Andrew was concerned, speaking out loud may have caused offence to the other passengers. For now though, he would keep his counsel and the peace.

The bus was nearing the city centre, giving Andrew time to gather his thoughts and remind himself of today's mission. First, he was going to secure a date for his visit to the château where he had no intention whatsoever of becoming a grubby farm-hand. God, he had been so insulted when the frog had suggested it the day before. What the actual fuck was he think-ing? No way was the lady of the manor's son going to work for a living, he was going to live it up for a few months and drink the cellar dry of vin rouge, that was for damn sure.

Second item on the agenda was to announce he was going to go back to university to continue his studies; his head was clearer and he knew where he was from, and all that psychoba-bble shite. Everything being equal, a freebie jolly in France, followed by a nice guilt cheque from Mother Dearest could be on the cards.

Third, was to see if there was any way he could worm his way into his big sister's life because from the sounds of it she had it cushy in Cornwall and maybe her husband was a bit of a soft touch too. If nothing else it was another holiday destination and Andrew quite fancied a spot of surfing and living in pasty-land.

The fourth and final vitally important item was a spot of carrot dangling and after yesterday's debacle, poor Mummy Nell would be gagging for a reprieve and guess what, that was exactly what she was going to get. Andrew would sit next to her at lunch, apologise for being a bit of a cold fish, blame it on nerves and being bombarded with so much information, but assure her that she was forgiven and he hoped – cue big blue eye moment, hint of tears – that they could start again.

Andrew actually laughed at his own cunning, a bit too loud, causing the guy seated on the other aisle to give him a funny look which he ignored. Thinking ahead to lunch caused Andrew's stomach to rumble as he imagined what delights he'd be treated to at the hotel. He could do with a good nosh-up after the session he'd had the night before with that tart from the flat above. Once his visitors had left, he'd dragged the carrier bags from under his bed that contained the food he'd stashed from the fridge and cupboards, along with the crate of beer he drank some of in celebration of a job well done.

Checking his watch, Andrew saw he was on time and concentrated instead on his phone, googling Provence and flights to Nice. He wanted to be fully prepared for the day his cash cow paid her dues.

Laurent led the way to the suite and while Jessica waited patiently, he inserted the key card into the lock, calling Nell's name as the door opened.

'Nell, we are here. Are you ready, chérie?'

Nothing, silence apart from the sound of the radio.

'Chérie, Jessica is here...' Laurent looked at his niece who shrugged and placed her bag on the sofa.

Making his way swiftly to the bathroom, Laurent listened but didn't knock because he knew something was wrong. Flinging open the door, he found Nell lying on the bathroom floor, her face drained of colour, lips slightly tinged with blue. He heard his own voice scream her name and then Jessica's, telling her to ring for an ambulance, quickly, quickly.

Lifting Nell from the floor and into his arms, Laurent cried and begged.

'No, no, no. Please stay with me, Nell, please wake up, my love, hang on, chérie, do not go, not now, please Nell, please.' But Nell remained limp, her eyes stayed closed, impervious to her husband's tears that poured onto her face.

Despite Jessica's pleading for someone to hurry, as he rocked his precious wife to and fro and the wail of an ambulance cried out in the distance, Laurent feared he'd left it too late and his precious Nell would not make it home. She would never see the fields of purple again. He had failed her.

Andrew was flanked by Wendy and Margaret as they entered the hospital and made their way to the ward. Wendy's incessant sobbing was beginning to grate on his nerves and he wished she would give it a rest. At least Margaret was in control and, fortunately, had been at Wendy's when Jessica called to give them the news, seconds after she'd rung him to say that Nell had collapsed, suspected heart attack, and they were en route to the hospital.

It wasn't often that Andrew was shocked, living the hard-luck life had toughened him up but he had to admit that for a second or two he'd been caught off guard as he stood on the pavement outside the bus station.

He was focused and in the zone, guiding Crying Woman by the arm and allowing Margaret to take the lead as she spoke to the nurse at the entrance of the ward. After a hushed conversation, the nurse scurried off and then Margaret turned, her face unreadable as she approached.

When they were inches apart, she spoke quietly, both hands gripping the straps of her handbag like she was going to open a fete, or name a ship. 'I'm so sorry, Andrew, Wendy, but we're too late, Nell's gone. She died in the ambulance. The nurse has gone to tell Laurent and Jessica we are here.'

The wail, when it escaped Wendy's lips, made Andrew recoil and wince before Margaret took over and begged her to shush, saying she would disturb the other patients. While Wendy sobbed and made strange sounds into her handkerchief, Andrew gathered himself and waited.

When a door a little way along the corridor opened, Laurent and Jessica emerged. Margaret nudged Wendy who, to Andrew's immense relief, desisted. Laurent walked slowly, staring ahead, his back straight and determined but the sag of his shoulders gave him away. Jessica followed, red-eyed and pale.

Once they were face to face, Laurent looked from one to the other, taking them in while his words settled on the polished floor. 'What do you want? Why are you here?'

Wendy spoke in a strangled, pathetic whine. 'I came as soon as I could, to see Nell, but I'm too late. I'm so sorry, Laurent, I truly am.'

The sound of Laurent's derisory snort made Andrew start. He hadn't prepared for this, death or the cold shoulder, so he remained silent, letting the scene play out.

'YOU are sorry? What for, Wendy? For turning your back on your best friend, for your vile words, your cruel actions?' Laurent then looked at Margaret. 'And why are YOU here, to gloat, to interfere, to cast another stone?'

Margaret straightened her back and looked indignant. Her pink painted mouth made the shape of an O but remained wordless. It was at this point Andrew knew Laurent was going to attack.

'And you, have you come to mourn your beloved dead mother, the woman you could not even hold yesterday, whose eyes you could not meet with one single ounce of kindness?' Laurent stared, his eyes burning into Andrew's.

It was the wheedling annoying voice of Wendy that broke his glare for which Andrew was most grateful.

'Please, Laurent, please don't be like this, I want to see her, say goodbye and tell her I'm sorry.' Wendy broke down once again.

The sound of her hysteria required Laurent to raise his voice a notch, speaking over her distress. 'You will not see my wife; you do not deserve to make your apologies or say goodbye. It is too late for that now. She is gone and she died with sorrow in her heart because of the three of you, the traitor, the ghoul and the gold digger. I never want to see or hear from any of you again.'

When the two women gasped, Jessica stepped forward and took Laurent's arm before speaking in a firm but gentle voice.

'Come on, Uncle Laurent, this is doing no good. Please, let's go back and sit with Aunty Nell. Wendy, you need to go home, there's nothing you can do here and you're just making things worse.'

Averting her eyes from the group, Jessica guided Laurent away but for a second he stood firm and focused on Andrew who had remained silent throughout.

The impasse lasted mere seconds where Andrew offered no condolences, showed no remorse. Apart from a curt nod and a brief flicker of a smirk to a grieving man, Andrew gave nothing away, then watched as Laurent was led back to his dead wife's bedside.

The game was up, Andrew knew that, but he would not be

cowed or shamed. He owed Nell nothing, Laurent even less. So rather than blot his copybook in front of the women with a slanging match, he took Wendy's arm and along with Margaret, shuffled her towards the exit.

As they made their way through the car park, Andrew took time to reassess the unfortunate situation. His cash cow was dead and due to his adoption, he had no claim on her estate.

That left Weeping Wendy who had Jessica to consider, but there was always a chance that, given time, he could wheedle his way in and extract some guilt money from his half-sister.

His attention was then drawn to Margaret, poor, lonely, childless Margaret who had latched onto her successor and appeared to have a hankering for her dead ex-husband. Margaret also had a nice home and according to probate records, a stash of money in the bank.

As he helped Wendy into Margaret's car, Andrew allowed himself a small smile. All he had to do was bide his time, make himself indispensable to the lonely widow, be nice to Weeping Wendy, and while he was at it, be the best brother Jessica could wish for.

15

Margaret stared into the mirror for a moment. She thought she looked younger these days, and she put that down to her live-in lodger, Andrew. In her head she thought of him as her stepson, but she never said it openly. She knew people would find that to be a joke, but she and Andrew had a closeness that gave her comfort in her mind.

So much of Mike was in Andrew, and she often found her memories drifting back to the early days of her marriage to the one man she would always love. It occurred to her more and more frequently that it had literally been early days of a marriage; he had quickly shown his true colours and became the man she had had no choice but to leave.

Although Andrew had never met his father, he spoke like him, he walked like him and he had a bit of a way with the ladies. Margaret frequently met unexpected guests at the breakfast table, but she could put up with anything to finally have someone to love.

Even when he was showing the sarcastic traits of his father, he did something that Mike had never done; he apologised and said he wasn't used to being cared for. Some nights they shared a pizza and a glass of whisky, watched a movie, had a conversation, and he was charm personified.

And now the day had come to act as if she had cared two hoots about Nell. Seven months after her death, Margaret was meeting the two women closest to Nell, Wendy and Jessica, and Margaret was going to have to pretend that she was missing her, that she had cared about her. They were going to have the wake denied to them by Laurent.

Andrew had said the previous night that he really didn't want her going to meet Wendy and Jessica, but she had insisted she had to do it, to raise a glass to the woman who gave birth to him, and a dear friend.

'But she wasn't your dear friend,' he had said, and she gave a brief smile of acknowledgement at his words.

'I know, but I knew her for such a long time, and as you get older, Andrew, you'll realise you have to act in a certain way, make it look as though you care when they pass over. That was Nell. And really, I'll be there to support Wendy, who has been devastated by her best friend's death. So I'll smile, I'll nod every time they speak of her with love, and I'll even pay for the champagne we use for the toast to beautiful Nell. You know, I admit I didn't like how close Wendy and Nell were, but I can pretend.'

'But I found you because of her.'

'Oh, Andrew.' Margaret blushed. 'You say the nicest things.' She picked up her cardigan and slipped it around her shoulders. He helped her straighten it, and then held her at arm's length.

'Gorgeous,' he said. 'And your carriage awaits. I've given it an extra polish in view of the occasion.'

She smiled at him. 'I'm sure it didn't need an extra polish, it only came out of the showroom three days ago, but you're a good boy. Is it everything you expected it to be?'

'It's an amazing car, Margaret. I'm so grateful to you.'

He opened the front door and escorted her down the path.

The blue SEAT Leon sat at the kerbside, and he opened the passenger door for her to get in.

'It matches your eyes,' she said with a laugh. Sinking into the comfort of the seat, the new car smell overwhelmed her, and she drank it in.

Andrew got in the driver's side and turned to smile at her. 'Taxi for Ms Cassidy. Where to, madam?'

'Oh, the Devonshire, by the riverside, young man. We've booked a table on the lawn, so hopefully the sun will shine all afternoon.'

'Sounds lovely. Wish I could stay with you, but ring me when you're ready to come home, and I'll collect you. I have to tell you, Margaret, that this past four months or so, since I moved into your home, has been the most settled and happy I've felt in years.'

He pulled smoothly away from the kerb, and Margaret relaxed for the journey, smiling without speaking.

Wendy was the first there, and she scanned the car park, looking for what she guessed would be a taxi. Owain had dropped her off, and she had left her return home open-ended. It was possible the three of them could share a taxi.

She saw the blue car drive in, and was shocked when Andrew jumped out and moved around to the passenger door.

Andrew helped Margaret get out, then closed the door before returning to his driving seat. Margaret waited until he had disappeared before turning and walking towards the lawned area, laid out with tables covered in crisp, white tablecloths.

She waved to Wendy, who held up a hand in acknowledgement.

'Hi,' Margaret said. 'Jess not here yet?'

'She's running a bit late. She'd had a bout of vomiting, and was sitting down for ten minutes to make sure it was over. Is that a new car?'

'It is. We bought it last week.'

'We?' Wendy said with a snort. 'Do you mean you bought it?'

'What if I did? It's my money to spend as I want. Now, back to Jess, and out of my affairs, if you don't mind. A bout of vomiting? Is she...?'

Wendy frowned. 'She's not said she is, but I wouldn't be surprised. They're happily settled in Cornwall, buying the house, and time is moving on. She said it was something she'd eaten, but I'm half expecting her to tell us she's pregnant.'

'Oh, that will be lovely,' Margaret gushed.

'Will it? Yet another continuance of bloody Mike Summers?'

Margaret's smile disappeared. 'You can't look at it like that! It's a continuance of you, of your family.'

'And his.'

'You hated him that much?'

'Didn't you, Margaret? You walked out on him because he had so many other women. He shouldn't have been allowed to live.'

It was clear from Margaret's face that she was digesting the words tumbling with some considerable venom from Wendy's mouth.

A waiter appeared at the table, and asked if they were ready to order. 'I think we'd like a cup of tea, please,' Margaret said. 'We're still waiting for someone to arrive before we decide what we want.'

He disappeared to return a couple of minutes later, bearing the necessary items for a drink, and during that brief hiatus neither woman spoke.

Wendy thanked him, then poured out the tea. She handed

one to Margaret. 'No more about Mike. We're not here for him. We're here for Nell.'

Margaret gave a brief nod, then sipped at her tea. 'This is very civilised, afternoon tea on the lawn of the Devonshire. Would Nell have liked this?'

'In her later years, I think she would. Not so much the time when she was travelling around the world, but after she met Laurent she seemed to grow up.'

Both women took a deep breath, acknowledging they had avoided a full-blown disagreement. Talking about afternoon tea was diffusing the situation.

Wendy was considering ringing Jess once more when she caught sight of her car pulling into the car park. Her car. Not a taxi.

Jess got out, locked the car and walked across to meet Margaret and Wendy, planting a kiss on each of their cheeks.

'That's totally French of you,' her mother remarked with a smile.

'It's in honour of Aunty Nell,' Jess responded. 'That's why we're meeting, isn't it? To honour Aunty Nell?'

'It is indeed,' Margaret agreed.

'Sit down, Jess. We'll order next time the waiter passes by. Are you feeling better?'

'Yes, it seems it was a momentary thing. I'm fine now.'

The afternoon sun beat down, and the three women were grateful for the shade provided by the large white umbrella overhead.

'I heard from Laurent this morning,' Jess began. 'He said he'd been to Aunty Nell's grave, taken her loads of lavender, and stayed a good hour chatting to her. I think he's accepted that nothing he could have done would have saved her, she was in full heart failure, but oh Lord, he misses her so much.'

'Do you think he would come for a visit if I email him?' Wendy asked.

Jess gave a slight laugh. 'Wendy, he blames you for Nell's death. He believes you exacerbated it, caused her to die before she got to see a specialist, you and your silliness about Andrew. So no, I don't think for one minute he'll ever see you again. He's coming to stay with me for Christmas, and Dan and I are going over to the château, probably for Easter. I'll take care of Laurent, don't worry about that.'

Wendy looked aghast. 'But he knows I loved Nell, have always loved her no matter that we fell out at the end. I would never have caused her harm... I can't believe he's holding me responsible.'

'But you did cause her harm,' Margaret said quietly. 'You did, Wendy.'

Jess reached across the table for the menu, and she heard her mother's intake of breath.

Key, wishing well, bell, house, heart – tiny charms on a bracelet given by her to Nell all those years earlier, and now around Jess's wrist; that couldn't be right. 'Where did you get that bracelet?' Wendy knew her voice was intractable.

'Uncle Laurent gave it to me. It was Aunty Nell's, and he wanted me to have it.'

'I bought it for her before bloody Laurent ever came on the scene. Give it to me!'

Jess took it from her wrist and dropped it into her handbag. 'Not an earthly chance, Wendy. It's been given to me, and with me it will stay.'

Wendy's temper was building by the second. How dare these

two women sit in judgment of her. How dare they castigate her friendship with Nell, a lifelong friendship that was leaving a huge hole in her life. Even the bracelet was no longer part of her memories, she didn't want to think about it now it was part of Jessica's jewellery box. And bloody Margaret! Margaret, who knew things about Nell's life, things that she had dropped into conversation, such as her meeting an Austrian called Hans with whom she had had a brief but intense affair. Margaret could only have known that by steaming open the letters Nell had sent to Wendy during that long year following Mike's banning of Nell from communicating with her. Deviousness that Margaret would never admit to, and she was turning on her!

The waiter approached, notepad in hand, and peace was momentarily restored as they ordered three cream teas, and a bottle of champagne. Jess asked for a small lemonade.

'Lemonade?' Wendy asked, as the waiter moved away.

'Okay,' Jess said. 'You've probably guessed anyway after my sickness earlier. I'm pregnant, and the baby is due in January. I won't be drinking the champagne, but I can toast Aunty Nell effectively with lemonade.'

Wendy stood and leaned across to kiss her daughter. 'Wonderful news, Jess. Congratulations to both of you.'

'And many congratulations from me too, Jess,' Margaret added. 'New year, new baby.'

'Just so you're aware, if it's a little girl we will call her Nell.'

Wendy's smile lit up the air around her. 'That's wonderful, Jess. I'm so pleased. Oh, I do hope, with everything that's in me, that it's a little girl.'

The afternoon tea was delicious. The three women worked their way through the various levels of food, and finally the champagne was poured.

'To Nell, our lovely friend,' two of the three women said, and raised their glasses. Margaret merely said, 'To Nell.'

And the Nell Appreciation Society meeting was almost over.

'I hope Nell's not meeting up with Mike,' Margaret said, busy tucking her credit card back inside her purse and unaware of the glare suddenly directed at her from both Jess and Wendy.

In that instant, after all the years she had known Margaret Cassidy and fuelled by half a bottle of champagne, Wendy recognised what the problem had always been with Margaret; massive amounts of jealousy, pure and simple anger that he could love other women.

Maybe the confession to killing that secretary who had been found to have committed suicide – Chris, was it? – in a wildly drunken moment one late night hadn't been the joke it was written off as the following day. Maybe the truth had been in the telling, not the retraction and the laugh.

'You evil bitch,' Wendy said quietly.

Jess looked across at her mother, at a face contorted by an anger so intense it was frightening.

'You absolutely evil bitch. Don't link my Nell with that bastard. If she's with him up there it won't have been worth it...'

Wendy's head was swimming. The lawn was undulating, seemed to be going around and around in circles, and she clutched onto the table in terror. Her mind went back to that same drunken night when Margaret had made her confession and she had made her own confession of being there at Paula's house, and hitting her with her car. What had Margaret said? *I know, I saw you there.* She remembered querying why Margaret was at Paula's house, and Margaret had smirked and said, *Mike was mine, I was watching her.* Had Margaret's been the car that had run over Paula? Not Wendy's at all?

'You killed her. You killed Paula.' Wendy's tongue felt thick, her mind felt numb, but she knew she was right.

Blackness.

The paramedic went on his way, happy to have diagnosed that the lady had been in the sun for too long, and she was fully recovered from her faint.

Jess was picking up her bag, ready for walking down to her car. 'Let me know when you're both safely home. Wendy, try not to frighten us like that again,' Jess said with a smile.

Wendy and Margaret nodded, knowing that lines had been crossed, that there was only one unanswered question.

Jess walked down the lawn, and they waved as her car disappeared from sight.

'Andrew can drop you off,' Margaret said.

'No, I've texted Owain and he's on his way to get me. This is over, Margaret. You've let me think I killed Paula all those years ago, and I didn't, did I? I'll never see or speak to you again.'

'No, you didn't kill her. I did,' Margaret said simply, a smirk on her face. 'I used to go to her house a lot, partly to see Mike because he went there all the time, and partly to plan how to get rid of her. I'd disposed of Christine; Paula was the next on the list. And then I'd get around to you. You presented me with the ideal opportunity when you hit her. She was starting to get up so you didn't even hurt her that much. I did. But this is my word against yours, and of absolutely no use in a court of law. I'll deny everything.

'I loved Mike with all my heart, and I was wrong to leave him, but he wouldn't have me back. And once he was dead, there wasn't much point killing you.' She paused and looked down towards the blue car entering the car park. 'Andrew's here. I'd better go now. He's picked up some flowers, so we're going to Mike's grave before going home. Doesn't it make you feel sick that Andrew is with me? Caring for me? Everybody is leaving you, Wendy... You'd better hold tight to Owain, because you sure as hell don't have me anymore, and you definitely don't have Jess.'

Wendy began to feel dizzy again, and she knew it was nothing to do with the sun. She was listening to a woman confessing to murdering two others, and plotting one more. 'I'll stay here a while and wait until Owain arrives. Enjoy your visit with Mike, but don't remember me to him. He'll not want that.' Wendy knew without any doubt that she could hurt Margaret with such an intensity, and she chose to follow the dark path.

'Have you ever been to his grave?' There was a seething resentment in Margaret's tone of voice.

'Why would I?' Wendy asked. 'I called down to the station the day of his death. I was supposed to be on my way to the hospital with my broken arm. I thought I had killed once, so knew it was possible to get away with it. It simply took a gentle push against his back; he never even saw me. But think about this, Margaret, if I hadn't thought I'd killed Paula, I would never have thought of killing Mike. But I did. And as you've made clear, it's your word against mine, and I'll deny everything. I killed the one true love of your life, and it was because you killed Paula and let me think I had done it. That's called karma, Margaret, karma.'

Wendy picked up the almost full glass of champagne that was left, tipped it over Margaret's head, and said, 'Cheers!'

16

You don't need my address anymore
Seven long months after losing you
My darling, darling Nell,

Yesterday, I met with Jess and Margaret to raise a glass of champagne to you, to say thank you for your life, your love, your support, and everything else about you, my beautiful friend.

I didn't cry until I arrived home, and then the truth of you not being there anymore bounces around my head, and now I can't stop the tears. These tears make those that followed your death look like streams; these are rivers of pain, turmoil and devastation.

I've spent all morning reading through your letters, the ones Mike couldn't destroy, looking at the many Christmas and birthday gifts you've sent me over the years, and I'm not sure I want to carry on without you. The thought that goes around and around inside my brain is if I had told Mike he had to go instead of you, that day following Jess's christening, you would have stayed instead of going to Israel.

I have to say sorry. You died after our last words spoken to each other were full of anger and vitriol, and although I am sorry, that word isn't strong enough, my Nell. I have loved you as a friend since the first day we met, nearly sixty years ago. We've laughed together, played together, and after I said I wouldn't help you meet Andrew, I don't doubt we unknowingly cried together, but nothing can ever bring you back and that thought is killing me.

Since you left me, everything in my life has changed, and I need to tell you about it because that's what we've always done. That was our promise to each other when you left that day to begin your great adventure around Europe. Nell, you may not be physically here, and I know you can't reply, but I have to talk to you one last time.

I'm losing Owain, I know that for sure. Oh, I don't think he'll ever leave me, he loves Jess too much to do that, but he's taken himself to a different plane, somewhere where he knows I can't follow because it's his plane and he decides who comes and goes. Does that sound stupid, Nell? It does to me, but it's the truth, nevertheless. The way I handled Andrew arriving in our lives made Owain see me in a different light, and I actually recognised that at the time but I couldn't do anything about it. Anger lived hard and deep within me.

The sense of betrayal because you had slept with Mike was so strong it became the overriding thing in my life, and I was determined you would never meet Andrew. It was punishment for you. I turned into judge and jury, and found you guilty.

I didn't believe you when you said Mike had raped you. I believed you had got on so well with him that the sex was by mutual consent, and that hurt.

But I have been reminded of how evil Mike was and although it has taken some time, I know you had stopped all the lying we've been doing over the years. The truth was there to be seen. He did rape you, and I let you down by not believing you.

Andrew is the embodiment of everything that was wrong in his father, and I suspect that is already being proved. I'm sorry, Nell, but I have to tell you he has moved in with Margaret, and he is happily spending her money. His feet are firmly planted there, and she treats him as if he is her son.

One day Margaret will find herself penniless and alone, as Andrew drives off into the sunset in a brand-new car.

Jess sees him occasionally, but he seems to have put his eggs into Margaret's basket, so I suspect even Jess, who hasn't a nasty bone anywhere, will eventually see through him and cut him out of her life.

I don't think his feelings on losing Jess will be anything like my feelings around losing my daughter. I have been an awful mother. Do you know she calls me Wendy? That says everything, doesn't it?

So I have nobody, but I do have a little hope. Jess is pregnant. Maybe I can grab at this second chance to welcome an infant into my life, to be a grandmother – no, a nanny – to my first grandchild. Jess said yesterday that if the baby is a girl, she will be called Nell. How wonderful will that be!

So we are at an end, truly. Oh, Nell, I miss you so much, and writing on 'our' notepaper has helped me feel a little closer to you. There is only one sheet left now, and I shall save that for writing a letter to welcome my new grandchild into this world. It is indeed an empty world without you, my beautiful, beautiful friend.

No matter what happens in the future, I will always love you and miss you.

Till we meet again, Nell,
Wendy

THE END

HOW THIS BOOK CAME ABOUT

In the beginning it was all about Messenger...

Trish: I'm in a right bad mood. Can't shift it either. No idea what's wrong with me. x

Anita: Write the mood out of your system and have a huge gin. We should write a book together, that would keep us laughing and do away with our bad moods. I'm snapping at everybody today, and I know it's because I'm not writing. I'm reading which stops me going on the computer and then I get umpty. Umpty Anita is not good to know, so Dave says. Xxx

Trish: Well, Brian's retreated into the garage. He's not even been in for a brew. I'm going to have a glass of red wine. And cheese and crackers for tea. We had KFC for dinner and I didn't enjoy it. I treated Harry as it's last day at grandma's before back to school. I've got an idea for a book we could write together. I'll tell you when I see you. I thought of it years ago.

Anita: Think we could do it? I wouldn't mind having a go. Think we're having cheese and crackers for tea. Xxx

Trish: I'll write down a brief summary of my idea. You will probably think it's poo. Have you got any ideas? I've always wondered how people write a book together. If they fall out about what they want to say. My idea sort of cuts out that issue. I'll do it now to get me out of my bad mood. And I'll make Brian a brew. Just to show willing. X

Anita: See? Mood lifting already! No ideas beyond two main characters, we take one each, one good one bad that maybe switch over by the end of the book. I am very open to other ideas lol. X

Trish: Great minds! Got your email. You're on, Waller!!! Let's do this. Take some time to think about it and we can have a brainstorming session. I bet you come up with some fab ideas. I agree with everything you've said. And also the best thing is we can tweak the plot as we go along. I'm rather excited now after my bad mood.

ACKNOWLEDGMENTS

We have lots of people to thank. Our families are the main ones, as always, but with this book they have been exceptionally supportive. They have cheered us on from the sidelines and encouragement has flowed around family, fans and readers. There are too many of them to name, but you all know who you are.

We also have a very soft spot in our hearts for our publishers, who said 'go for it' when we first mentioned the idea. We actually had already gone for it, and Trish was in the throes of detailed plotting! So thank you Fred and Betsy at Bloodhound for your faith in us, and for the wonderful comments when you first had sight of the completed manuscript.

The full team of Heather, Alexina and Tara at Bloodhound have been equally supportive of the idea of a co-authored book, Bloodhound's first, and we are truly grateful.

Morgen Bailey, our editor, also deserves our gratitude; a superb editor.

We both have a team of ARC (advance reader copies) readers, and without them taking the trouble to read our books and review on publication day, life would be so much more difficult.

A big round of applause to both teams, and thank you so much for your continued support.

This book was written because one day at the end of August 2019, Trish felt off, and a little bit down.

Et, voilà! Two and a half months later...

Trish and Neet
November 2019